THE
Lovers'
ROOM

Steven Carroll was born in Melbourne and grew up in Glenroy. He went to La Trobe University and taught English in schools before playing in bands in the 1970s. After leaving the music scene he began work as a playwright and became a theatre critic. Now a full-time novelist and reviewer, he has twice been short-listed for the prestigious Miles Franklin Literary Award—the richest literary prize in Australia.

Steven
Carroll

THE
Lovers'
ROOM

MIRA is a registered trademark of Harlequin Enterprises Limited, used under licence.

First published in Great Britain 2007
MIRA Books, Eton House, 18-24 Paradise Road,
Richmond, Surrey, TW9 1SR

© Steven Carroll 2007

ISBN 978 0 7783 0146 2

59-0507

Printed in Great Britain
by Clays Ltd, St Ives plc

To Fiona

Acknowledgements

My thanks to the following people for their advice and assistance in the writing of this novel: Eiko Sakaguchi, formerly of the East Asian Collection, Melbourne University Library, now the curator, the Gordon W Prange Collection, Marylands University, Washington, USA; Yuki Tanaka, formerly of Department of Political Science, Melbourne University, now Research Professor at the Hiroshima Peace Institute; Les Oates, formerly of Military Intelligence, Australian Army, and later an academic at Melbourne University.

Thanks also to my agent, Sonia Land and all the gang at Sheil Land, to my publisher, Sarah Ritherdon, to Catherine Burke, and to my editor, Robyn Karney, for her superb work.

Finally, my thanks to Fiona Capp for her constant help and suggestions—and for supplying the title.

Prologue

Melbourne—June 1973

If he could have gone back and changed the order of the afternoon, he would have. Would never have gone out into the cold and the wind, would never have entered that wretched staff room, and he had regretted it from the moment he sat down on the soft black departmental chair. Even then he could have slipped out and nobody would have noticed. But he didn't, and chance, coincidence or just plain bad luck had done their work and nothing could change it now. If he were more of a superstitious person, he might even believe something like fate had called and he had answered. But, no, it was just rotten luck.

The garden light hovered like a full moon over the lawn, the black staff that supported it invisible in the gathering darkness. Allen Bowler, dressed in a tweed coat and brown felt hat, stood on the footpath, staring at the light, at his illuminated garden, his illuminated house, until the cold made him shiver. The street, opposite Melbourne University, where he had taught for most of his life, was empty. It was the shortest day of the year, dark by five. There were no other lights on in the rows of Victorian terraces except those in the corner milk bar, which glowed invitingly for the last of the day's custom.

He had just walked back from a staff meeting at the university to bid farewell to some old colleagues. A meeting that had dragged on into darkness. Allen Bowler, Professor of English, was an established figure at the university and was often invited to university functions. Generally the invitations went straight into the wastepaper bin, but this afternoon, out of a mixture of obligation and sheer restlessness, he had gone along and had sat in a stuffy staff room, listening to endless speeches, and anecdotes he'd heard once too often.

'Professor Bowler?'

The voice was as crisp as the air he now stood in. So much so that he could have sworn he could hear his name even now, as though somewhere out there, in the dead of winter darkness, he was being called. Unusually, he'd gone to his room after the meeting to gather some books, and had looked up from his desk to see a young Asian woman standing in his doorway. She seemed to have materialised from nowhere—he had no recollection of seeing her in the corridor, yet there she was, addressing him in the light, casual manner of an old acquaintance. The accent was English. London—he was a regular visitor to the city. The eyes, Japanese. Her face told you one thing, her voice another, and the disjunction of signs had been oddly disturbing. Indeed, he was grateful that he had been leaning forward, palms on the desk, and head down, reading over some old notes, when he'd looked up in response to the inquiry. It was a simple situation, he told himself afterwards. Mundane, even. No need to dwell, and he was a good dweller. A student had simply asked if he were Professor Bowler and he had looked up from his desk and nodded that he was. That was all. But there was nothing simple about the jumble of emotions he had felt then, and which he felt now.

The front gate squeaked open and he stepped in. It was ridiculous, but as much as he told himself he was not going to be held emotionally captive to some silly fancy of his, as he knew he was prone to do, the fact was that she'd stirred something in him that had lain dormant for a long time: she had stirred the young man buried inside the older man. And he'd have preferred things to have stayed the way they were, thank you very much, he reflected, slamming the gate behind him with sufficient force to sound a metallic clang through the otherwise quiet evening air. He should never have gone to the bloody meeting in the first place. But he had, and now his day was buggered—and for the most insignificant of reasons.

Annoyed with himself, he made his way along the narrow concrete path that ran beside his miniature garden, past the silver birch, the kumquat tree, pruned and shapely, the Japanese maples, the azaleas of the rock garden and the low ferns whose fronds shone under the garden light. As he mounted the steps that led to his front door, he stopped and idly scanned the garden. It was always a satisfying moment, the tranquillity of the garden acting like a natural balm whenever he returned troubled about something. And the house, too, was a sanctuary, closing the front door tantamount to locking the world out. But tonight the greeting of the young woman still echoed in his ears, the garden's calming powers were wanting and he was aware of something or someone following him in off the street, entering with him and violating the sanctuary of the house. The young woman, the face, the voice. That, and all the little things he couldn't even begin to put a finger on, disturbed him the way a sudden gust can disturb a pile of neatly raked leaves and toss them into the air.

Suddenly he was a young man again, and all the dreadful insecurity of the young man he once was came rushing back to claim him. The snapshots of his memory were thrown up from that neatly raked pile of memories he'd long ago hidden in some distant corner of his mind where they wouldn't be disturbed. And, thrown up, too, in this general disturbance, the name by which he'd once been known and which he hadn't heard in over twenty years: *Spin.* He dwelt on the sound of it, both strange and all too familiar. Then he whispered it softly to himself as he stood on his doorstep, as if, indeed, he were greeting the ghost of his former self. *Spin? Is it you? Are you back?* The question was spoken as if it were addressed to a past that belonged not just to another self, but to another body, another man altogether, who had lived another life that he knew about in the same way that he knew the lives of characters in books. As though this, indeed, were the figure that had followed him in from the street. Uninvited, yet with an air that it had every right to be there. But it wasn't someone else. This 'Spin' belonged to him— *was* once him—and the effect of speaking his old name again, however softly, was immediate, its power undiminished by time. As he paused, fumbling with his house keys, he was suddenly quiet, jolly, incidental Spin again. Nature's gentleman. Such was the absurd power of the word. That, and everything else that had followed and which came in its train.

Once inside, he took off his overcoat and placed his fedora on the hall stand alongside an impressive selection of other hats—borsalinos, Stetsons and the peaked sports cap he wore at the races. The stand was oak, its dark grains and knots gleaming from years of regular polishing.

He had been engaged to be married soon after the war, but had ended the engagement only weeks before the wedding date. The act shocked both sides of the family and still divided those who spoke to him and those who never forgave him.

There were no mementoes of the engagement in the house: no photographs, no letters, no candles from the cake carefully wrapped in tissue and waiting to be rediscovered one rainy Sunday afternoon. All that remained of the engagement was the hall stand. They had found it one Saturday morning in a second-hand furniture-and-book shop.

Since then there had been a long succession of what he still referred to as girlfriends, even though it felt odd to be talking like that at sixty—his birthday, the previous month, had been a quiet affair in a local eatery. But he was always being told he was the Peter Pan of the university staff, appearing to his colleagues to live an emotional life that belonged to another time. The jar of pills in the medicine cabinet for the faulty valve in his faulty heart, however—which only he and his doctor knew about—proved the contrary: that Peter Pan does not live for ever and looks can, indeed, deceive. His current companion was a lecturer in Shakespearean studies, but she was now living in Brussels and they rarely saw each other, except on trips, one of which—his long-awaited sabbatical—was coming up in a few weeks.

Allen Bowler draped his scarf across his overcoat, glanced in the hall-stand mirror, smoothed his hair and stepped into the study. He was a man who read. Everything. Or at least he used to. These days he seemed to flick through books more than anything else. His passion for reading was once such that he could sit for hours on end in his favourite armchair and barely move apart from his fingers turning the pages and his eyes following the print. Some of his most deeply satisfying memories were of reading when his passion for it was at its peak. As a student he had consumed *Anna Karenina* and *Middlemarch,* one after the other, without stopping for meals or even sleep, or so it seemed in recollection. But the passion had gone and he was more of a browser than a reader now.

All the same, the study was where he lived and its walls were lined with books: volumes on the Oriental languages that he once studied and the literature he eventually came to teach. The works of Matthew Arnold, J. S. Mill, Austen, Eliot, James and Conrad were prominent on the shelves, along with a section devoted to an almost complete set of *Scrutiny.* At Cambridge he had attended lectures given by Leavis, and *Scrutiny* was a legacy from that time. Following the Leavis lectures, along with other enthusiastic young students, he often attended afternoon teas at the luminary's house. Many of the old hard-backed volumes, early paperbacks and autographed first editions dated from that time. Underneath the set of *Scrutiny* were rows of other journals collected over the years, and manila folders filled with newspaper clippings as well as correspondence he had conducted with the authors.

He poured himself a whisky and settled down in his padded leather armchair. The shelves contained the gift of literature, the solace of poetry. The right works that, read in the right way, could nudge the world into greater tolerance. Bowler had taught literature for most of his life and had come to believe in it at a time when there was nothing else to believe in; not religion or country or politics, or any of the other discredited faiths. And he had clung to his faith with the quiet desperation of someone who dared not look back on his past or test his convictions too closely. Throughout the rainy Monday tutorials, the repeated lectures and the dull departmental meetings, he told himself again and again that he was doing what he did best and that that was all there was to be done. At least, if he followed that simple philosophy, his life would not have been wasted.

Allen Bowler had arrived at Cambridge in the spring of 1937 and often joined his college friends when they played cricket, sometimes to look after the score book, but mostly to watch and chat. The company was always interesting, the cricket absorbing. He loved cricket. Not that he could play. He'd been laughed out of too many school matches to think otherwise. Perhaps because of this he loved the game all the more.

One day he had been standing on the boundary line, not watching the game but staring at the deep green of the oval, the correctness of the rolled pitch and the sun on the clubhouse where teacups and sandwiches had been set out for the change of innings. All the time he was idly tossing a cricket ball in the air, its seam revolving in flight, then falling back into his palm like Newton's apple. A fellow student who had been observing him suddenly called out, 'Hey! That's what we'll call you. Spin. Spin Bowler.'

There was general laughter along the boundary line and the name had stuck, become synonymous with those first few years at Cambridge. He had carried it with him into the education corps of the British army, when many of his fellow students suspended their studies to enlist. In 1942, after the bombing of Pearl Harbour and the fall of Singapore, somebody mentioned that Spin spoke Japanese and he was transferred to Intelligence, where he stayed throughout the war. The name was distasteful to him now, but, since he had very few friends or acquaintances who had survived those days, he rarely had the displeasure of hearing it, and certainly avoided remembering it. Until now.

If only he hadn't tried to escape that general, indefinable sense of restlessness by going to the staff meeting. He could have stayed home and passed the hours harmlessly enough in his study and might never have encountered the young woman. It had ruined his day, destroyed his equilibrium, for, with that encounter, with that rush of memory, had come the name. He poured another whisky from the decanter and saw the young woman again, standing in his doorway.

As he sipped his whisky, he lingered over her image, wondered again where on earth in the building she'd emerged from and played this odd encounter over again in his mind.

'Professor Bowler?'

He'd nodded, outwardly composed, but inwardly struggling to find even the simplest response, and so he left it to a nod and to silence, while he waited for her to go on. Her winter coat was open and she stood with one leg forward; while he waited for her to speak, he stared, suddenly hypnotised, as she shifted the weight of her body from one foot to the other. Dreamlike. As though everything out there beyond his doorway and his room had suddenly dissolved, the world was suddenly an extension of his mind and his mind was no longer his.

She had then given her name, which he had immediately forgotten, as he usually did with students. She was English—just visiting, she said. Chatty. Both oblivious of her effect, and yet fully aware of the measure of it: at once innocent, and all-knowing. Her eyes told him that. At least, her eyes told his instincts and his instincts had taken over. She hovered in the doorway, waiting to be invited in. He sat, reluctantly. And the more she spoke, for all the innocence of her inquiries, the more his mind took the counsel of his instincts and the more he was convinced that she was fully aware of this thing that was happening to him. But why? She had appeared at his door, uttered a handful of words, and he was suddenly thrown, stirred, tossed.

She was studying the depiction of colonialism in literature. They all were, he thought. She rattled off the title of her thesis, but he didn't so much forget it as simply never bother to register it in the first place. Besides, he was too busy trying to calculate her age: mid-twenties, not much more. She went on. It was increasingly the case now. Nobody studied writers any more. They studied things like colonies, and their depiction in literature. Colonies, she was saying, they're either shoved aside—turned into a footnote or a small-talk reference—like the bad side of a dream that the book doesn't really want to know about. Or, they *are* the bad dream from which a hero walks away, all the better, all the 'rounder', for the experience. What did he think? Even if his mind had been functioning properly, he still wouldn't have understood what she was talking about.

'Why don't you speak to someone a little younger? Someone who knows more about these things?' he'd finally said.

'Because they'd only agree with me. I want someone who won't.'

'An old fogey?'

'C'mon…' She grinned, as if to say, don't play the old fart with me because we both know you're not.

She mentioned Conrad. That was his field, wasn't it? At least, she was told it was. Spin nodded, vaguely aware of a thesis that he'd abandoned in mid-sentence years before and never returned to. And it was while he was wondering why, that she said she was only here for another few days and could they talk properly soon. And, before he knew it, they'd set a day and a time.

And then she was gone, floated away. His door was open, the corridor outside silent, no sound, not even the footsteps of the young woman departing. She had dematerialised as suddenly as she had appeared, but the effect of her presence remained; her skin, her cheeks, peachlike, had been near enough to touch if he had stood and reached out, and something told him that he could, for he had touched that skin before. He sighed deeply, feeling the sheer weight of his memories and suddenly he could see it all again, plain as day. Suddenly, he stepped back into it all, was in the midst of it; those days of overheated military offices with their sickly scent of bubble-gum, cigarettes and stewed coffee, along with the image of the windswept, desolate streets of a defeated Tokyo outside. That, and everything else. By which he meant Momoko. Momoko. And it was disturbing, or just bloody maddening, that even now, after another lifetime, he still couldn't bring himself to say her name straight out. Even silently to himself in the privacy of his study. The phrase 'That, and everything else' had first come to mind. Only then had he pronounced her name in his head, as he would have all those years ago, lingering on each syllable. Mo-mo-ko.

On a shelf in the corner of the study, almost hidden behind a vase, sat a Japanese doll dressed in what had once been a light-green kimono. Now, the thin material of the dress was faded and the amateurish dabs of paint that once coloured the face were almost completely gone, revealing the bare, beaten tin underneath. A matchstick umbrella rested across one shoulder and, although its rice paper had yellowed over the years, it was still intact. He imagined the young man who made the doll scurrying along footpaths and picking up matchsticks dropped by strolling GIs. He would have measured the success of his day by the number he found, along with the discarded tins, string and paper.

He picked up the doll, examined it from different angles, then turned it on its head. There was a metal lever underneath it and he wiped the dust from the mechanism. Constructed out of rubble, it was a marvel, a monument to its maker's ingenuity. Slowly, he turned the lever, completed two revolutions, then let it go. For ten seconds a sparse, single-string folk tune played in his hand and he was Spin again. He closed his eyes, feeling like a reformed alcoholic risking just one drink for old times' sake.

But the sudden image of a young woman with blood running down her chin intruded into the music. Her eyes stared directly at him, whether in reproach, pity or anger, he couldn't be sure. All that mattered was what the look said: *Now, you join the rest.*

Part One

Chapter One

The autumn wind was cold and the runway slippery with rain and spilt fuel. Giant American transports landed at regular intervals, avoiding the bomb crater in the middle of the tarmac, then slowed and queued to deposit their cargoes before flying out again. As soon as the doors were opened Japanese ground workers began unloading crates and boxes of food, clothes, munitions, paper, typewriters, ink and rubber stamps.

They worked quickly, supervised by healthy, well-fed American soldiers. Calls of 'Hubba, hubba' were heard in relays as the unloading progressed. In the middle distance a detail of soldiers walked to a line of waiting buses, their uniforms pressed and cleaned, boots and buttons polished. Their pea-green helmets shone like the oily water on the runway.

Atsugi had been a kamikaze base during the last months of the war. All around the edges of the airfield, the shells of Japanese fighter planes, bombed on the tarmac before they could take off, were beginning to rust where they had been bulldozed and dumped.

Beside the hangars a parked B29 was being repaired. With its silver fuselage, its graceful, curved lines and glass-nosed cockpit, it could have been an exhibit of the Bauhaus school, a pleasing combination of form and function rather than a machine that, for the last six months of the war, had fire-bombed Tokyo into rubble. A mechanic strolled across the wing and casually began dismantling an engine. On the side of the fuselage, painted in red, were the words *Texas Rose*.

Spin stood beside the transport that had just delivered him, his bag at his feet. He watched the Japanese workers, most of whom were still dressed in uniforms displaying their former rank. They worked in silence, staying stooped even when they ran back to the opened doors of the planes.

After an intensive course at London University, Spin had spent the war translating Japanese documents that had been relayed to army intelligence, or decoding German diplomatic messages. For most of the time he had been cooped up in a basement office near Piccadilly, watching the passing feet of commuters on the pavement above him and listening to the hushed conversations of the cryptanalysts with whom he shared the office space. Consequently, he knew the uniform of the Japanese soldier only through newsreels. From the darkness of the city's cinemas he had watched that uniform riding on bicycles, five abreast, along solid, British-built roads down the Malay Peninsula, standing in triumph outside Raffles Hotel and entering Manila. Week by week the newsreels followed their progress across a black-and-white map of the Pacific. The army of the sun seemed always to move under darkness.

He watched that once-proud army now as it ran back and forth, bowing and obedient, carrying cardboard cases and wooden boxes, gathering the rubbish and papers blown about the airfield. This is the way an Occupation begins. For most of the Occupation's soldiers it was a dull job, a bureaucratic procedure. Spin followed an American private across the tarmac. The United States flag, quickly hoisted above one of the hangars, was damp with the autumn rain and flapped stiffly in the wind. This is the way it begins, he thought. This is the way one country occupies another, almost indifferently. Behind him a plane landed; another, emptied of its cargo, rose from the end of the strip, over the cornfields and out towards Tokyo Bay.

Atsugi was over twenty miles from Tokyo. Spin sat with the private assigned to look after him on a grimy bus with most of its windows broken. The wind blew through in gusts and they lifted their coat collars. Travel was slow and they passed few points of interest along the flattened landscape between Yokohama and Tokyo. The young American commented upon them like a guide conducting a particularly forlorn tour bus. As they neared the centre of the city and turned off towards the Imperial Palace, the private pointed towards a large, six-storey building untouched by the bombings. Spin, gazing at the palace walls, turned when the young man spoke.

'That was the Dai-Ichi Insurance Company. It's headquarters these days.'

Spin looked around at the imposing grey building on his right.

'That's where Mac hangs out,' the private told him, referring colloquially to General Douglas MacArthur.

It was noticeable that most of the city centre had survived the incendiary bombings. Some modern structures near the Imperial Palace had suffered no visible damage, not only because the buildings were made of brick but also, as Spin well knew, because the Allied strategy had long been to preserve the palace and the emperor inside it. Even before the war was over, the post-war politics had already been planned.

There were signs of re-emerging social life on the streets: department stores open, the odd café and bar, and street stalls selling noodles, sweet potatoes, fish, dolls and trinkets. He watched one of the noodle vendors standing by his stall, looking about and shuffling his feet in the gathering chill. A young man—Spin's own age, he guessed—he was dressed in army trousers with a civilian shirt and coat. Six months before he might have been fighting on one of the islands. Or had he spent the war in the suburbs of Tokyo, watching the city burn and waiting for an invasion that never came?

He turned from the passing cityscape to the American private, whom he guessed to be no more than eighteen or nineteen.

'Where are you from?' he asked him.

'Montana,' the private answered, looking out through the broken windows. 'Butte, Montana.'

'You're a long way from home,' Spin commented, unconsciously slipping into a tone that suggested seniority.

'Yeah. Everybody's a long way from home in this place.'

'You like it here?'

'Kinda.'

'But not much.'

'It's spooky. I mean, they're such nice people. Aren't they? Nice folks,' he added, shaking his head and studying the backs of his hands. 'They'll go out of their way for you. Makes you wonder what it was all about.'

'The business, you mean,' Spin said casually. The young man stared at him, clearly puzzled.

'The business? Is that what you call it?'

Spin looked the young man up and down, not sure if it were merely an innocent question or whether he'd been ticked off. Until then he'd simply looked upon him as a fresh-faced kid, but, of course, he wasn't. Chances were that this kid, whose clear skin and wide-eyed stare implied an innocent world of milk shakes and Midwestern Saturday nights, had learnt to kill on the way to fetching up here. And the island war Spin had just referred to as the 'business' had been fought by kids like this one seated in front of him.

'Silly phrase, really. Funny how these things stick.'

The young man nodded without replying and Spin quietly contemplated the twists and turns, the economic imperatives, the accompanying intrigues, the human error, the urgent last-minute peace missions and the ultimate diplomatic failure that had brought a teenager from Butte, Montana, to the walls of the Japanese Imperial Palace.

He was pulled from his reverie by the bus's arrival at the wide roadway that led into the barracks at Yoyogi Park, rows of curved, temporary huts that looked like dissected soup cans. Spin mentally pronounced the words *Nissen huts*—they'd been everywhere in Britain during the war and seeing them almost made him feel at home.

The private showed him to his quarters. 'Welcome to Washington Heights.' He grinned, extending his hand.

Spin shook it, thanked him and watched the young man stride purposefully back to the bus. Then he lifted his bag and entered his new home.

Chapter Two

One evening a week later Spin was walking around the remains of the Shibuya district. Before the war this had been a busy residential centre, filled with restaurants, geisha houses and the regular comings and goings of trams loaded with shoppers and visitors.

Now most of the place was flattened, with only the odd structure standing out here and there against the sky. There were few lights and, it being a windless night, virtually no sound. Tokyo was a city of silences. There were no motor cars to be heard, no trams at this hour, nobody on the streets; only the distant hum of a transport passing over the coastline.

Spin stopped in front of a door that led to nowhere, an odd, surreal sight amidst the rubble. He stared at it, then started to slide it open. Where there had once been walls and a roof, there was now a clear sky of stars.

He thought it so odd that the door and the front of the house should have survived that he turned to take it in one last time before reaching the bottom of the street. He followed the tram tracks, listening to the sound of his boots as the heels hit the road, then suddenly he stopped.

How it came to be there so soon after the general destruction was difficult to comprehend. Perhaps it had simply survived. But it was definitely a restaurant, there among the gutted and flattened buildings. The flags proclaiming the name of the establishment hung above the low doorway and the distinctive red lantern that denoted the less expensive eating houses hung at the front of the building. The windows were made of frosted glass, rendering the interior invisible, but it looked clean and well lit, and would be warm inside.

After deliberating for some time about whether he ought to intrude upon that world, and struggling to overcome his natural reserve, Spin crossed the street, slid the door open and stepped inside. There was a brazier by the window, and although there was some evidence of damage, the room was as meticulously cared for as he'd imagined it would be. There was a counter at the front of the restaurant and a number of low tables. The restaurant was indeed small and could have looked cluttered, but the tables had been artfully arranged to convey the illusion of space. The owner and his dozen or so customers looked up from their conversations and stared at this officer of the occupying army, a pistol at his hip, as he slid the door closed behind him. It was ironic, Spin reflected, that having gone through the whole of the war never carrying a gun or firing a bullet, he should, after persistent advice, be wearing one now.

The owner emerged from behind the counter, bowed, and Spin returned the bow. Then the owner said hello in English and pointed to a free table. Spin sat down uneasily and ordered tea. Conversation slowly resumed around him and he was glad he had ordered in English, for he could now listen without attracting suspicion. The man at the next table was moving to the country to join his wife and two children. His friend was complaining about the cold. Everybody talked about food. Nobody spoke about the scores of transport planes that flew daily over the city, or the well-fed occupying army that had commandeered its best remaining buildings. Nobody spoke about him nor did they look at him. They simply carried on. Spin was not sure whether to be relieved or insulted. It wasn't as though he had been graciously accepted; he simply had the distinct impression that, apart from the attentions of the owner, he didn't exist. But, all the same, there was an air of reassurance about the place. The flag with the name of the restaurant painted upon it, the lighted red lantern at the front door, the ease of the owner as he welcomed Spin into his establishment, proclaimed that normality had resumed. Whatever may have happened had now passed, and commerce, communication, drinking and laughter could begin again. Indeed, two men playing dominoes occasionally broke into loud laughter and were joined by their friends, who were observing the game with keen interest. In the midst of the rubble the miracle of the restaurant appeared as an affirmation that all would be well again. The owner had beer, almost a luxury outside the Occupation army bases and, glory of glories, this man had fish. Fresh fish.

When the tea arrived Spin bowed, said thank you and took out a Japanese translation of *Macbeth* that had been completed soon after the Meiji Restoration. He sipped tea and began making notes in the margins. He had begun official work two days after arriving— interpreting, translating letters and documents—and had volunteered to contribute to the cultural re-education programme. When he had suggested *Macbeth* be produced for radio, there had been grumbles that this wasn't exactly the BBC, but they let him do a shortened version.

A voice addressed him and he looked up to see the owner bowing slightly before him and holding a square, wooden platter of sliced tuna. Beside the fish was a porcelain cup that Spin knew would contain sake. He had not ordered it and it was immediately apparent that this was a gift, a gesture of goodwill on the part of the owner. The activities of the restaurant had stopped and Spin knew that the eyes of everybody in the place were on him. Surprised and flattered, he was halfway through a sentence accepting the dish when he realised he was speaking Japanese. There was a sudden hush in the restaurant and the owner spoke again, as if his ears were testing what they had just heard, that the young Englishman—for Spin was wearing the uniform of the British army—spoke Japanese. And not just spoke it, but spoke it well.

The owner pointed out the various ingredients on the platter— the fish, the sliced ginger, the dark sauce, the green mustard—as if talking to a ghost. When Spin lifted a slice of the raw fish to his mouth, deftly held by the wooden chopsticks, swallowed it and pronounced it wonderful, the owner smiled and bowed, acknowledging the praise, and the mood of the restaurant relaxed. But when Spin casually asked how it was that the owner could serve such fresh fish the atmosphere suddenly became tense again, and the owner paused uncertainly without answering. Spin quietly reassured him that he was merely curious and the man eventually replied that his brother was a fisherman.

'And the beer?' Spin asked, clearly in admiration.

'That,' the owner said, with an air of mystery, 'that is business.'

Spin told him that the establishment was a marvel, and the owner backed off, accepting the compliment, and tended to the rest of his patrons. To Spin their mutual suspicions had been broken down, if ever so slightly, and there seemed to be a genuinely puzzled look in

31

the eyes of those around him, as if they were entertaining the hitherto unthinkable possibility that things might not be so bad. That the invaders might not be barbarians, after all.

The next morning Spin stood in a production booth at National Broadcasting. The recording studio was crowded with actors, and through the studio speakers he heard loud, stirring music that was like a Hollywood soundtrack and probably was. It was familiar, and he was idly wondering what it was when the music suddenly stopped.

'The Japanese people must now hear the names of the war criminals.'

A man in a suit, white shirt and tie stood close to a microphone, reading from the script he held in his hand. Behind him five actors, all formally attired in Western dress, stepped forward to a separate microphone.

'Yes, yes. We must know. What are their names,' they chanted, like a Greek chorus.

The narrator waved his hand dismissively, sweat running down the side of his face, and silenced them.

'Wait, wait.'

'What are their names?' the chorus repeated.

'The Japanese people need wait no longer.'

'Give us the criminals' names.'

'Yes, yes. Here are their names.'

In the production booth the Japanese producer sat hunched over a desk, watching intently. At his side his technical assistant monitored the control board as the disc revolved and the recording equipment gave off a slight humming sound. Behind him, the production assistant leaned against the wall, watching the actors, a clipboard in her hand. Spin looked around the booth and noticed that the woman with the clipboard was staring at him, puzzled. When he caught her eye she quickly looked away.

The recording finished. Spin turned to check the producer's reaction and saw the woman staring at him again with the same puzzled expression. This time, when he returned her gaze, she didn't look away, but spoke to him in impeccable, polished English.

'Excuse me. I didn't mean to stare, but I'm sure I know you.'

Spin studied her. 'I'm sorry…?'

'London. Just after everything started.'

He stared at her, puzzled.

'You must think I'm mad,' she said, smiling briefly. 'It was a government building of some sort. I've forgotten.' She laughed. 'And I've forgotten your name. I'm dreadful with names. But I am good with faces.' She leaned forward slightly.

Spin looked back at her, still confused. 'My name's Bowler,' he said. 'Allen Bowler.' She looked puzzled again. 'But they call me Spin.'

'Yes, Spin,' she said, a smile returning to her lips.

'And you?'

'I'm Momoko,' she said quickly, before being summoned by the producer for advice on a point of translation in the script. There were only a handful of reliable translators in the city, and often the scripts written by the Civil Information and Education Section contained curious phrases. One sentence seemed to be particularly bothersome and Spin, his brow still creased and puzzled, watched as this young woman rewrote it for the producer, making it more accessible to the Japanese listener.

That night, in an old five-storey building, the converted restaurant that served as a press club in the city centre, Momoko reconstructed, in astounding detail, the evening when they had first met over six years earlier. They had, in fact, met twice, but over time the two meetings had fused into one. Still, Momoko's memories were vivid. It was the first time she had accompanied her father, Toshihiko, a diplomat, to an official function and she'd felt quite adult. At first Spin had been bemused by her recollection, but her descriptions of the night brought it back to him. Yes, of course. But she'd been a chubby-faced teenager then, not the elegant young woman with him now who had, he learned, arrived in London with her family at the age of seven and left at seventeen when her father was recalled. During that time she got the best, the City of London School for Girls, where she was top in History and English Literature. Her English was as impeccable as her Japanese. She had—and this was a sentiment she often repeated—two cities. Two lives.

The sounds of the press club swirled all around them, jukebox music, laughter and shouted greetings coming in waves and sudden gusts. But gradually the sound of clinking glasses, the laughter, the greetings and the popular songs faded to a low hum as Momoko relived the past.

Soon, she was back in Knightsbridge, where her family had lived throughout their time in London. Her father was seated in front of her. With his pinstripe suit, his spectacles, his short hair parted to the side and his grave expression—a flicker of irony forever behind his tired eyes—he seemed to resemble the Son of Heaven himself. She closed her eyes and leaned back in her seat a moment, for the memory of the night she met Spin was now so clear. 'Why,' she could again hear her young voice saying, 'do they call you Spin?'

'My surname is Bowler.'

'As in the hat?'

'As in the man who stands at the end of a cricket pitch and rolls his arm over.'

'Do you play?'

'No.'

'Shouldn't you?' she remembered asking, then watching Spin as he gazed about him and answered without looking at her, 'Your name, it means peach. Does that make you edible?'

'I never said any such thing.'

Momoko glanced briefly around the club then turned and looked directly at him, the hint of a playful smile in her eyes. 'When you're seventeen, and a young man tells you you're edible, I can assure you, Spin, you remember it.'

It had been a small dinner for British and Japanese departmental staff, as well as their academic advisors. There'd been talk of the 'phony war', the blackout, getting lost in once-familiar streets, China and the death of Yeats the previous winter. At some stage during this the two interpreters had been introduced. Throughout the evening when they weren't talking he'd watched the delicacy of her hand movements as she lifted a spoon, sipped from a glass or arranged her napkin. She was self-conscious but assured. Her skin had all the clarity and smoothness of a young girl's, and images of dolls, of translucent porcelain and paint had risen in Spin's thoughts. And by the time the dinner had been completed he'd transformed her into something at once sensuous and brittle.

What Momoko didn't mention about that night was that she'd come away with quite a crush on this young lieutenant. And, if she'd got it right, this young lieutenant had spent the night trying to impress her.

Spin had little knowledge of women, and virtually none of Japanese women. But he knew enough to recognise that ten years in London had left its mark and that Momoko didn't conform to anybody's idea of what a young Japanese woman ought to be.

'Then my father was recalled,' she said, her mood darkening, 'and we came back to Tokyo.'

To lighten the mood, Spin told her what he knew about the club. It was even more crowded and noisy than when they had arrived, and he took pleasure in being able to point out some of the characters of that world: diplomats with their wives or mistresses, journalists, intelligence officers—both American and Japanese—as well as an Australian novelist with a notepad in hand, on to which, from time to time, he scribbled his observations. There was even displaced royalty from the subcontinent, and an assortment of dodgy types who'd been up to heaven only knows what during the war and were now seeking either to get out of the country or reinvent themselves as good, solid citizens.

Spin ordered drinks, and they talked about London before the war, finding points of common interest. Momoko reminisced about the old family house in Knightsbridge and speculated as to whether it had survived the bombings.

'Did you like London?'

'I loved it. I grew up there. I've got two homes now. Not that I saw enough of London,' she added wistfully. 'My parents were very strict about where I went. I was never allowed to use the underground or the buses.'

Spin, eager to share some of his life with her, spoke of his time at Cambridge. He'd topped Classics at Melbourne and one of the few departmental scholarships had taken him to Cambridge. Even though he came from a family of shopkeepers who had little time for books (there was no exchange more central to his father, who ran a mixed business, than the daily exchange of goods), his local minister had recognised the scholar in Spin and encouraged his reading. In time, it wasn't just the texts but the books themselves that Spin came to love: the style of print, the illustrations, the jackets and the feel of the paper. And the smell of them. Some were fresh, their pages crisp like a roll of new pound notes still smelling of ink. Others were pleasantly musty, the paper brittle, the corners folded by previous owners. These books evoked the sense of a whole community of readers, and to read them was to take part in a continuing and enlightened dialogue. The local minister's study was, more or less, a private library, and all four walls, almost to the ceiling, were lined with categorised shelves, the books alphabetically placed, as if the room, in its order, were a model of how the universe ought to be.

Spin, an only child, came to regard this study as a second home. He would ask about a particular book and the old man would bring the wooden ladder round, climb to the specified title, and while still perched on the steps give a brief dissertation on its contents and style. He would finish with an evaluation, then snap the book shut. It was at these moments that Spin learnt to appreciate the sound of books. Some closed like a dull clap in an empty theatre, the larger volumes with a weighty thud.

'I went to Cambridge intending to study Classics,' he said, his tone more serious than he really intended, the echo of old books still in his ears. 'I always thought that literature was something you kept for your leisure hours, but when I arrived there the best were studying it. It was an enormously exciting time. We weren't just enrolling in a discipline, we were inventing it.'

'You make it sound like a religion.'

'Yes, I suppose I do. It's hard to believe in anything now, isn't it?'

Momoko gave a slight shrug. 'I haven't thought about that for a long time.'

Spin caught what he thought to be a slight dismissiveness in her manner. 'You think I'm talking nonsense?'

'Good heavens, no.'

'Most people just live from day to day. Don't laugh, but—'

'I'm not laughing, honestly,' she assured him.

'But people could turn to poetry as a kind of faith. Is it so ridiculous to believe that reading a book, or a single poem, even—the right words at just the right moment—can make you a better person?'

Again Momoko noted that controlled but infectious fervour in his voice, that undergraduate bounce in his walk when he went to the bar. Those affected mannerisms she had noticed in London— the impatient tapping of the cigarette end and the thoughtful pause—returned to amuse her. Even the cowlick in his hair was still there. Only now he was far more practised and the mannerisms could even have looked natural, except that she had seen them when they weren't. He was a little older, a little subtler, but she was pleased to realise that he was still trying to impress her.

They leaned towards each other. Momoko was aware that she hadn't allowed herself to think in this manner, let alone speak in it, for a long time. They were throwing words at each other. Only words. Were they both talking nonsense? Probably. She told herself she didn't care. Spin watched the delicate gestures and hand movements he had all but forgotten and found himself remembering the dinner at which they had met more clearly. Momoko's hair was now brushed back from her forehead in the American style and held by a dark clip that matched her bracelet. Spin watched it catch the glow of the makeshift lights.

She had never been in the club before and was constantly being distracted. Twice she had turned from him while he was speaking. When it happened again Spin was forced to repeat himself, overcome by a feeling that his conversation had been far too ponderous for the occasion.

'Do I go on too much?'

Momoko turned to him and reached out a reassuring hand, catching her dark bracelet on the cuff of his sleeve. 'No. No, you don't,' she said, disentangling her bracelet, then settling back in her chair.

'You're sure? It's a bit of a pet topic,' Spin said, suddenly feeling awkward and uncomfortable, not sure what to say now, and convinced that her interest in him had vanished, that he *had* gone on too much. Laughter broke out from the bar and Spin watched Momoko's face light up as she smiled at the Americans.

Why weren't they laughing, too? He should be able to amuse her. But he hadn't and her attention had wandered. His earlier ease had left him and he concluded that it would be forced to attempt humour now.

She left when two Americans joined them. Spin watched her go, picking her way through the tables, and only vaguely listened to the latest talk the two Americans offered.

At home, Momoko stood by her window and watched a branch of a sycamore rising and falling outside in the street. It was casting shadows on to the wall of the building opposite, playfully waving like a cut-out figure from a children's book. She smiled. At first she wasn't aware of the fact that she was smiling, and she didn't know how long she'd been smiling for, but she felt as though it was the first time she'd really smiled in years.

Her sleep was restless and she recalled the evening in fragmentary dreams. Once again she sat with the young Australian, the noise of the club a background babble. A cowlick fell across his forehead and she woke briefly in the act of brushing it back, the warmth of his forehead still on her fingertips. She even looked drowsily about her room in her half-sleep as if he might actually be there, then fell back on to her futon.

Spin caught a lift with the two Americans back to his hut in Yoyogi Park, where he lay on his bunk, mulling over the night. It was Momoko's calm, a calm beyond her years, that he now recalled from their first meeting all those years before, for it was still there, as was the delicacy of her movements—the way she lifted a glass or smoothed her hair. At one time, when their conversation had flagged and she was watching the rest of the room, he had been free to observe and speculate. After studying the peculiar blue and green of her eyes and the line of her eyebrows, his gaze came to rest on her jet-black hair, shining under the press-club lights, tied in a bun and fastened with a deep-brown clip.

On the drive home, he had convinced himself that he'd made a botch of the evening and he fell asleep rewriting the whole encounter and wondering how her laughter would have sounded.

Chapter Three

The following day Spin looked for Momoko at the studio, but she was out researching material. As he stood staring at the rain from the cover of the doorway at Japan National Radio, a woman wove round the people in front of him, then stepped out on to the footpath, dodging the puddles as she went. Spin clutched his dripping umbrella, glancing now and then at the sky, waiting for a sign of a break in the weather.

The woman didn't notice him and he didn't recognise her at first. It was only when she was walking away that he saw the hairclip, saw the loose strands of hair falling over the back of her coat collar, and he knew who it was. He could have stopped her, he could have called out her name and she would have turned and spoken to him. But the awkward feeling from the previous evening overtook him and he stood still. He didn't call out and she didn't turn.

It was always the same. He always missed his moment. He stared after her, knowing that it was just plain silly to watch her go and not say anything, and he decided to follow her. He put up his umbrella and listened to the rain falling on the black cotton. But when he next peered out from under the rim, she was gone. He hadn't waited long before following her, and although she was walking quickly he didn't think she could have disappeared so soon. He slowed down as he passed the street stalls and looked through the doorways of the few shops in the city that were open, but he saw no sign of her. He stopped at the corner, then turned and retraced his steps.

In a break in the crowd he saw her standing on the opposite corner and wondered if, during the time he had been looking for her, she had been watching him. She seemed to be waiting for someone. Her navy coat was open and she wore a light dress underneath. One leg was forward and he watched her body as she shifted her weight from one foot to the other. Because of the way she was standing, he could see the crease of her knee in the folds of the dress, as well as the line of her thighs.

He watched her for a little longer, feeling more and more convinced that she was waiting for someone, then turned and walked away. She had been waiting, he was certain, and while he absentmindedly merged with the crowd, he reconstructed events in his mind so that instead of walking away he crossed the street and became that someone.

In her room that night, on a hilly street in Kojimachi, Momoko looked through an old photograph album. The curved Edwardian chair she sat in, brought back from England, was in need of repair and creaked when she moved. The one lamp in the room cast a dull light and she squinted, rubbing her eyes as she studied the images of that other world she'd known as a teenager; the back garden in

Knightsbridge that her father had patiently tended, herself in front of the City of London School for Girls in the deep navy blue of her uniform—a disjunction of signs, the uniform speaking one language, her face another. She was young, still carrying her puppy fat, and with an easy smile that was years removed from the weariness that she now constantly felt. She reminded herself that she was only twenty-four, after all, but it didn't help. She still felt weary beyond her years. The album contained page after page of fresh, youthful images, all set against the backdrop of a world that seemed far too solid to admit even the possibility of change, let alone upheaval. Now it was almost impossible to believe that world in the photographs had ever existed. And yet, meeting the Australian translator lent substance to the past. She turned the pages and looked at herself as he would have first seen her. At the same time she felt the faint shiver of that teenage crush as if it had never really gone away.

Momoko knew she was lucky to have a room in such a part of the city. In fact, it was a combination of good luck and good, American planning, for she now knew that Americans had deliberately not bombed the area near the Imperial Palace. And it was no coincidence that within days of the Occupation the finest houses in the area—and there were many—had already been commandeered by the officers, the families and the high-level bureaucrats who had been flown in from Washington.

Consequently, Kojimachi still bore all the signs of the affluence of the Meiji nobility who had built their mansions there. The head of the emperor's special guard had lived nearby in a large house with broad gardens. Expensive apartment blocks had followed and Momoko's apartment, a tiny, single-room affair, was part of one. Elsewhere, across the remains of the city, two, or even three, families lived crowded together in one room. People gathered tin and

43

corrugated iron, pieces of metal and steel, rocks and bricks, then loaded them on to makeshift carts and pushed them back to places that had been cleared in the rubble. These remnants were greatly valued, as was anything that hadn't been burnt or melted in the months of incendiary bombing that had levelled Tokyo.

She had watched Spin that afternoon, walking up and down the street in the rain, smartly, almost urgently, as if he had been late for an appointment and was desperately trying to find the person he was meeting. The day's work was finished and she was waiting for a friend, but she soon forgot about her friend and watched the young Australian who looked and sounded like an Englishman. She had listened as he spoke to one of the producers in the studio the previous day and noted that his Japanese was academic, a little rusty, but good.

His light, curly hair and pale skin stood out on the street and she had watched him come to a stop on the corner. She stared in his direction for a moment, then looked away, studying the sky and rocking back and forth on her feet. She could have been waiting for him, and any moment now he would cross the street, join her, and they would walk off together unconcerned by the rain. The next time she had looked, he was gone.

Chapter Four

You meet someone a dozen times, Momoko thought, and you can never remember anything about them from one occasion to the next. Their face, their voice, their name, even—nothing stays with you. Then you meet someone once and remember everything.

Wearing one of the last of her English dresses, Momoko sat opposite Spin in the restaurant he had discovered in Shibuya. He seemed to have barely aged since their meeting in London that first year of the war. His hair was still unruly, as she remembered it, and the skin of his face was soft. It wasn't a hard face like all those she'd known over the last few years, made severe by worry and constant anxiety, grown old from the sheer effort of fighting a losing battle. Spin's was not only a comfortable face that had never known defeat, it was a confident one that had never seriously entertained the possibility. It was her face that had changed and aged. She had watched it happen throughout the last year of the war when she worked long hours at the Defence Department, translating captured American documents. Most of the documents, however, had been captured in the early years of the war. There was nothing much new that she ever saw and her work was a waste of time. But, as unrelenting as the hours had been, the job had kept her out of the munitions and arms factories that were nightly being razed by American bombers. It was only when the end was in sight that she was plucked from the department and dropped into radio. Radio, she was told, would be crucial for the Occupation that was surely coming, and translators would be as scarce as rice.

When she was with Spin, though, she felt her tiredness dissolve, her muscles relax. There was an enthusiasm and liveliness in his speech that almost made her believe that something good could happen again, that all the good times hadn't been lived after all. He had energy and passion, she thought. The sort of passion that assumed there would be a tomorrow. She sat there looking at him, at his quick eyes, and hearing the almost childlike enthusiasm in his words and gestures. The memory of that schoolgirl crush, combined with actually daring to imagine what might be, was a thrilling and potent cocktail of nostalgia and desire that left her feeling more alive than she'd been in years.

But she also felt something else, something he couldn't possibly share: the experience of that last year of the war, with the constant worry, the weariness and the eventual numbness that was more than just physical. She knew things he never could because he had never been defeated. He had had his blitz, but he hadn't had this. He didn't know what it was to undergo almost total annihilation and then to submit to the unconditional surrender that followed it. That was a special kind of knowledge, and with it came a strange sense of moral superiority, an odd sense of power.

* * *

The bombings had begun in winter, the coldest anybody could remember, colder than any of her London winters. For over a month the temperature stayed below zero and during the nights the pattern was always the same. Formations of American B29s flew unchallenged over the city, first dropping the incendiary marker cylinders, the Molotov flower baskets that left the sky ablaze with spring flowers. Next would come the short, rhythmic bursts of thunder and the horizon would light up.

Then, early in March, on the night of the ninth, a date she had circled carefully in her diary, a strong wind blew through the city. She had waited throughout the day, wondering if the Americans would come again during the night, fearful of what the wind would do.

By midnight she heard the first sound of engines and a few moments later the flower baskets began to light the sky. They came close to the family home that night, but their destination was the industrial district of Fukagawa in the east of the city. For three hours Momoko stood at the window watching formation after formation fly over, until at last they retreated, leaving the eastern sky incandescent.

Shortly after three the door slid open and her father entered the room, dressed in a heavy English overcoat, thick trousers, a hat, boots and carrying a first-aid kit. Momoko turned from the window and studied him for a moment.

'Wait,' she said, then left the room and re-entered carrying a heavy coat and woollen hat.

Toshihiko inspected her. 'You'll need a scarf. For your face.'

At the front of the house her mother was waiting and the three of them climbed into the old Mercedes and drove towards the fires, comforting themselves with cautious small talk. But as they neared the flames they fell silent. Sirens whined occasionally in the distance as they stepped out of the car and the first rush of heat hit their faces. They tied their wetted scarves about their necks and stood looking helplessly at the scene. A lamppost flared suddenly like a giant match. A building exploded into bright, yellow flames, further intensifying the firestorm that almost scorched their faces even from where they stood. Entire houses ignited and became part of the general glow. The street was barely recognisable under the rubble, the broken glass, the craters and the splintered, burning wood that the bombs had thrown up.

Momoko glanced at her father, who stood staring into what had once been a modest working-class neighbourhood. He knew this district well. For centuries it had been famous for its timber merchants, warehouses, wharfs, and for its many teahouses, the speciality of which was eels soaked in oil, soy sauce and salt. It was also a district known throughout the city for its raffish geisha houses, where the geisha provided more than the traditional skilled entertainment. As a student Toshihiko had sometimes come here, drunk warm sake, eaten oysters and mussels, then walked to the hill places, as the unlicensed pleasure quarters were called.

He also knew it was an area familiar with disasters. The Arakawa, which flowed nearby, had often burst its banks, and during the earthquake of 1923 it had been the first area to be razed. If it wasn't flooding, it was fire. But none of that compared to the spectacle now before them.

Tucking his first-aid kit under his arm, Toshihiko looked at his wife and daughter and shook his head. He ushered them back into the car. Sparks and ash fell constantly. Momoko could just distinguish the bodies lying half-submerged in the rubble or sprawled on the ground. Then, directly in front of them, she saw three figures stumbling from the heat and the light towards the welcome darkness where the flames would no longer surround them. There were two adults and what appeared to be a child, all three of whom suddenly dropped to the ground as if they had been shot. Momoko was convinced they had been and turned in disbelief to her father, who shouted in response to the question in her eyes.

'It's the air. There is no oxygen. You can't breathe out there.'

He started the engine and they backed away from the firestorm, Momoko not taking her eyes off the three figures now lying face down in the ruins.

The next day she heard other accounts, like the story of the women on the gutted tram, still sitting in their seats clutching handbags and bundles of possessions, waiting for the regular stop. Momoko would later read about that night and be numbed by the clinical precision of the statistics. More than three hundred B29s had flown over the city, each carrying eight tons of the new fire bombs. By the end of the night seven hundred thousand bombs had been dropped on Fukagawa, ten times greater in weight, she learned, than all the bombs dropped on London in the September Blitz. In one night Fukagawa ceased to exist. And although it was impossible to count the dead, they were generally agreed by the statisticians to number more than seventy-two thousand.

When the bombers returned in daylight, their engine vapours trailing across a blue sky, their silver bodies shining in the clear spring light, entrancing, almost beautiful, Toshihiko decided to move to the country while the war played itself out to its inevitable conclusion. He loaded the car, its white paint now yellowed by the heat of the flames, and quietly slipped out of the city, driving south to Nara.

Toshihiko never saw Tokyo again. Never saw the streets lined with

Imperial soldiers facing the shopfronts and buildings, their backs turned to the roadways in deference to the convoys of American and Allied troops that had begun to occupy the city. At first the Americans Momoko met had been wary of the gesture, until she had explained to them that it was, in fact, a mark of profound respect.

In front of her Spin turned his glass in circles. He was telling a story, but she had missed the start, and she interrupted to ask him to begin again. She sat back, only vaguely listening, staring at his face.

When closing time came Momoko swirled the remains of green tea around in her cup.

'Next time I could show you where I live. It's in the posh part of town.' She suddenly looked up, smiling. 'Posh, where do these words come from? I haven't had a visitor in so long. We could drink English tea. Would you like that?'

Spin nodded and stared openly across the table at her, made suddenly bold by his uniform, the uniform of the occupying army. He knew that the directness of his look would have been impossible only a few months earlier, given the circles he was used to moving in. Spin didn't give women the eye. He wasn't that sort. He was, he knew, the shy type, the only child who had inherited his father's diffidence around women. In fact, when he thought of him, he wondered how his father and mother had ever got together. So, as he stared, he waited for Momoko to laugh and shatter the fragility of what he felt was a transparently silly expression of desire, for he was certain now that he wanted her. But she didn't laugh, she returned his look. Spin shivered, looked about the room and noticed that the small brazier by the wall had gone out.

Outside, they decided to walk for a short while before going their separate ways. It was late and they were the only figures in a still and silent landscape that was almost lunar. When one of the few evening trams appeared Momoko took it, promising to open the packet of tea, a gift from England, when they next met. She waved from the stuffy, overheated carriage, noting Spin's easy walk as he strolled away.

He made his way back to the barracks, once again mulling over the fact that he had only been with a woman on a few occasions since leaving Cambridge. He had always wound up being more of a friend than anything else to the women he admired, but as he walked through the still streets and the silence, broken only by GIs on leave, he felt that here he could be someone else.

At home, and in England, a pattern of behaviour was expected of him, and, even though he disliked it, he invariably conformed. There, Spin was the bookish one, the quiet one, always removed in people's minds from the world of romance and action. He knew he was probably viewed as more head than heart.

Here, he told himself, there were no expectations. Here, he could be someone else altogether and express feelings, reveal qualities, that had hitherto remained stifled. Here there were no constraints, no expectations, no patterns of behaviour to conform to. He could step out of the shadows and re-create himself. It felt possible.

Closer to the barracks, groups of GIs passed him, Jeeps and army trucks drove by. Overhead a giant transport flew out to sea. Inside him and all around him, something momentous was happening. Whatever he had been, however he had been perceived, was all part of a past that now seemed impossibly far away. He was like an actor who has suddenly stepped out of his accustomed role and felt the thrill, the intoxicating rush, of not knowing what comes next. And once he'd felt that, once he'd felt that glorious uncertainty, he knew that he was free for the first time in his life.

* * *

In her room, Momoko lay curled up on her futon under a quilt. Outside, a dark wind whistled over the vacant lots and somewhere in her sleep a giant yellow lantern tumbled over temple and palace like a truant moon at play on the currents of air, freed for the moment from all her accustomed gravity. Momoko clasped her hands together, then drew her knees to her chest as if she were drawing a lover towards her.

The next evening they took the tram back to Momoko's flat and she served him the tea she had promised the previous night. Spin, standing on the floor in the brown slippers that Momoko had provided, looked about her home. Most of the window was made of frosted-glass panels. Only the top section was clear and this was the only view on to the street outside. Inside, the room was a world unto itself and Spin had the distinct feeling that whatever lay beyond—streets, trucks and people—was an illusion and only the room was real. And although Spin was not a tall man, he noted from the moment he stepped inside that the low ceiling made him instinctively feel inclined to stoop.

There were a number of paintings and prints on the walls, a mixture of Japanese and Western. And just above a low, small table, a series of what he guessed were family photographs: Momoko in her school uniform in London, Momoko with her father, grinning back at the camera beside a young man in a white summer suit, Momoko with a short, squat woman he took to be her mother.

Still standing, idly wondering who the young man in the photograph might be, his eyes fell on a superbly lacquered sake jar.

'May I pick it up?'

'Yes.' Momoko smiled, standing beside him. 'Please do. It's not a museum piece.'

Spin turned it round in his fingers. 'Is it old?'

'Not very.'

'Do you use it still?'

But Momoko wasn't looking at the jar now, she was looking at Spin's hands as he turned the jar and didn't hear the question.

'Do you use it?' he asked again.

'No. It's a decoration. I don't know where it came from. An uncle somewhere.'

'So intricate.' Spin ran his fingers over the surface of the jar, reading the Braille of its design, while Momoko stared at his face. She was aware that he was speaking again, but his words were distant sounds, like conversation coming from another room. Then, without thinking, she reached across to him, brushed the cowlick back from his forehead and let her index finger descend, running across his temple, his cheek and down his neck.

Spin, halfway through a sentence, stopped and watched her hand as she reached out to him. Her eyes were steady, but they did not catch his. She brushed his hair back with the palm of her hand and touched his temple and cheek. And when her fingers slid slowly down his neck, they reminded him of the first droplets of condensation down the side of a cooling drink.

He could remember the first part of the sentence he had been speaking and could remember how it was to end, but there was no point in finishing it now. They had touched, and the words belonged to another time. Before that moment of touch he could merely conceive of knowing this woman; now he was about to. They'd crossed over, and whatever he might have been about to say was now irrelevant. To continue the conversation would be an absurdity, like clinging to the manners and speech of an order whose time had clearly passed.

They touched again, slowly, lingeringly, so as not to miss any of the sensations that the following seconds, minutes and hours would yield. They would touch and explore each other again after this night, but they would never again do so for the first time—and first-time touch was a sensation that lived only once, and fleetingly at that. Looking back, years later, Spin would wish, time and again, that he'd known all that as he dropped the sake jar on to a cushion and entered fully the closed world of Momoko's room.

He ran his hand along her thigh as she lay facing him on the futon in the corner of the room. There were goose bumps along her hip, stomach and arms, but she lay quite still, watching his hands touch her as if she were a spectator of her own lovemaking.

She didn't know where the impulse to brush the hair from his forehead had come from, and she had certainly never done such a thing before, but from the moment she touched him she knew that something in the order of things had shifted dramatically. She knew, too, from the look on Spin's face, that he had been unprepared for it, that she had surprised him as much as she had surprised herself. Suddenly she was watching the progress of her hand through the air as if it belonged to somebody else. Perhaps, she mused, she had spent the last four years of restraint preparing for just such an act. Just such a liberation.

Yet she could not help thinking of the woman downstairs who had watched her walk in with the British lieutenant, staring know-ingly at Momoko as they passed her. Spin had looked quickly over his shoulder to ensure nobody else had seen them. They were fra-ternising. When she impulsively brushed his hair back from his fore-head she was fraternising, and when Spin touched her thigh or ran the backs of his fingers across her stomach he was doing likewise.

But, without a word being said, it was understood that regulations did not exist in Momoko's room. Here there would be no laws, no taboos, other than those they invented for themselves.

Spin looked about the room, seeing it already as a sanctuary, feeling its seclusion. From now on the rest of the world could go hang, just as long as he could stay exactly where he was. He took her in his arms again, kissing her neck, and casually whispering some lines from Donne about the room being an everywhere.

The lines, he hoped, had been said as if this sort of thing happened all the time, as if his mind were so drenched in verse that poetry flowed naturally from him. But as he lay there, he realised it was true. The poetry he had once committed to memory had flowed from him naturally and spontaneously and now had a life of its own.

Momoko lay still and watched him. She had no doubt that, for all his nonchalance, he had more than likely spent hours memorising all sorts of literature so that, if the chance arose, he might impress some girl. What did it matter? She closed her eyes, smiling, remembering once again that this was what fun felt like.

Later that night Momoko moved about the low-ceilinged room, searching for articles of clothing. Spin watched her from underneath the quilt, speaking her name silently to himself and lingering on each syllable: Mo-mo-ko. He studied the fair colour of her skin, the two long, blue veins that ran like rivers into her hands and fingers, the fine, dark hair that he knew curled out from the coffee-brown skin around her nipples, the flat of her stomach, the dark dot of her navel and the black, matted hair of her sex as she turned and faced him, dressing gown in hand.

I know that body now, he said to himself as he recalled the feel of her calf and the curve of her back. He knew it now and, he mused, each day he would make new discoveries, revaluing the sense of touch which he had never thought that much about before. Before Momoko, that is.

He had somebody. For the first time in his life Spin had somebody. She was his. In the following weeks, as he went about his daily affairs, translating proposals on agricultural reform and the standing of postwar Japanese industry, or examining documents suggesting the possibility of a national rice shortage that coming winter, he would occasionally stop and stare out of the window, knowing that for the first time in his life there was somebody to go to when the work was finished. It was an utterly new feeling that would often cause him to pause mid-sentence, savouring the deeply thrilling knowledge that there was somebody out there after all.

From now on he would formulate his plans in plural. Over the next few weeks he would, for the first time in his life, use the words 'we' and 'us'. Even his own name sounded different now. He had always disliked the name Spin. Although given in affection, it seemed to him condescension. It wasn't a serious name. It was a name given to someone never to be treated with complete earnestness, who would remain for ever something of a plaything. Above all, it was the type of name given to a bachelor—somebody whom everybody felt sure would always remain single: who arrived at dinners alone and left alone, mulling over the evening in the closed silence of his car. He would have dropped it, but upon arriving in Tokyo two English officers he'd known in London addressed him as Spin and very soon everybody else did, too.

But all that was changed now. His name had taken on a new solidity, as his very self had done.

Chapter Five

Major Adler, formerly an advertising executive in California and now one of the senior administrators of the Civil Information and Education Section, was a large man, rapidly going bald. He flicked through a freshly typed manuscript as he spoke to Spin. It was, he explained, part two in the series of broadcasts exposing warmongers and profiteers, the first of which Spin had witnessed being recorded in the studio soon after his arrival. More war criminals would be named and further details of Japanese aggression revealed. Spin had two days to complete the translation.

'I want the actors with this script in their hands by Thursday. Can you do that?' Spin nodded as the major passed the manuscript across the desk. 'Then there's the music. We all favour that piece from *Gone with the Wind* here. Something stirring. But that's not your concern,' Adler said, indicating the door.

Spin worked for two days without rest and when he finally fell asleep in Momoko's room he dreamt, for the first time in his life, in Japanese. He woke feeling as if he were emerging from a trance. Light poured in through the frosted glass of Momoko's only window, hitting two watercolours—one a mountain landscape, the other a nude study of a young woman with only a dark bracelet about her wrist. He leisurely examined both of them, concluding that the landscape was well executed but cold, while the study was invested with something more personal. Its lines were good, and he decided that whoever had painted it not only knew his craft, but also his subject.

Below the watercolours were two stacks of books, a mixture of Japanese publications and hardback English productions with familiar imprints on their spines. From where he lay on the futon, he could make out what appeared to be the complete works of Tanizaki, as well as Auden, MacNeice and Eliot. There were other poetry anthologies, some forgotten novels and a few pre-war histories of Europe, which he guessed would now be sadly out of date.

In the room above, the daily sound of a man's hammering began.

'How did you get this place?' Spin asked, ignoring the noise.

Momoko looked up from making tea. 'We've always had it. I pestered my father to let me live in it when we returned from London and he did. The building survived. Not so many bombs around here, too near the Imperial Palace.' She looked around her. 'It really wasn't so shabby then.'

Spin watched the precision with which she unfolded, then refolded, the paper containing the precious leaves of English tea. Like origami, he thought.

'When did your family come back?'

She put the packet of tea in a tin. 'Not long before Pearl Harbour—well, I say it like that now. We were suddenly called back. I've forgotten what the official reason was, but my father knew what was happening.'

The water boiled; she lifted the kettle and filled the teapot. 'I remember those last few days in London. I rode the buses, looking at everything twice. I took the underground for the first time. Can you believe that?'

Spin shook his head.

'I did. And I took some sandwiches one day and sat by myself in Trafalgar Square and ate them. It felt like the end of the world.' She arranged the pot and two cups on a tray and carried them to the futon. 'I'd made all sorts of plans about the future. I'd already chosen Oxford over Cambridge.' She grinned. 'Then we came back and suddenly it felt like there wasn't going to be a future.'

Spin brushed her wrist briefly with the back of his fingers as she poured tea.

'And your father?'

'He's dead,' Momoko said softly, looking down at the leaves still swirling at the bottom of her cup.

'The bombings?' he asked quietly in the silence that followed.

'No, it was nothing like that. It was a matter of—' She stopped. 'I'm not sure what it was. He belonged to a different type of Japan. My father was that rare thing at the time, a Japanese liberal. You see, when we came back and the military had taken over and the police were, well, invisibly everywhere, it was like coming back to a different country from the one we'd left in 1929. We'd been away for over ten years. At first my father was appalled at what he found.' She put her cup back on the tray. 'My father was a very quiet man, even when he was angry. His anger was quiet, but deep. He argued with people, he protested, but he eventually withdrew. There was

59

no use for him any more. His type had been useful for a time, but his time was over. He was so deeply ashamed of everything.'

Momoko was silent for a while, watching the light shining on the watercolours. 'When the bombings got bad my parents moved to the country, to Nara. My father was from the area and his parents had passed on a lovely little…cottage, I suppose you could call it. He spent his time cultivating the little garden. He was a very good gardener and was pleased with his efforts. He seemed happy enough. One day, when he'd done all he could, when he'd planted all the plants and shrubs and flowers that were available, he brought out a special garden chair he'd made and sat down in the sun. He sat there all afternoon looking at his handiwork. Later in the day my mother went out to call him, and thought he'd fallen asleep. At first she didn't want to disturb him, but the sun was low and it was getting chilly so she prodded him, and that was when she found he wasn't sleeping at all.'

She looked down, holding her hands tightly over her knees, then folding them again and again. Somewhere deep inside her, out of public view, tears were falling. Eventually she looked up at Spin. 'You ask how he died.' She sighed and gazed about the room. 'Idiotic as it might sound, I think I can truthfully say he died of a broken heart. People do, you know.' She paused, then nodded to herself. 'We buried his ashes in that garden. He never said as much, but I think that's what he meant all along.'

When Spin eased himself off the futon and moved towards her, Momoko held her hand up to check his progress. That's very kind of you, the gesture said. Considerate as a lover should be considerate, but no. She would prefer simply to sit still for the moment and try once again to absorb the fact that the father she loved was no longer living and that her life would always have some part of it that would remain empty. She would be laughing, content with her work, happy with her love, yet she would suddenly feel sad and not even remember why for a moment.

Spin watched her from the edge of the futon. For the past few weeks Momoko had shared her thoughts, her emotions, her body with him. He was hers, she was his. It was understood, without ever having been spoken. They reached into each other, and in love they became part of each other. There was, it seemed to Spin in those first few heady weeks, no part of each other they couldn't eventually reveal. But here, before him, was a Momoko he knew he would never reach: a Momoko who would always withdraw from his touch, from his comfort. A Momoko who would always be a mystery.

They were daydreaming on the tram to Arakawa-ku. The winter sunshine caught the edges of the collapsed buildings and the bull-dozed rubble in the vacant lots. A group of children had taken advantage of the sun and were playing baseball on a bomb site, im-provising with a bat fashioned out of a tree branch. Spin leaned back in his seat and closed his eyes, catching the smell of fresh fish and vaguely registering the conversations around him.

The tram was slow and when it stopped and people brushed past him to leave, he opened his eyes again and turned to Momoko. Her head was resting against the window.

'How long?'

She opened her eyes and smiled at him.

'Not long. You'll like it there. It was never bombed.' She corrected herself. 'Hardly bombed.'

As the tram laboured on, the landscape changed. Grimy, bulldozed lots, burnt-out apartments and gutted factories, neglected since the war, gave way to clean, swept streets and small, almost ornamental lanes.

They stepped off the tram near a line of cherry trees. Only a handful of old leaves clung to the branches, but in a few months, he thought as they walked in the sun, blossoms would cover them like layers of snow and the pavements would be lined with flowers.

At midday they ate sweet potatoes and noodles on the steps of an old Shinto temple. A group of children sat on the steps, but when Spin and Momoko sat down they moved away and whispered to each other at a distance, occasionally glancing back at Spin, at the uniform of the foreigner, but not daring to come near. Sometimes laughter erupted from their circle and Spin felt that the sounds they made were different from those of the children who played in the bleak ruins or behind the disused factories. The sound of the children here seemed pleasantly musical.

Then the little group suddenly stood. A small boy produced a brown paper hat—like a GI's—and pulled it down over his forehead the way he'd seen the Americans doing. He took the arm of the girl beside him, and, much to the amusement of their three friends, paced up and down in front of them like an adult couple. By now both Momoko and Spin were watching, only Momoko wasn't smiling.

'What are they playing at?' he asked.

Momoko hesitated, sighing softly before answering. 'They're playing at being a GI and his prostitute. It's a popular game. They're all playing it this year.'

Spin suddenly leaned forward, frowning. Momoko caught his frown and shook her head at him.

'No frowning.'

He laughed and his face relaxed again.

'They're just children,' she added. 'It's a miracle they're playing anything at all.'

Spin leaned back on the steps, watching the winter sun on Momoko's hair. She brushed his ear with her hand.

'Happy?' she asked him.

'Very.'

He was smiling at her. It wasn't a broad smile and it wasn't an open smile. It was, Momoko concluded, a contented smile. She grinned and he looked at her quizzically.

'What are you grinning at?'

'The way you look.'

'And how do I look?'

'You look at ease, soldier. You look at ease. I told you you'd like it here.'

'I love it.' And at that moment, warmed by sunlight and laughter, he could also have added, 'And I love you,' but he juggled the different ways of saying the thing so that it would feel natural, and by the time he felt he had arrived at the right combination of words, gesture and tone, the moment had passed. There would be other times. There would be time for Spin to tell her about this thing that had transformed his life and turned him from an observer of life into someone who lived it; for whom there was now a before and an after. There was a life before Momoko and there was a life after Momoko. In between something momentous had taken place, and when the moment was right Spin would tell her.

They rose to leave and one of the children suddenly burst away from the others, ran towards Spin and touched him lightly on the sleeve. Just as suddenly the child ran back to the security of the group. Spin turned to Momoko.

'They're curious,' she said. 'You're a conquering hero, and they want to touch you.'

Perhaps they just wanted gum. Spin fished in his coat pockets, but there was none there. He never chewed the stuff, but sometimes he carried it for occasions such as this.

Years later the taste of sweet potato and the smell of noodles would work on his senses, reclaiming a memory in the same way, he imagined, that Proust's teatime madeleine had done.

When he got back to the offices of the Civil Information and Education Section Spin found a Captain Boswell waiting to meet him. During the drive back to the barracks Boswell outlined the schedule for the following couple of weeks. Spin had been amused to learn his name, half-fancying himself as a latter-day Johnson with the affable Boswell by his side.

'We're going on a school raid into the country, day after next,' the captain yelled, the wind fanning his face.

'Why?' Spin asked as they drove down the tramlines.

'School teachers,' Boswell sniffed. 'They're still fighting the war. Especially out in the sticks. I don't trust 'em. Never have. Who do you think taught all this Nazi stuff in the first place?' He tapped his temple with his free hand. 'In their heads they're medieval. Like the whole fucking country.'

They slowed to negotiate a series of potholes in the road.

'What do we look for?'

'Guns. Spare parts. Ammunition. Grenades. You name it.' Boswell swerved to avoid a particularly large hole in the road. 'But we'll do the looking. You do the talking—and the listening. Especially when they think you're not listening.'

Later, lying on his bunk, Spin could hear a group of GIs talking to children and handing out sticks of gum, the children speaking the only approximations of English they knew, 'Gumu, Joe. Gumu.'

Over the sound of two languages mingling, Spin considered the factors that had brought him to this place.

He had come home from school one day—his parents, wanting him to have the privileges they never did, had sent him to a famous private school in the heart of the city—dropped his bag on to the polished floor of the shop and waited as his father took one of the large jars from the counter and offered him liquorice. Spin had just turned thirteen and was a fish out of water at the elite, expensive school. He found it impossible to make friends and spent most of his lunchtimes reading. He glumly chewed the sweet, but kept his misery to himself.

Sometime, during one of those long, lonely lunchtimes, however, he'd conceived the notion that the trick was not so much to be liked as to have something no one else did. To be interesting—needed, even. Then one day he came across a magazine advertisement for a sea cruise promising discovery of the 'mysterious Orient'. It pictured a woman dressed in a light-green kimono kneeling in a rock garden, a waterfall tumbling behind her. This, he intuitively recognised, was new, different. Apart from his aunt having a penfriend in a place called Osaka, he knew nothing of Japan.

He made inquiries, and by the following Saturday morning was sitting in Japanese classes at MacRobertson Girls High in South Melbourne. It was, he later came to realise, a precociously mature decision for a thirteen-year-old, but it had seemed perfectly natural at the time. This accomplishment would be something that he, and nobody else at the school, had. It would mark him out as different. Interesting. He would no longer be the dull, quiet boy from a shopkeeper's family who played no sport. He would be the boy who spoke Japanese.

Every Saturday morning his tram took him past Albert Park

Lake, where crowds would be queuing to enter the football ground while he was mentally reciting Japanese phrases and memorising the characters. By the time he was nineteen he had entered Melbourne University where, alongside Classics, he continued his Japanese as part of an extension programme. His fascination with a foreign culture he had never experienced, a country he had never seen, continued and intensified like a long, chaste courtship.

Spin lounged back on his bunk, clasping his hands behind his head, contemplating what in life constituted an accident, what was by design and what happened 'accidentally on purpose'. It seemed odd that so much should result from the simple act of reading a travel advertisement. The decision had brought him no friends, and to the students of Melbourne Grammar he had simply remained the dull, quiet boy from a shopkeeper's family who played no sport. But what did it matter now? His chosen path had finally led to this country, this city, this bunk. His decision had eventually come good, for there was somebody out there after all.

Chapter Six

Momoko was laughing in the last of the afternoon sun, laughing at nothing in particular, doing the things she hadn't done since before the war. She was leaning against one of the wooden bridges that forded the moat and led into the Imperial Palace gardens. As she looked down into the moat she noted with amusement the overfed fish, staring up at her, mouths gaping for food. Some things were constant. The fish had lived on, oblivious of the war, the fall of imperial rule, the bombings, the fire and death. They had come through it all—and so had she. She drew breath, contemplating that single, extraordinary fact. Thousands had died, and she had lived. Life was all the more precious for it, she thought, as she stood smiling down into the moat, and swore not to forget that. Behind her, the trees of the eastern garden of the Palace swayed gently in the breeze. Spin's camera clicked as she laughed again and the winter sun lit her hair, black like the feathers of a crow.

Spin pocketed his camera, she took his arm and they strolled off through the debris of the city to find a tram. Occasionally people stared at them, their disapproval barely concealed. Mostly, people looked the other way as if Momoko and Spin didn't exist. It was odd, then, to feel innocent, but she did. If a little of her innocence had survived everything, why not? They were lovers, after all, she told herself. Lovers. And in spite of everything, like all lovers, they carried their innocence with them wherever they went. They strode through the wreckage to the tram that would take them back to the sanctuary of her room, where they would forget about everything and live every moment for the gift it was.

At the tram stop they watched as a GI gave a chocolate bar to a man wearing an old, dark suit that had probably once been his best, who was clearly overwhelmed by the offering. He bowed repeatedly to the soldier as he expressed his gratitude.

'Thank you, awfully,' he said. 'Thank you, awfully.'

But the GI couldn't understand and the man continued, bowing, smiling and thanking him. Eventually, seeing the GI's perplexity, the man stopped bowing, dipped into his pocket and produced what Momoko knew from the cover to be a popular English phrase book. Still smiling, the man opened the book and pointed to the relevant phrase.

'Thank you, awfully!' the man said again.

The GI grinned, at last understanding. 'Don't mention it, old sport,' he said, affecting an upper-class English accent.

The man put the phrase book back in his pocket and the GI backed away, waving to him. Momoko and Spin crammed into their carriage, and as the tram started up Momoko looked back and saw that the man was still waving to his benefactor, his lips still moving as he stubbornly endeavoured to master that awkward foreign phrase.

* * *

In her room, once again, Spin gazed at the sleeping Momoko. Every day he made a new discovery about her, like the feel of the dark hairs at the base of her spine. When Momoko dozed off after their lovemaking, Spin would always sit up, staring at her and marvelling at the novelty of it all.

So this is what a lover does, he thought. He sits in an unfamiliar room, on a dishevelled bed, watching the other sleep. He allowed his gaze to shift to the intricately carved wooden chest, which he knew contained Momoko's accumulated memorabilia. He contemplated the clothes he had only ever seen before in public, now revealed in their private ease, hanging from the door, draped on the only chair in the room or unapologetically lying on the tatami floor where they had been dropped a few hours before. A lover notices the little things, he mused, like the frayed lining of a dress mended with contrasting cotton, the safety pin in place of the missing button, the make-up tumbling from a small cosmetics bag on the floor. He is privileged to see the reality behind the performance, to go backstage to witness the shedding of character, and to see the mirror by which she dresses before assuming that character again.

Other people would only ever know the things she chose to let them know, whereas Spin knew all of this. He had pierced the world of appearances and had entered the private reality beneath. He was a lover.

Beside him, Momoko stirred and rolled over on the futon, mumbling a word in Japanese that he couldn't understand. She had no sooner turned over than she was breathing in the slow, regular rhythms of sleep again.

Spin wondered for a moment what the word might have been, shrugged his shoulders and turned his attention back to the room.

He took nothing in it for granted. The details were all important and needed to be filed away for that inevitable day when the room, everything it contained, and all that had taken place inside its walls became a memory. As he looked about him, he was mindful of the fact that he had never been happier and would possibly never be this happy again. All of which made his happiness bittersweet. He was Donne greeting the good morrow and he whispered the lines from the poem to himself, very slowly and deliberately, luxuriating in their richness as if he were writing rather than reciting the words, and the act of remembering tantamount to creating them. The words were his. He was Donne. Why not?

Quietly, without disturbing Momoko, Spin rolled off the futon and began dressing by the rice-paper lamp while staring idly at the group of family photographs: Momoko in her uniform, with her father, with both her parents, with her mother. He looked at the four portraits again. Then again. Odd. The photograph of Momoko and the young man in a summer suit was gone. Spin had merely assumed the young man to be a cousin or a family friend, but then why take his photograph down from the wall? Why replace it? Unless the young man was something more than that. No, he smiled to himself, she was just bored with the usual photographs and had decided to rearrange them like people do. He was buckling his belt when Momoko awoke. She peered at him through sleep-blurred eyes.

'You're leaving already?'

He looked down and smiled. 'It's late.'

'Why didn't you tell me?' Checking the clock by the futon, she rolled on to her back, yawning. Spin watched her, knowing she would be sleepy and warm under the quilt, and longed to stroke her skin once more and feel the heat it radiated before leaving. She turned her gaze towards him, a mock-look of childish indignation on her face.

'You should have woken me.'

'Why?' He smiled. 'You were happy. I was happy. Why disturb things?'

'What were you doing?'

'Looking.'

'At what?'

'You. The room. Everything.'

Momoko swivelled off the futon and slipped into her dressing gown. 'You know you're going away tomorrow. You should have woken me. And don't tell me I was happy asleep. You can't be happy or unhappy when you're sleeping. You're just sleeping.'

She secured the waist of her gown and brushed her hair back with her fingers. Spin wanted to ask her about the photograph, but couldn't muster a casual tone so he let it be. Instead, he watched her hair fall back across her eyes and felt an ache in his heart. He put an arm around her as they walked to the doorway, where he put on his boots.

'Thank you for a lovely day.' She grinned, a smile in her eyes like that of a comic privately enjoying a joke just before telling it. 'Thank you, awfully!'

He kissed her and brushed her lips with his fingers. Momoko slid the door open for him and stood shivering in the evening chill as he went downstairs. When he had gone she closed the door behind her and touched her lips lightly where his fingers had been as she studied the family portraits, impassively staring back from the wall on the other side of the room.

It was an icy night and all along the seemingly numberless platforms of Tokyo Station—which looked to Spin like a city unto itself—families, groups and solitary travellers huddled under blankets or wrapped themselves in their coats, waiting for trains that were already days late. Spin, Captain Boswell and two GIs picked their way through the crowd, the Americans leading the way and ignoring the children who ran up to them.

There was a special carriage waiting and the four of them stepped on to it with the eyes of the platform following them. Spin had expected a battered carriage, something like the bus that had taken him from Atsugi to Yoyogi that first day, but it was in excellent condition. And far from being cold and draughty, the compartment was overheated and stuffy. They sat, opening their greatcoats and turning their collars down.

Boswell passed around a flask of whisky before they retired to their bunks. Throughout the night, on the slow journey to Kyoto where they would connect with their train to Nara, ice gathered on the windows, and whenever the train stopped, Spin would be woken by the sound of voices and running feet along one dark platform after another. But they were always distant voices, comfortably removed from him. And when any of the civilian travellers came too near their carriage, Spin would hear the guard who looked after their compartment saying, 'Americans only, Americans only,' and the noise would retreat.

In the morning it was sunny. As they pulled into Nara on a small, rattling train, they saw a town untouched by war, as though word of it had never filtered through. The buildings, most of which were wooden and coloured with the same dark-brown stain, were undamaged. Snow rested on the roofs of the shops and temples, as well as over the gardens of the town. It seemed impossible that the town had ever been at war, and as the four men drove through the small main street in an army Jeep Spin noticed that all its shops were open.

When they stopped outside one shop to check their bearings, he admired the care with which the windows and doors had been polished. Images of his father's shop returned to him, the faint scent of packaged teas, the sweet smell of the lolly jars that lined the counter and the suggestion of kerosene fumes on cold days. As Spin stared at the shop the door slid open and the owner stepped out, catching his eye, and the two men exchanged looks before the Jeep moved on. As on the day of his arrival, Spin had the feeling that they could have been a group of tourists, and even as they entered the school he had a vague sensation of being on holiday.

They stood in the gymnasium while the headmaster bowed and explained that the boxes in front of him contained nothing but sports and art equipment. Spin watched as two students overturned box after box of harmless articles: uniforms, kendo masks, paintbrushes and bundles of paper. When the GIs had finished sifting through the pile a group of students put the contents back into the boxes. Boswell looked at Spin.

'They've been tipped off. We're too late.'

The headmaster bowed again and said something to Spin. Boswell watched, irritated, then stamped his foot on the hard gymnasium floor.

'What's he saying?' he demanded.

'That there's nothing here,' Spin replied.

'He's a liar.'

Boswell looked from the headmaster back to Spin. 'They'll smile and they'll bow,' he said, in a knowing voice, 'but don't be fooled by any of it. They're thinking something quite different from what they're saying.' He paused, then threw a chequered Go board on to the floor. 'Scratch the surface with this crowd and you're back to the Dark Ages. Believe me, I know.' Then, quietly, without show, he touched the revolver at his hip. 'I've had this thing since '43. I don't let it out of my sight. You've gotta get past all the bowing and smiles and nice manners with these people and get *underneath*.' He tapped Spin's shoulder. 'Underneath.'

For the next three hours Boswell, the two GIs and a small group of students upturned every crate and opened every cupboard and box in the school, but there were no arms or militarist literature to be found in any of them.

They left without speaking any further to the headmaster, and on the way back through the town Spin sat quietly in the Jeep listening to the arguments about the afternoon's raid. They passed a young woman in the street, her hair brushed back and pinned up, and his mind moved to Momoko, wondering what she was doing. He noted the fading afternoon light, checked his watch and calculated that she would soon be leaving work for home. And as they pulled up at a requisitioned hotel near the station he wondered where her parents' house might be.

A little while later he strolled round a pond close to the temple. The light was fading, lamps had been lit in the houses surrounding the lake and daubs of red and yellow light played on its waters. Three of the deer that had wandered around the town for centuries like herds of sacred cows huddled together for warmth near one of the benches that lined the lake. He was entranced by it all, but only half-happy, and as he walked back to his lodgings, he swore that he would return to this place with Momoko.

Chapter Seven

The grubby, unstamped envelope had been slipped under the door. Back late from the studio, Momoko eased her shoes off by the door, dropped her bag on to the floor and stood looking at it. There was nothing written on either the front or the back. She slit the envelope, using the letter opener she had salvaged from her father's desk.

The note inside contained only an address and a small map outlining how to get there. Momoko studied the handwriting, then slumped into her chair. She remained like that for some time, half in shock, half out of exhaustion, until it occurred to her that she might be imagining things. She was tired, and this could be a trick that tired minds played on themselves. The script on the envelope was utterly unfamiliar and somebody had made a mistake, slipping the letter under the wrong door. That was natural enough these days.

But when she looked again she knew there was no mistaking the distinctive style of the script that she hadn't seen for almost four years; the flowing, graceful lines of the characters, spontaneous yet assured, even when executed with an American ballpoint pen. The work of an artist.

The address took her to the district of Shinagawa, an industrial area that she had rarely passed through and barely knew. When the tram departed, she was left standing on the pavement with the letter in her hands. She crossed the tramlines and walked along a vacant lot, hoping to find her bearings, but none of the markers on the map were visible.

Eventually she stopped someone and showed him the map. He pointed back in the direction of the better-class suburb of Shiba and Momoko soon came to a corner with a cherry tree and a small shop, as the directions indicated.

It was a large, wooden house that sat at the very end of the street. Somehow it had survived the fires, as had most of the houses around it. The front door was unlocked and she entered. There was a line of slippers in front of her, and as she looked about it occurred to her that the house had the appearance of an inn. Unsure of herself, she called out and a woman appeared from a small room to the right of the doorway. Momoko bowed, spoke to her quietly, and was directed upstairs. On the stairs she passed a young woman wearing lipstick and American nylons. To her left at the top of the stairs an old man and two young children were sitting cross-legged in the corridor playing a game. They sat like figures in a frieze, and as Momoko approached the children looked up and stared openly at her. She stopped at the second door on her right and stood staring at it, afraid of what was behind that door.

Before she knocked, she reassembled the face that had departed over four years earlier, at the same time preparing to meet the one that had just come back. She closed her eyes, remembering a young man's face, a face with a joker's smile, one that could almost have been called chubby, with quick, intelligent eyes and a constant, mischievous grin. The war had only been a few months away when they met, but it was always as if the dark events taking shape around them had been turned to black farce for their exclusive enjoyment. Those were the last of the frivolous days before the war and they had been determined to find all the fun in them that they could. He was a young artist who couldn't stop painting and sketching, and she'd loved his passion for life from the very start. He constantly carried a sketch pad, amassing drawing after drawing of people and places, a record, a chronicle of the time, he said. While she stood waiting at the door Momoko spoke his name, Yoshi, and her body relaxed with the sweet, familiar sound of it. Then one day, she remembered, Yoshi was suddenly a soldier, too.

Momoko finally knocked, and stood listening to her heart while she watched and waited for the door to slide open.

For the first time since arriving in Japan Spin was eating steak. They were the guests of an American major stationed in Nara, who had provided genuine Midwestern beef fried in butter. There was also fine Japanese beer on the table and the four visitors savoured both.

Their host jabbed the air with his fork. 'They knew! Before you were halfway up the line they knew you were coming.'

Boswell looked up from his plate. 'Who would have told them?'

'The stationmaster, the guard, the ticket collector,' the major said dismissively. 'Who knows?' He sliced his meat. 'You've got to catch them when they're not ready. Don't announce your destination, just get on a train and let them know when you arrive.' He looked at Spin. 'And you should be watching as well as listening. You know what an artist does, don't you?'

Spin stared back, unsure if it was necessary to answer.

'He gets below the surface,' the major continued. 'Right? And if he doesn't he's not an artist, is he?'

'No,' said a puzzled Spin.

'It's the same with interpreting. Listen to what they say, but watch for what they don't say, for Christ's sake. You might speak Japanese, Lieutenant, and you might know their culture. And I respect that. But there are different kinds of knowledge. We fought them, and believe me, you learn a lot about a people from the way they fight a war.'

There was a silence, and it seemed to Spin that he was being unfairly reminded that he had spent most of the war in an Army Intelligence office in Piccadilly, not in Guadalcanal or Okinawa. "I'm sure you do,' he said calmly.

Boswell nodded and the conversation resumed, mostly about the camaraderie of the war. Once again Spin was the outsider, the bookish one who had spent the war decoding documents with only the camaraderie of cryptanalysts recruited from Oxford and Cambridge.

Momoko and Yoshi sat side by side on the floor, holding hands. Neither spoke. The afternoon was fading and the light on the wide, frosted window that faced the street was turning orange. Yoshi's hair was cropped, his face had thinned and the smile was gone. He was sitting cross-legged, something like a Buddha, in a white shirt and an army coat and an old pair of pinstripe trousers that would have been reserved by their former owner for special occasions.

Momoko had taken his hand quite naturally, like one child consoling another. There was a light and a lamp, but no heating in the room other than a small brazier, and at first his skin had felt cold.

Gradually, the chill had left his fingers, for her hands had still been warm from having been plunged deep into her coat pockets. They didn't look at each other. Thoughts and impulses were signalled through their fingertips. It was as if the act of holding hands and exerting the tiniest pressure was the most intimate exchange imaginable, an extinct order of emotion from a more innocent time being miraculously recovered.

She looked at her watch, noted how late it was, gently released his hand and rose. Her legs were aching and her dress was creased from kneeling. Yoshi hadn't moved. He sat with his head down as she smoothed the material. When she finally straightened she looked around the room. It wasn't large, but it wasn't small, either. It was a good size and in good condition, if bare—only a small table by the window, some cooking utensils and a bag of rice.

'What is this place?'

Yoshi looked up. 'It was an inn. There are no tourists or travellers any more, of course. The woman who runs the place took in tenants. I was lucky.'

'What do you do for food?'

Yoshi shrugged. 'I get what I can from the stalls and the black market. Last week I travelled to Sendai and brought back a sack of rice. I knew a farmer from the war. He sold it to me.' He moved his feet. 'It was very good of him. He could have made much, much more on the black market.'

The light in the window dulled.

'How long have you been back?' Momoko asked.

'A month. Lucky again, I guess.'

'And you didn't think to contact me sooner?'

'Yes.' He looked down. 'I thought about that very much.'

She turned a slow circle, once more taking the room in, before leaving. As she stood in the doorway she ran her fingers down his hollow cheek. She hovered there for a moment, tense with unspoken questions, but knowing that this wasn't the time to ask them.

'How we've changed,' she said in a low voice.

For the briefest of moments the smile returned to his face. 'Yes. How we have.' His face hardened again as she turned back to the stairs.

'Tomorrow,' she promised.

'You don't have to.'

'I know I don't. I'll be here tomorrow.'

Spin and Momoko mounted the stairs under the dull light of a bare globe. It swung on its cord in the cold wind that entered the building with them. Upstairs a door closed and they both peered up to the second landing.

A young man wearing slippers, a faded army shirt and a soldier's coat came downstairs towards them. He wore no hat and his hair, which had once been cropped, was growing back on top but still thin at the sides. He carried a hessian sack on his shoulder.

Passing him on the landing, Spin turned suddenly. 'What do you make?' he asked.

The man stopped and turned, his eyes darting from Spin to Momoko, clearly surprised to hear Spin speaking Japanese.

'Dolls,' he said finally, repositioning his sack. He stared nervously at Spin's uniform.

Momoko watched silently as Spin looked the man up and down and continued in the relaxed, affable tone of an interested observer, 'You're a toy maker?'

The man shook his head. 'A carpenter.'

'Ah, I see.' Spin smiled and pointed to the sack. 'What's in here?'

Looking alarmed, the man lowered his sack from his shoulder and opened it. 'My dolls.' He bowed. 'I take my dolls to the stalls and I sell them.' Momoko turned away as Spin bent forward and peered into the sack.

'May I see one?'

The man nodded, eager to please, and lifted a doll out. Spin admired the painted face, the light-green kimono, the carefully crafted use of discarded tin and wood.

'Look,' he said to Momoko in English, 'it's very good.'

She nodded stiffly, only glancing at the doll.

'We could buy one,' Spin suggested.

'If you want.'

'But do you want to?'

Momoko shrugged. 'All right, let's buy one. He'll be very pleased. Besides, it's cold here.'

Spin turned back to the man, who had been growing more and more uneasy as he listened to them talk. 'How much?'

The smile returned to his worried face as he thought for a moment before replying. Spin reached for his wallet and the man added quickly, 'That's a special price. It's much more on the street.' He took the money and carefully dropped the coins into his wallet, then retrieved the doll from Spin and turned it upside down. 'Let me show you.'

He wound a lever at the base of the doll and handed it back to Spin. The spare, clipped sounds of a Japanese folk tune played briefly on the landing. Then, taking his sack, the man disappeared downstairs and went out into the street.

In her room Momoko watched Spin unbuttoning his pressed army shirt. 'Why did you do that?' she asked.

'Do what?'

'Interrogate that man.'

Spin stared at her, puzzled. 'That's a bit melodramatic, isn't it?'

'You tell me.'

He stood still for a moment. 'There's nothing to tell.' His tone was now indignant, slightly hurt. 'I was interested. I just wanted to see what he had and he was pleased that I was interested.'

'Do you think so?'

'Yes. What's the matter with you?'

'It didn't look that way.'

'Well,' he said, peeling his socks off, 'it was that way. Don't forget, I come from a family of shopkeepers. It's in my blood. We understood each other perfectly.' He lifted his singlet above his head and dropped that, too, on the chair.

Momoko looked at the smooth, white skin of his arms, the freckles across his neck and shoulders and the fine brown hairs curled across his chest. He unbuckled his belt and shed his trousers and stood naked in front of her. Just a boy, she thought. What was she making such a fuss about? He was just a boy with milky skin whom she took into her bed.

Later, when they were lying under the quilt, drowsy and clinging to each other, she said again in a softer voice, 'You *were* interrogating him. Even if you didn't know it.'

'I told you, I wanted to see what was in the sack.'

Momoko broke into an impish grin. 'I'm in the sack, old chap.'

'You know what I mean,' he said, laughing, and looked across the room at the painted doll standing in the corner against the wall. 'It's really very good, considering.' He turned his gaze back to Momoko. 'Aren't you glad we stopped to look?' She nodded as she stroked his arm. 'It's for you,' he added.

Momoko ran a finger along his shoulder to the freckles at the base of his neck, her other hand still retaining the faint sensations of pressure and release, as if somebody else were still gently squeezing it.

They drifted off and when Spin woke Momoko was lying with her head back on the pillow, sleeping. He was free to watch her and dwelt on her face with luxurious indulgence, but somehow guilty, as if he were part lover and part voyeur. The more he stared, the more entranced he became, and knowing that he risked disturbing her, he lifted his arm slowly and stroked her cheek. Without waking, she stirred at his touch. It was then that he heard her speak. Her head moved slightly from one side to the other, and she murmured something indistinct. He waited for her to say it again, but she settled back into a still sleep.

Suddenly he was wide awake, looking at Momoko differently. He couldn't tell what she'd said. It was whispered, too soft to be heard properly. But, for no particular reason other than it had sounded as if she were addressing someone, he became convinced it was a name. And having concluded that, he speculated about whose name it might be. A friend. One of her parents. Someone from years before, all but forgotten and recalled in dreams. Perhaps, even, an old lover? And he had no sooner contemplated this when—in what seemed an instant—the image of the young man in a white summer suit returned to him. Had they smiled like lovers or friends in the photograph? If they were merely friends, why, he asked himself again, why take the photograph down?

He knew it was silly, absurd even, to be speculating like this, but, having brought the idea to life and toyed with it, he now found it difficult to dismiss. Within the space of a minute he had gone from contemplating her cheek, to contemplating her past. They had never spoken much about her private past, and perhaps this was the reason. She'd never raised it, and he knew intuitively that it was none of his business. He was suddenly convinced that Momoko had had other lovers, but what did that matter? It was the past, after all. All the same, he found himself thinking about other men who might have stroked her arms and legs as he did; imagining other fingers travelling along the contours of her body. And on that first night they slept together, hadn't she started things? She had brushed the hair back from his forehead and stroked his cheek like someone skilled in little tricks. She had. Of course she had. And with that realisation came the first twist of the knife, between his sixth and seventh ribs just beneath his heart—or so it seemed—warning him that her love might be less than total.

He sighed in the dark, annoyed with himself. So what? What a fool he was. What did it matter if there had been someone before him? Did he care? Did Momoko? Of course not. But as soon as he asked himself, his unease started again. Why would she whisper the name of somebody unless she still thought of him? And once again the devil entered his head and he shook it, shaking himself free of its madness. He was happy. He was lucky. He was in love. He looked up to the rice-paper lampshade on the ceiling above him. She could be whispering anything, anything at all. He smiled to himself and put his crazy thoughts down to the darkness and the lunar silence of the city outside. He was on the moon, no wonder he was thinking crazy thoughts. He turned his head to the side, his gaze lingering once again on Momoko. What a fool he was to even think such things. What a fool. It was all very simple. She was his now, and he was hers. He lay still and relaxed, remembering her lips on his eyes earlier that evening, and how she had closed his eyes with kisses.

After Spin had gone, Momoko lay in the dim light, wrestling with the events of the past few days. Eventually, she decided to wait until the right moment came along before saying anything about Yoshi.

Chapter Eight

A few days later Spin watched the morning sun break through and hit the leaves of an indoor plant somebody had left in the barracks. The night before he had given a talk on 'Sweetness and Light' to a small literary society in a dull and draughty hall, otherwise used as a gymnasium. With quiet passion he had discussed the role of the critic in establishing standards of excellence in literature, and on the role of literature in improving the spirit of the individual. He had spoken for an hour and a half and the small audience had listened politely. In dark times, Spin said, it was art that provided solace and light, and to contemplate rebuilding the country without regard to this was to condemn the whole enterprise to failure and the present to being a mere repetition of the past. From the walls, photographs of pre-war judo and karate masters looked down on him as he stood at a desk, glancing nervously from time to time at his notes.

He hesitated, rearranged his notes and sipped from a glass of water on the desk. 'Sweetness and Light—Jonathan Swift's phrase, not Matthew Arnold's,' he said, quickly clearing his throat, 'is a phrase that has too often been misunderstood, too often been used as a stick to beat Arnold with. For when the latter spoke of Sweetness and Light he had in mind beauty and intelligence, a "well-tempered nature, a nature not given to extremes".' Here Spin paused for emphasis. 'Or violence,' he went on. 'A nature achieved, in part, by the highest possible scholarship and reading, for great poetry and morality are inseparable.'

Shuffling and coughing in the audience was becoming more noticeable and Spin, feeling his time was up, skipped three pages and finished.

All in all, he had been pleased with his talk and almost wished his old local vicar had been here to hear it. He smiled. The vicar had always greeted Spin at his house in the same way: cigarette in hand, smoke rising in the hallway, an air of satisfaction at having just finished a good book. 'It's amazing the things people will share with total strangers in the pages of a book,' the vicar had once said. 'Things they'd never say on a tram or a train, not even to a friend. But, in the end, it's just one story, and we're all in it. You see, it's all happened before. That's the wonder of this room…' he smiled '…it's all here.'

A fresh band of sunlight hit the plant in the barracks and dazzled Spin once again with the intensity of the plant's greenness. For a moment the spring green of the college cricket fields came back to him and he stared out the window, lost in a satisfying inner landscape. But as the clouds outside reassembled and the light on the window faded, he had the distinct sensation of being a colonial missionary suddenly missing the summer twilight.

The late afternoon, that indeterminate time between the end of the working day and the beginning of the evening, had over the last few weeks become the time that Momoko associated with Yoshi's room. When she left the radio offices she took a tram through the potholed streets to go to him. The sky was clouding over, but the passing view showed that the rebuilding was moving quickly and Momoko wondered what the city would look like when everything was finished. At least, at the moment, she could still imagine how it was. But a new city was another city. It would become normal and soon expunge the old one. In time, the Tokyo she knew would only exist in the photographs and words of those who thought to record it before it disappeared. Then she forgot the landscape. She thought instead of Yoshi and was suddenly aware of her emotions quickening, and once again felt the delirious anxiety of being nineteen and visiting her lover for the first time.

They had met in the summer of 1941, a year after her parents had returned to Tokyo. From the start they had done most things together—things that other couples didn't do, because they weren't just another couple. She carried with her a Western assurance unusual among the Japanese women he knew, and he had flair and a sense of fun completely lacking in most of the dull young men she met.

Yoshi's family was from Kyoto and they had been introduced when Momoko accompanied her father on a visit to Kyoto University. When it became clear that the young people were lovers, Momoko's father said nothing about it and remained silent in the manner of enlightened fathers, remembering sadly that it was almost two years since he had scolded her for lingering in a London cinema and being late back from school. Now, she had a lover. She had always been educated to be her own woman and, he told himself, it was time to stand back.

She and Yoshi had their own pleasure quarter and often, in that last autumn before the war, they would walk through the narrow, willow-lined streets of Shimbashi, with its latticed windows, past swaggering businessmen and hesitating husbands contemplating a night on the town. They had always walked as a couple, holding hands, an unusual spectacle that drew stares.

But there was another presence on those streets, one that let everybody know that their indulgences were frowned upon by the austere new order. The pleasures of the floating world—customers arriving on barges on the river under bobbing white lanterns, the flowery scent of the streets, the wine and late nights—those passing moments of sensory delight, were now clearly in contravention of the new dispensation. Uniformed observers moved regularly through the crowds in twos and threes, watching and warning.

One evening Momoko and Yoshi had been drawn to a small crowd gathered in front of a house in a lane. Soldiers were walking in and out carrying silk screens and tapestries; an old man, an artist of the district, sat in the doorway of his house and watched helplessly as the soldiers made a pile of his work. When a lieutenant, the officer in charge, took a box of matches from his coat pocket, Yoshi pushed through the crowd, protesting. The officer turned, casually looked Yoshi up and down, noting the style of his clothes and the manner of his speech, and framed the tone of his reply in response to the conclusions he had drawn about Yoshi's social standing. 'Keep moving, please. We know what we're doing.' The officer smiled, and repeated himself in firm, reassuring tones.

Yoshi moved forward slightly, challenging the quiet certainty of the man's gaze, then observed the two armed privates behind him at the same time as he felt the tug of Momoko's hand on his sleeve.

When the officer finally lit the bundle of silk, cloth and canvas, the old man raised his head and watched the images of courtesans and reclining figures, of life behind the licensed quarters of the city, succumb to the flames. Smoke was fanned into the air to mingle with the smells of fish and pork and spices. Momoko and Yoshi walked down to the river and waited for a barge. Although they did return to Shimbashi often after that night, their pleasure district was never the same again.

Momoko was not a woman who made friends easily. In England, even though her fellow students had been very polite, she was always the Japanese girl, and as much as she copied their upper-class accents and mannerisms—often sounding more English than the English—she remained the Japanese girl. In Japan, she had no doubt, she was the woman with the English manner, English clothes and sudden English turns of phrase. The women, she imagined, half-admired her, were even in awe of her command of Western language and style. The men, for the most part, were silent. She was never invited into the houses of acquaintances: it was as though she might be a disturbing influence, as if those liberal English ways she had so obviously acquired, along with the fashions and the make-up, might somehow rub off on the women.

She was aware of her difference wherever she went. Then she had met Yoshi, and he was different, too. He, too, had few friends, and in those last months before the war they continually drew stares on the streets, Yoshi in his bohemian attire and Momoko in her English dresses. Now, whenever she walked in the street alongside Spin, she felt those stares again and heard their silent censure.

The tram laboured its way to Yoshi's suburb. She felt her anticipation gather, then intensify, as she mounted the stairs for what had now become their weekday rendezvous with the past.

In his room she listened to the slippered sounds of his footsteps as he came up the stairs from the communal kitchen below. She turned from the window as he entered the room, carrying an army saucepan filled with boiling water, the steam of which trailed like an aeroplane's vapour as he crossed the room. She noted that his hair was growing back and that it would soon need cutting.

'It's not real tea. But it's moist and warm.'

She knelt on the floor with him, taking his hand in hers.

'When we travelled to Kyoto to tell your parents about us,' she began, 'we went to the cinema the night before. Do you remember?'

'I do. Quite clearly.'

'What did we see?'

He looked at her for a moment, smiling. 'You don't remember?'

She shook her head. 'I was thinking of it this afternoon on the tram. I remember what a warm night it was and how hot the theatre felt. I remember the striped tie you wore for a joke, like an English public-school boy. But I don't remember the picture. What was it?'

He grinned, deliberately teasing out the moment. '*Smith Goes City,*' he said finally, giving the film its Japanese title.

She looked at him, baffled. 'What?'

'No memory of it?'

'None.'

His grin grew wider as he broke into English. 'How about *Mr Deeds Goes to Town?*'

She burst into laughter and he joined her. At some stage during the journey on the tram back to her place she would note that this was the day they had laughed.

'Why ever did we see it?'

He shrugged his shoulders. 'For fun.'

She looked down for a moment. 'Yes, fun was hard to find.'

'I liked it,' he said, pouring the tea. 'It was very amusing.'

Yes, she thought. This was the old Yoshi.

They were both silent then, Momoko looking about the plain white walls of the room and remembering when Yoshi had painted her. She had posed as a courtesan, her face turned from the canvas so she wouldn't be recognised. How daring, she now thought. How daring we were. She had reclined on a cushion, wearing only a dark bracelet, the weight of her body supported by one hand as if it were a classical pillar of white marble.

But her memories were interrupted by Yoshi handing her a cup of tea, poured from the army saucepan.

'What do you do during the day?' she asked. 'Do you get about much?'

'Sometimes. When I hear there's work available. Every couple of weeks I go back to Kyoto and my parents give me a little money to help me out.' He clicked his tongue. 'We're lucky, you and I.'

'When will you start painting again?'

He drummed his fingers on the small table he had recently acquired. 'I'm not going to.'

'What?'

'I'm not painting any more.'

Momoko scrutinised him, as if he had suddenly become a stranger. 'Why not?'

He caught her look and shifted uneasily on the floor before answering. 'It's not important to me any more.'

'But you can't just stop,' she countered, her voice rising.

His calm suddenly broke and he spoke with an intensity and bitterness unfamiliar to her. 'You expect me to just go back to the old life as if nothing has happened.'

'Of course not.' Her voice was almost a whisper.

Yoshi closed his eyes and was silent a moment, regaining his lost calm. 'Once it was everything, now it's not. Like falling in and out of love.'

She was amused by the comparison. 'When have you gone falling in and out of love?'

But he wasn't amused. 'It was an example.'

'You'll miss it. You say this now, but you'll miss it.'

'No, I won't. Once it was part of everything I did, now it's not—it's like an indulgence. Can't you understand that?'

She shook her head. 'But you were always sketching and painting. Everywhere you went.'

'That wasn't me. That was *him*.' Yoshi ran his hands through his hair, staring down at the floor. 'We did things,' he went on, quieter now. 'In the war, we all did things that make painting irrelevant now.'

Since his return there had been a forced equanimity in his speech, Momoko had noted, a tone that suggested he was gamely trying to pretend their world hadn't really exploded, that their old lives hadn't been completely shattered. It was as if he were afraid to acknowledge, too soon, what had happened. But now Yoshi had said the 'war', and this was the first time that a confessional tone had entered their conversation. Momoko waited for him to continue, but he didn't. She silently asked the questions she longed to ask, but couldn't. Whatever Yoshi had seen or done, she would have to wait for him to tell her.

A long silence followed. Yoshi sat, it seemed to Momoko, hunched under the weight of some unbearable knowledge. To break the silence she suddenly found herself talking of Spin.

Yoshi looked up, suddenly alert, and stared back at Momoko in the semi-darkness. She saw the anxiety in his eyes.

'He makes me laugh,' she said. 'He's almost innocent.'

'*Almost* innocent?' Yoshi suddenly grinned, but only briefly.

'Yes.' Momoko watched in half-shadow as the grin on Yoshi's face faded. 'Is anybody really innocent any more? Sometimes I can't believe anybody will ever be innocent again. But when I'm with him…' and here she gave a short, bitter laugh '…I feel like it's almost possible.' Then she turned serious. 'You're the only person I've told. You know what people are.'

'Those sorts of people don't matter.'

'I know they don't, but you know what I mean.'

He nodded, and let go of her hand. 'I know,' he said, absorbed in his own thoughts. 'But you must promise me something.'

She stared at him. 'What?'

He closed his eyes, exhaled slowly, and opened them again. 'You must not mention me to this man. You must not speak of me even in passing.'

'But why?'

He stared past Momoko to the window. 'This is very important.'

'The war is over now, Yoshi. Done. You were a soldier, you went to war and you've come home. There's no guilt in that, is there? Everybody went. On all sides.' A faint, pleading tone entered her speech.

He listened, letting her finish. 'Momoko—'

'Momo,' she corrected, reaching for his hand and clasping it to her mouth.

He felt her lips on the tips of his fingers, then withdrew his hand. 'Momo, this isn't my uniform.'

'What?' She looked at him, suddenly frightened. 'Whose is it, Yoshi?'

'That's not important.'

'Whose uniform?'

He didn't answer, and they were silent while the implications of what he had just said made themselves felt.

'I stole it. The man I stole it from was dead.'

'What happened?'

He closed his eyes again. 'It will take time to answer that question. And I can't now. I need time to think.'

Momoko looked at his hunched figure, then glanced hurriedly at her watch. Yoshi noticed.

'If it's difficult for you to visit me, if you don't have the time…'

She closed his lips with her fingers. 'I'll always have the time.'

He nodded. 'But you must promise never to mention me.'

'All right, I promise,' she said slowly. 'I won't mention you.' She moved to stand up, but he stopped her.

'This is very important,' he insisted.

'I know. You have your promise.'

Yoshi breathed a sigh of relief. 'Good. Thank you.'

He looked at her apologetically, aware of the difficult nature of his request. Momoko rested her head on his shoulder. 'Oh, Yoshi. Don't be a stranger with me. Don't be strange.'

She left him standing by the door, where he cast a faint shadow across the floor of the landing. Contrasting patterns of darkness and light played upon his face, making it momentarily unfamiliar. As if, for a terrible, passing moment, he could have been just anybody.

Momoko sat on a crowded tram, checking her watch, knowing she was late and that Spin would be waiting. Or, perhaps, had even given up waiting. She stared out the window into the dark remains of the city, knowing that she was looking at the past, knowing that one day it would have given way to some as yet unformed future, and wondering if she would approve of its shape when the change took place—or even feel the moment when it did.

Chapter Nine

Spin had let himself into Momoko's room and was sitting on the futon, waiting for her. He leaned back against the wall, smoking and looking at his watch. He had spent the afternoon looking at his watch, waiting for precisely this time of day, in this room. But Momoko was late, quite late. And he was still looking at his watch. She had been late a few days before, but not like this. He stubbed out his cigarette and lit another one, aware that time was precious. Momoko also knew that time was precious, yet it was now dark outside and still she hadn't come. Restless, annoyed and worried, he snapped to his feet and began pacing about the room.

When the door finally slid open and she stepped in, he looked hard at her, pouring out all the pent-up emotion of someone who has been waiting too long into two words: 'You're late.'

Momoko shuffled her shoes off, still mentally in Yoshi's room. 'I know. I'm sorry,' she pleaded.

'I was worried.'

She sighed briefly as she crossed to Spin and relaxed against him, feeling his arms fold round her. 'I'm sorry I'm late, and I'm sorry you were worried. But you don't *have* to worry.'

'I do, though.'

She looked up, kissed him and stepped back, smiling. 'Poor Spin.'

'I've been waiting,' he said, barely concealing the irritation in his voice. 'You know what it's like when you're waiting. You imagine all sorts of things.'

'I'm here now.'

He stood still, hands in his pockets, playing impatiently with some coins. He didn't know it, but it was a gesture that annoyed Momoko because it belonged, in her mind, to the GIs who jangled all they were prepared to offer the young girls in Shinjuku Park— their loose change.

He took his hands from his pockets, the jangling stopped and he held out his arms to Momoko. She embraced him as she always did, under the low ceiling of her room, and the room was still their refuge from everything outside them, but something was different. And he couldn't say what. Was it his imagination, or were her eyes avoiding his?

'You look tired.'

'I know.' She let go of him and knelt by a small kettle.

'What have you been doing to make yourself so tired?'

She shrugged, busying herself with the teapot. 'The usual.'

'Where have you been?' he added, trying to sound casual.

'Working,' she said quickly. 'Just working. We ran overtime on a long speech. All the actor had to do was read the lines out.' She gave a half-hearted laugh. 'You'd think that would be pretty easy.'

There it was again. She was chatty, she was light. She was all the things Momoko had always been, but something was wrong. She hadn't looked at him the whole time she'd been speaking, and there were silences between her words. When she spoke, he tried to dismiss what was said and listen instead for what wasn't being said, as well as noting the manner and tone of her speech—like he would if he were on duty. And, suddenly, he realised he *was* on duty. It was no longer *his* Momoko speaking. He had stepped back and was now paying attention to her with the eyes and ears of an impartial observer. Even a stranger. She was speaking to him now, but her words were distant.

'I was worried. The nights can be dangerous.'

'It's my city.'

'Is it?'

She looked at him, a sudden ferocity in her eyes. 'What do you mean by that?'

He hunched his shoulders. 'You've never called it that before.'

She handed him a cup. 'Well, it is. So you don't have to worry for me. And as for looking tired, I've been tired for years.'

For the first time since they'd become lovers, she just wanted him to go.

'I didn't think you'd be coming back,' he said. 'Isn't that odd?'

'Yes.'

'I thought, this is it. All over, she's not coming.'

'Aren't you funny?' she said without smiling.

He kissed her on the forehead and she held him for a moment. But when he attempted to kiss her again she spun round on the worn soles of her slippers and whispered, 'Please, no.'

He stepped back, checking his watch. 'Perhaps I should go.'

'Perhaps,' she agreed.

Her voice was soft with regret and Spin nodded. Everybody had their moods. Everybody had to be alone sometimes. There was no point making a fuss.

At the door Momoko promised to show Spin some of the old Tokyo the following night. 'That is—' she smiled '—if I can find it. Till tomorrow,' she said. 'We'll do things properly.'

But suddenly Spin found himself saying that he wasn't free the following night. This voice was telling Momoko that Spin was busy, was working late. A report that everybody wanted finished right away. Did she mind?

'No,' she said. 'No, Spin, I don't mind.'

He kissed her, she smiled once more, and then she slid the door shut. As Spin walked away he cursed himself for being such a fool, such a bloody, childish fool. But there it was, it was done now, and he would have to wait twice as long to see her again. But what played on his mind as he entered the street and walked to the Jeep he had cadged from the Americans, was the way she had said no, she didn't mind. For it was clear she didn't. She could have said it was a shame, she could have looked sad. But as he slumped into the Jeep behind the wheel he had the inescapable feeling that she was happy. And for the first time since they'd met, her happiness made him miserable.

In her room Momoko heard Spin's Jeep growl into life and slowly disappear into the silence of the city. That silence could be unnatural, a constant, nightly reminder that things weren't right out there and there was no point trying to live as if they could ever be right again. At other times, though, it was good to simply sit on the matting floor in her room and listen to it.

But not tonight. The silence only accentuated the rattiness of things and all the talk of the day kept coming back to her, again and again. Yoshi with his demands that she promise never to speak of him. How many times had she been made to promise before he believed her? And then Spin. Spin had lied to her, she was sure of that. It was a silly lie, a pointless lie. It was the kind of childish lie she'd told her classmates at school in London when all the time she knew she was desperate for company and desperate to go to whatever party she'd been invited to. The kind of lie she told when she was feeling left out of things, when she was sure she'd only been spoken to out of obligation. And so, to show them all that she, Yamada Momoko, had something more important to attend to—which she didn't— she had lied. So, too, had Spin lied. She sighed, smiling faintly to herself and shaking her head from side to side, for in that lie she felt the weight of his love.

Once familiar streets were hard to find now because the landmarks weren't there any more. Momoko would sometimes be walking, by herself or with Spin, through anonymous ruins when her progress would suddenly be arrested by an old, familiar fruit shop and she would realise that she knew the area well. She could even reconstruct places as they once were, like a photographer superimposing one image over another.

Occasionally, she wouldn't even have to do that. Pockets of the old life were dotted all over the city, and when she stumbled across them she would always have to remind herself that none of it was normal any more, that ruin was normal, and these pockets were nothing more than the scraps of a way of life that would never come again. But sometimes, like now, it was so seductive to stand on one of these islands that the bombs and flames had missed and imagine that nothing had changed after all. There was no war, there were no bombings and she still had a father.

Spin and Momoko had just pushed their way through the rows and rows of black-market stalls on the Shimbashi Bridge. The stall keepers, open and brazen in their trade, were unconcerned by what Spin or anybody else thought, for they had paid their dues to the various clans that constituted the Tokyo Mafia and were confident that nothing could touch them. Spin was curious about the old city and Momoko had gravitated back to her old haunts.

They entered a small lane near the Tsukiji fish market and came to a stop. Red lanterns glowed in the early evening light along the length of the lane and baskets of flowers—flashes of bright red, pink, yellow and green—hung from the small terraces of the restaurants, shops and houses. And because the baskets had been freshly watered, both sides of the lane glistened as drops of water fell from the terraces to the ground.

She knew the place well, but hadn't been here since the days when she and Yoshi strolled lanes like these together. The area had not only survived, it looked preserved, unchanged. The fires had burned to the very edge of the lane, then inexplicably stopped, leaving the lane's modest two-storey wooden houses, restaurants and bars all intact. Momoko hadn't spoken since she and Spin came to a standstill and she couldn't tell how long she'd been lost in her own silence. There was even a part of her that imagined Yoshi, as he used to be, standing beside her, and played with the notion that they could pick up their lives where they'd left them and stroll down this tiny lane as they always had. Odd, so odd to think that the very stones she now walked on with Spin she had walked on with Yoshi. At moments like these even her bones ached for the impossible.

Eventually she gathered herself and turned to look at Spin, relieved to see that he was as captivated as she was at their find. It was he who broke the silence.

'Was it all like this?'

'I never knew the area,' she heard herself saying, then added, 'Or, not well.'

'It's ridiculously beautiful.'

'It is.'

Why the silly lie? She was being as silly as Spin. She could only say to herself by way of explanation that she had suddenly felt as if she were trespassing on the past, treating it with scant respect by returning to it arm in arm with Spin and walking the very streets she had walked with Yoshi. That, with every step they took, they were trampling on a sacred place. And her only defence was to keep private the part of her that knew the area and all that it meant to her. In that way the past remained private, she remained true to its memory and there was no travesty in her being here with Spin.

But her heart sank when Spin stopped them after taking only a few more paces. The lantern suspended at the front of the restaurant was new—a bright red orb, the establishment's own personal setting sun—but the door, the windows, the small terrace and hanging baskets were exactly as she remembered. She resisted the idea of going in, suggesting it wasn't quite what they were looking for.

'Not at all. It's just the ticket.'

His enthusiasm could not be dampened and he could not be diverted. He was, she was beginning to notice, pigheaded like that. It was almost a matter of no surprise at all when the aged but still-familiar face of the same owner greeted them at the door. He looked from Momoko to Spin, then quickly back to Momoko. He bowed, they returned the bow and he bowed once more. He then welcomed Momoko back to his establishment and Momoko turned to Spin, quickly speaking in English.

'I'd quite forgotten I'd been here,' she said by way of explanation, her eyes bright with emotion as she spoke to the owner. 'Odd what time does. You get things muddled.'

There were few other patrons in the restaurant and the owner looked after Momoko and Spin all evening, proudly bringing Spin the simple, home-cooked dishes that had always been their speciality. He apologised profusely for the sweet potatoes. There was no rice, he explained. Not today. He couldn't get it anywhere, not even in the 'free' market, and if they had no rice, nobody did. Momoko tried to explain that it didn't matter, but the man was deeply ashamed. Potatoes, his gestures seemed to say, were peasants' food. Momoko soon realised he would not be consoled on the subject of his lack of rice, and so she concentrated instead on praising his fish. Eventually, he left their table, pleased enough with his efforts.

At the end of the meal the owner returned to their table, asking again if everything had been satisfactory, and although Spin wanted to thank the owner he was reluctant to come between him and Momoko, for all his questions were directed at her. And while he asked what work she was doing now Spin gazed idly about him; a couple chatted nearby, a man sat contentedly by himself, while the woman Spin assumed to be the owner's wife prepared food behind the counter. But Spin returned to their conversation when he heard mention of Momoko's young friend, thinking the owner was referring to him. Then he heard the words 'amusing young man' and 'artist', or at least thought he did, and realised the owner wasn't talking about him. The man was about to share a particularly fond memory of those days, but before he could finish his sentence Momoko suddenly swung round to Spin and spoke loudly and clearly to him in Japanese.

'All this talk about the old days. You must be bored.'

The owner suddenly looked up at Spin as if acknowledging him for the first time and quickly backed away.

Spin paused, puzzled, looking in turn from Momoko to the owner and back again.

'Not at all,' he said at last, but his mind was already elsewhere. He had been distracted while he was looking around the restaurant and he was now trying to piece together what he'd heard and what he thought he might have heard. And he actually hadn't minded all this talk of the past. It was harmless, pleasant chatter. But Momoko was suddenly jumpy, and talking in that nervous, strained way people do when they've got something on their mind that they'd rather not discuss. And so they talk and talk and talk the way Momoko was talking now.

He had only half-heard what the owner had said and it probably wouldn't even have mattered, had it not been for all the fuss. Suddenly, he was tense and alert. The excluded one again, the outsider. Watchful and distrustful. And so, once again, summoned by the jittery small talk, the owner's silence following Momoko's question, and the warning bells of those words he felt sure he heard— 'amusing young man' and 'artist'—the devil was let loose in Spin's mind. And nothing that was said after that could shake it free. This imp that wouldn't shut up was chattering away inside him again.

Spin had always thought of himself as happy-go-lucky enough. The old, black dog of despair had always been an incomprehensible part of other people's lives, or just a literary pose that had always bored him. He even thought there might be something deficient in his nature because he never grew depressed, as if this meant that he were somehow not serious, didn't have a mind large enough to summon it all up. But now he was discovering how easy it was to feel the lightness of your being sink without a trace. Had he heard right, or was this place just sending him bonkers? Was she his Momoko, or was only a part of her his? And were there compartments—cunning corridors and sliding doors leading to other doors inside her—that he would never know, and she would never reveal to him because he wasn't the one to have all this mystery bestowed upon him? Suddenly he felt like a plaything, kept in the dark, and was tormented by knowing beyond doubt, beyond hope, that whatever she revealed to him from now on, it would never be everything. Never enough.

All the way back, in the streets, on the tram, Momoko talked and Spin brooded, agreeing with her without listening, nodding every now and then without hearing. She was familiar with her father disappearing into his black moods in those last years, and she could see it in Spin. She talked to stop him from drifting into the sulks, but the more she talked, the more he slipped away from her, and they eventually arrived at Momoko's flat in silence.

Inside, in that other world of Momoko's room, his mood lightened briefly. He loosened his tie and looked about. Here he possessed her, here he knew she was his, as she always had been. Throughout the autumn he had removed her clothes as if removing the layers of her self, and they had given in to each other, melted into each other without holding back. This was their room, their fortress, their own private world, and always would be. Here, he could touch and hold a Momoko that nobody else ever saw or knew because she did not choose to let them.

Now, he gently pushed her back against the wall, the buttons of his uniform caught momentarily by the lamplight. She smiled briefly as she let her head rest against the wall, but the journey back hadn't put her in the mood for any of this.

'What are you playing at?'

'Me? Playing?'

She looked away. His antics were out of character. She didn't particularly like it and she wasn't amused. Then he opened her coat and pressed his body against her.

'Come off it, Spin.'

'I'm not playing, but if you'd like to…'

He smiled, held her face still and kissed her on the lips. With his other hand he reached for the buttons that ran down the front of her dress. But she suddenly pushed him away and he staggered back, startled.

'Stop it, Spin!'

He forced her body back against the wall with his and kissed her again, tasting her lipstick. This time when she pushed nothing happened. The last few days suddenly welled up in him: the anxiety of waiting for her hour upon hour, only to be sent packing like a troublesome schoolboy; the insult of being told she was too tired for him; the innuendo and the half-finished sentences left dangling before him like a torment; the jittery talk tonight, and now this. Stop it, she had the nerve to say. Stop it! Who did she think she was talking to? Some kind of creep she didn't want around any more? A bore whose amusement value had run out and who could now be dismissed back to his old life without so much as a kiss? Is this what it had all come to? The usual brush-off?

Without even being aware of the fact that his arm was reaching out, or that he had made contact, or that he was even touching her, he wrenched Momoko from the wall and threw her on to the futon.

It was the loud, tearing sound of the front of her dress coming away in his hands that stopped him. He looked incredulously from his hand to the torn material of the dress, then fell dramatically to his knees by the futon.

'Get out!' she screamed at him.

He held his hands up as if to explain. 'Please, it was an accident.'

'An accident?'

'I didn't mean it.'

'Yes, you did.'

'No, I thought, perhaps, you were bored with…' he was stammering now and felt as if he were being called upon to justify someone else's actions and not his own '…with us. With *me*!' He swung his head back and looked up to the ceiling where the circle of lamplight hovered above them like a faintly amused moon in an unfamiliar sky. 'God knows, everybody else is. Everybody I've ever known has ended up bored with me. Before I knew you I'd spent my whole life going out with women who told me they were tired at the end of the night. Now you.'

He then lowered his gaze and discovered that Momoko hadn't moved since falling on to the futon. He saw the torn dress, the incredulity in her eyes, and he wasn't even sure she was listening. He clenched his teeth, imploring her to understand what had just happened. 'The day before when I waited for you all afternoon… By the time you arrived, I'd given up. I didn't think you were coming. And I thought, that's it. It's all over.'

His head slumped and he sat staring at the floor, his hunched figure, Momoko thought, somehow smaller now.

'Do you understand?'

She shook her head slowly, beginning to sit up. 'I wasn't bored, Spin. I was tired. I can't help it if you get things wrong.'

'I'm so very, very sorry,' he said, now staring at the dress. 'Is it badly damaged?'

She fingered the torn cloth. 'The dress? No, the dress isn't badly damaged.' She looked up. 'That can be fixed.'

'I'm dreadfully sorry. I am. Believe me.'

He was the familiar Spin again, but as Momoko sat on the futon, watching him, she wondered if he could ever be her Spin again.

'I dare say you are,' she eventually said, 'but now I want you to go.'

'I'll see you tomorrow?'

Sighing, she said, 'I don't know. Let me think.'

'Shall I ring you in the morning?'

'Spin,' she said, closing her eyes. 'Will you just go?'

'Shall I? Ring you…?'

She nodded, realising that he wouldn't leave until she agreed. Then he was gone and the room was hers.

She lifted the dress above her head, dropped it on to the floor, then leaned back against the door, staring vacantly across the room. It wasn't till then that she realised she was exhausted, that she was too tired to think properly. Too tired to think at all. Perhaps, tomorrow, she would be able to see that it had all been a mistake after all. Perhaps tomorrow she would be able to put everything in perspective. Perhaps they'd just picked a lousy time to meet, with everybody still hard and coiled and ready to spring at any moment. Perhaps while she'd been worried for Yoshi, she should have been looking to Spin.

She gave up thinking as she curled up under the quilt and fell asleep.

Under the yellow, fan-shaped leaves of the ginkgo-nut trees in Shinjuku Park, GIs walked with their Japanese girlfriends. An easy distance from the base, it had seemed like a good spot for Momoko and Spin to meet the next afternoon. Now, Momoko wasn't so sure.

As they followed one of the park's many paths they could see a couple pressed up against a tree in a nearby wooded area and Momoko once again regretted her choice of venue.

'I thought it might be more tranquil during the day,' she said.

They passed a small forest of towering pines and maples and the sun was blotted out as they followed the shaded path. Neither spoke, and all around them they could see and hear the giant, black crows of the park fluttering from branch to branch and constantly calling to each other. It was a windless autumn day, but nothing was still in the park. The closer Momoko looked, the more she noticed the couples, the GIs and their call girls, up against the giant trunks of the pines and maples, or lying at the foot of them, partly submerged in beds of scarlet leaves. She felt like a botanist lifting a log or a branch or a rock and becoming suddenly fascinated with a species of life she'd never really encountered before. She knew the park: it had always been a meeting place for lovers, for prostitutes and their clients, but only in the evenings. Now it was a bright, crisp day with a clear sky. And all around them, amongst the greenery and low foliage, she caught flashes of khaki figures shifting from foot to foot and young girls with bright red lips and floral dresses.

As they left the wood the park suddenly opened out on to a vast expanse of dazzling green lawn. Reaching a fork in the path, they walked towards a large pond, leaving behind them, at the very edge of the wood, a GI sharing a cigarette with a young woman on a bench. On a distant section of the lawns GIs were playing football and every now and then an egg-shaped football described a high arc across the open autumn sky.

'You frightened me last night, Spin,' Momoko finally said, coming to a halt at the large middle pond. In summer it would be covered by water lilies with leaves as broad as dinner plates, but the flowers were gone now. As she peered into the murky water, schools of overgrown, overfed goldfish swam to the edge of the pond, their mouths opening and closing as if gasping for air rather than food.

'I didn't mean to. You must believe that. Do you?'

Momoko looked straight ahead across the pond. 'I'd like to.'

'I can't quite explain what happened myself. I was tense. I was muddled. I thought you were fed up with me.'

Momoko, looking at him at last, slowly shook her head.

'I suppose I don't know much about love,' he said.

'Who does?' she replied, flicking a leaf on to the pond and watching the fish descend on it.

She moved off, following the path around the pond, and Spin followed a pace behind, hurrying to catch up to her as he spoke. 'I hurt you and I didn't mean to. What happened, what you saw…that's not me. I don't hurt people. I don't do things like that. And I'd never want to hurt you. I love you,' he called across the cinder-path gulf between them.

It was then she stopped, turned and stared directly at him. Spin stopped, too, and sought the love in her eyes, sought its return in her look, but could discern only disappointment, sadness and something that—in spite of everything—he could only call a kind of gratitude. And at that moment a part of him wished he'd never fallen in love at all. Not like this. He wished he'd bungled into first love the usual way, falling into it and falling out of it and moving on. Not like this. For something in Spin told him—even then—that he would only ever love once. And that he had been granted that love when he was too inexperienced to know how to keep it.

Momoko turned back to the pond and folded her arms against the chill.

'Perhaps we shouldn't be talking about love.'

'Momoko,' Spin said, a pleading tone entering his voice. 'I never wanted to hurt you. It was a mistake, a dreadful mistake.'

She studied him as he stood hunched in his uniform, hat under his arm. The afternoon light was dying and behind him she could see couples and soldiers straggling through the park.

When she finally put her hand out to him a smile lit his face, open and disarming. A few weeks earlier she had thought of Spin as just a boy, a soldier playing at war. But as they walked away, leaving the park to the gathering nightfall and all that it brought with it, she was now aware of another Spin.

Chapter Ten

By Christmas, Spin was used to the sight of crowded railway stations and restricted military trains kept waiting especially for the detachments he interpreted for. He barely noticed the crowd as he pushed his way through to his carriage with Captain Boswell and two other GIs.

As the train drew out of the city snow began to fall, like heavy rain at first, then floating like apple blossom on the wind. There was a small brazier in their compartment, the boarded-up windows had been repaired and the group was reflected in the shiny, new glass. Outside, the light thickened.

Boswell was sipping brandy from a flask and discussing the American football season with the GIs.

'The Bears,' he said, in reference to a forthcoming game. The GI disagreed, favouring the Cleveland Rams. 'No,' Boswell insisted. 'The Bears. It's their year.'

He passed the flask and Spin took it, inwardly noting that all fond literary associations with Boswell's name had long disappeared.

* * *

In the morning, having slept with their greatcoats draped over them for blankets, they arrived at Sendai, a seaport north of Tokyo. Some of the old parts of the city had been destroyed by bombs, but as they arrived the only immediate signs of the war were two sunken freighters still visible in the harbour. The snow had stopped, but the wind blew in from the Sea of Japan.

This time they were not raiding a school, a library or a station, but interviewing the richest family in the prefecture, who not only owned more land than most people in the country, but also controlled the thousands of people who worked on it. Schoolboy images of the three-field system came to Spin as he left the station and mounted a Jeep with Boswell and the GIs, all armed with handguns and automatic rifles. If only that whole, medieval past could be swept away in the next few years, he reflected, then a few good things would have come out of the war after all. It was a world still living in some dark past that time hadn't yet eradicated, but soon would. And as their Jeep pulled out of town and on towards the landowner's residence, Spin had the distinct feeling of being on a mission.

The three heads of the family clan, the father and his two sons, stood outside waiting for them. One of the sons reminded Spin of his London bank manager—gaunt, stooped and glum. The father, bald and bespectacled, looked like General Togo himself. Apart from investigating the land and the commercial concerns of the family clan, Boswell was interested in the possibility of finding large stores of gold hidden in one of the many warehouses on their property.

Upon entering the house Boswell snapped his orders for everybody to sit down at a large table and Spin automatically translated the directives in the same snappy tones.

The youngest son outlined the size of the family's landholdings and wealth, and the four soldiers stared at each other in disbelief. The morning's examinations continued in stops and starts, with Spin translating the questions, often raising his own voice in response to the force of Boswell's invective. Throughout this the three family members sat impassive. They left long pauses between questions, forcing Spin to repeat himself two, often three, times, and they always conferred in low voices before replying.

'No muttering,' Boswell yelled at one such moment, and Spin translated, hitting the table top with his fist for emphasis.

But they simply looked at him, only mildly interested by his intrusive but irrelevant noise. Spin frowned. They were playing games, he thought. They had bowed on greeting the party, they smiled and nodded while the introductions were made, but their expressions remained distant and they didn't acknowledge the soldiers' presence or authority any more than they acknowledged the Occupation itself. They toyed with their interrogators, only answering questions when they were ready, after long silences that rang with contempt.

The balance of power shifted from one side of the room to the other, as if the war were still being fought on a subtler and more cerebral level; as if defeat had never occurred and the emperor's call to endure the unendurable had never been made.

At the end of the morning the father made what amounted to a short speech in defence of his family's wealth. When he had finished Boswell turned to Spin for the translation.

'He says you must realise that they love their sharecroppers and would never do anything to harm them. They have been with them for generations. If their crops fail, they help them. They love them like parents love their children, and they return that love.'

Boswell looked the father up and down with barely concealed contempt in his eyes and was on the point of saying something to the old man, who carried in his bearing and attitude precisely those Old World assumptions that Boswell blamed for causing all the mess. But, in the end, he grunted, as if that was all the old man deserved and as if it were befitting of a conqueror to dissolve the old dispensation in all its iniquity with nothing much more than the accompanying gesture of a grunt.

Boswell and his two GIs searched the warehouses, but found nothing. Once again, as in previous raids, Spin sensed that they had bungled in too soon, without properly understanding the situation they were entering.

As they left, Spin translated Boswell's directive that, according to the land reform bill, the family's land would be sold. The three men nodded, looking, Spin thought, almost as if contingency plans for its purchase through phantom buyers had already been made. They bowed, and stayed bowed until the army Jeep turned the corner.

Spin returned, determined to get things back to the way they had been with Momoko. But the whole time he'd been gone he had imagined her slipping away from him. He imagined her at work, at parties, at social gatherings, laughing easily in the company of other men and enjoying their talk, as free with her smiles as she was with her laughter. And all the time he was gone he could visualise the smooth, easy-talking types that would make her laugh, that made all women laugh. Spin had learned over years of watching that everything began with laughter, and while he was away he loathed the very idea of it. He found nothing to laugh at in his travels and looked upon all those who did with suspicion, as if they had come from Momoko's side.

During the journey back to Tokyo, he felt as heavy with brooding as the sodden trees outside were with rain. She wouldn't want him like this, but he simply couldn't shake off his misery. He was convinced that while he was absent her days had been filled with light and freedom. Yes, freedom from him. But now he was bringing the black cloud of his miserable love back with him, knowing it could blot the sun from the sky, the gleam from Momoko's eyes, the joy from a table. He would be the one that everybody wished to see go. He would know it, but be incapable of stopping it, and wherever he went the black cloud of his misery would trail after him like a balloon on a string. He would wear her down. She would tire of him. Perhaps she already had. Perhaps the day was not far away when he would turn to her and her look would tell him that she was thinking of someone else.

The effort of putting all this behind him seemed almost physical to Spin as he took the tram to Momoko's work, but the anxiety he felt at seeing her kept him alert, although edgy. Until now they'd only looked at each other in the glow of love, which excuses all imperfection. Now they had to discover each other all over again. As he walked through the revolving door of Japan National Radio he had the distinct feeling that he was meeting her for the first time, that all their nights together now counted for little or nothing. He would know if she still wanted him from her first glance, and he prepared himself for the worst.

But when she turned from a script she was working on and walked towards him with a rush in her step and a smile in her eyes, it was his Momoko. Likewise, when she placed her arms around him and allowed herself to be drawn into his embrace. And when she turned back to the studio to check that nobody was watching and kissed him, it was his Momoko, too. All was well again, and he felt the string running out between his thumb and forefinger as he released his cloud, allowing it to float away like the last image of a bad dream.

The smallest things mattered again as they had at first. Holding Momoko's hand in the street, feeling her long fingers entwined in his, occasionally squeezing his hand, gently increasing and decreasing the pressure of her grip. Then the rush of small talk that suggested she hadn't been speaking to anybody much, let alone showering strangers with her laughter and smiles, and the sidelong glances as she asked about what he'd been up to. Everything was as it had been, but surely better. All was well. They'd regained the paradise of each other's unspoken trust. Even the silences were reassuring.

As they turned a corner on the way to the tram they stopped at a fruit shop. It hadn't been there the week before—they would surely have noticed. In the time Spin had been away it had simply popped up. Most miraculous of all was the row of buckets at the front of the shop filled with flowers. There were only a half-dozen or so, but the footpath seemed to be a blaze of red and yellow. All around them the city was mending itself. They paused to marvel at the blooms, and when a small, middle-aged woman emerged from the shadows at the back of the shop, Momoko bowed, then picked up a red rose from the nearest bucket. It was, Momoko thought, inspired, for the city cried out for flowers as much as it cried out for rice and she had no doubt people would buy them to light their rooms.

A low sun spilled over a vacant lot that had been cleared by bulldozers. Pools of muddy water suddenly turned golden. Momoko waved the flower under Spin's nose, but he could only stare at her.

'Don't move,' he said.

She didn't. It seemed oddly daring to stare directly into Momoko's eyes, but he did. And for a long time he hesitated over the question of their colour. Were they green or blue? He eventually decided they were a kind of bluish-green. A colour all their own, not seen anywhere but in Momoko's eyes. And the more he stared the more intense the experience became. He remembered those times before he knew her as well as he did now, when he could only glance at her, catching quick glimpses, and he remembered how much he had longed to lose himself in her eyes. Now he could. She was familiar and strange, excited and calm. And the very act of staring at her for so long was itself both tender and obscene, an affirmation of the extraordinary love Spin brought to her and a violation of that love. For while he stared at her with the tacit permission of a lover, he also did so with the effrontery of a stranger. Intimate and prying. And all the time Momoko openly returned his gaze, occasionally aware of the people passing round them, and conscious of the fact that they were a spectacle.

Momoko then took his hand and they strolled on through the crowds, past the bulldozed blocks, the charred remains of buildings already overgrown with weeds and wild flowers, and on to the tram stop.

Her room was once again their sanctuary. They lay on the futon, talking quietly in the muted glow of the lamplight. Only a passing Klaxon reminded them that there was a world out there. On the floor beside them were two plates containing the leftovers of the tinned ham Spin had brought with him. They shared the last of their rice wine from the lacquered sake jar he had turned round in his fingers the first night they'd spent together. That night seemed impossibly distant now, and he was so utterly changed that when he contemplated it he felt as though he were looking back on some childhood self, and not the man he was a mere two months before.

The silliness, the misunderstanding that had nearly destroyed them was never mentioned. If not forgotten, it was now just one of those things, one of those muddled moments that get out of hand. It was done. It was over. Once again Momoko looked at him with the bright eyes of a woman in love. She had just told him that she had never felt as transparent as she had in those first weeks of their romance. Her skin had a translucence she'd never seen before, and her eyes a clarity they'd never possessed before. And everybody, she was convinced, everybody knew. For it was there to be read in her eyes as clearly as the morning newspaper. It was there in her eyes now, and Spin was invulnerable once more. And, as in those first few weeks together, he had no doubts about that love or any fears for it. Nothing could touch him, and the devil that had been loose inside his head was banished with the dregs from the sake jar.

No one wrote about happiness, he thought a few days later, moving quickly through the crowds to Momoko. Possibly because they were too busy simply *experiencing* it. Happy people didn't spend their time wishing they were somewhere else, or someone else. They neither looked back nor forwards, but lived every moment. No wonder nobody wrote about it. Besides, one's happiness was dull to others. Or worse, a painful reminder to too many people that such a state could exist.

As he brushed through the crowds, his eyes on the footpath, he was remembering how his circle of Cambridge friends had laughed at happiness. He wondered now if any of them had known it, for it suddenly seemed so much easier to be dismissive of happiness when it belonged to someone else. When he looked up, Momoko was walking towards him from the doorway of Broadcasting House. The late afternoon had closed in and low clouds sat on the jagged skyline. She smiled, and he noted that the rush hadn't left her step. Nor had it left his. The night was theirs. He'd waited for this all day and was intensely aware that, from now on, his sense of ordinary time would dissolve: if he were not careful the night would be gone before he'd had time to savour everything properly.

Spin had been dispatched to wander the hilly streets around Kojimachi for over an hour. Momoko didn't say what, but she had a surprise for him. And, like all good things, it would take time. So, out he went, intrigued, sniffing the cool, brisk air like a man taking a turn around the streets before his evening meal. Surely, only food could take this long, and while he walked he warmed himself with images of sliced fish, eels and sweet sauce, pickles and pork. So vivid were the images that, for a moment, he swore that the air carried with it a faint hint of ginger. Luckily, the low clouds that hung on the sky brought no rain, and it was not cold enough for snow.

In the entrance hall, he shook the cold off him along with his greatcoat and left his shoes by the door. Eagerly, he slid the door back but there were no smells of cooking and everything was quiet. Intrigued, even wary, he looked about the dimly lit room, at first seeing nothing.

Then, there she was, kneeling on the floor beneath the window, eyes lowered. The shock was almost physical, as though a hard, extended hand had suddenly hit his chest, arresting his progress, stopping him in his tracks. He stared at her. So, this is what takes so long. Slowly, still feeling the imagined pain in his chest, he, too, knelt on the floor, in front of her, unsure whether to speak or to remain still and silent. He was only aware of having entered a game, the rules of which he was unsure of, and so, not knowing what came next, he sat, watching and waiting for something to happen.

At last Momoko lifted her face and Spin found himself staring, for all the world, into the eyes of a stranger. And not just a stranger, but smack-bang, as his American colleagues would say, into the face of a strange land. The effect was immediate, its sudden impact breathtaking and utterly unexpected. Precisely the kind of unguarded moment in which lives can turn. His reading had taught him that people fall in and out of love in the bat of an eye. Young girls recognise their destiny in the eyes of strangers in a split second, husbands decide upon leaving their wives in between striking a match and lighting a cigarette. It happens, and—out of nowhere—Spin was sure that this was one of those moments. He was like a traveller who, having wandered off the beaten path, suddenly stops and looks about, wondering where on earth he is and how he could have been so careless.

The anxiety of that traveller suddenly gripped him, pumping through his veins to his feet and fingertips. In an instant his palms were sticky, his head light. And it was then that the word 'lost' popped into his mind: not a stranger, not a foreigner, but simply lost. And the more he wandered into this unknown, uncharted territory, the more lost he would become. What had he been thinking? What did he really imagine could become of all this? This woman whom he knew as Momoko was no quaint doll to be twirled around in your fingers, no magazine photograph to be gazed at and speculated upon from the comfort of a lounge-room chair now thousands of miles away. No, he was in her world now, and as much as he dared not admit it even to himself, his first impulse was to put it behind him. To be gone—to go before he was in too deep to find his way out. And this shock was all the more powerful for being in *their* room, for being so intimate.

And so, coolly and deliberately, he looked at her face, clinically taking in the distinctive features of a Japanese woman. To see, not *his* Momoko, but the woman in front of him now and all she brought with her. The sensation, he imagined, was like those moments in an expatriate's life when the view from the window is suddenly wrong, the landscape alien, and the wind carries a disturbing inland dust. He was not so much a lost traveller, as one who contemplates a point on a map, then dismisses the idea, thankful in retrospect that his common sense has prevailed and spared him a sticky experience. But what if his fear were merely excitement, and her exotic aura, her difference, that which he had always craved? And so this very strangeness drew him in, even as it turned him round; one Spin was urging him to go back, the other refused to listen and stepped forward, oblivious of all danger, entranced by the sheer foreignness of the tableau before him.

Her hair was brushed back, woven into a tight, ornate bun, and held by a large, mother-of-pearl pin, and the face that she lifted to meet him was not the face of his Momoko, but a white mask. The effect was extraordinary. There was no sign of that soft, clear skin he'd once, in his imagination, transformed into porcelain. Her eyebrows and lashes were black, her lips a bright, painted red. The eyes that looked out from the mask were at once familiar and utterly strange, the two impressions constantly alternating, leaving Spin uncertain as to just whose eyes he was staring into: those of his Momoko, or this other. Her make-up was moist, and her now white skin, her red lips, shone in the light of the candles placed on either side of her. But, much as he was entranced by the sheer spectacle of it all, he longed for the simplicity of the delicate lips and natural skin that he knew—not this face that she now wore, which was not to be kissed or stroked, but only to be looked upon. As a child he'd kissed his overpowdered aunts, who wore their make-up like theatrical masks, and left him with an unwelcome taste of rouge, powder and cream on his own lips. As he gazed upon the doll's face in front of him, that taste was with him again.

He lowered his eyes and took in, fully, the splendour of the heavy silk kimono that she had carefully, painstakingly, wrapped about her while he was walking the streets, savouring the expectation of an evening feast. Was her kimono red, purple or burgundy? He couldn't decide. Eventually he concluded it was all three. A colour he'd never seen before. And the rich and swirling art-nouveau pattern, which seemed to his eye to be of nothing in particular, ran over the shoulders and down the long, meticulously stitched and lined sleeves. And, as he stared at the pattern, he realised it was not nothing in particular, but a glorious butterfly, poised as though preparing to take flight. The obi, which she had tied at the front, pushed her breasts up, while the lower half of the twelve and a half yards he knew it took to make a woman's kimono fell about her on the floor like a late Empire ballgown.

There seemed to be barely enough room in Momoko's small flat to accommodate the garment. It filled the room, and so, inside it, did Momoko. Still, they hadn't spoken and, already, Spin had lost all sense of time; he had little idea of how long it was since he had entered the room, or how long he had been kneeling before this painted creature. It was surely less than a minute, but it could have been five. Or even ten. And it wasn't the splendour of the thing, the sumptuousness of the garment, that had done this, but the woman who wore it. It was the fact that she could manufacture this display that was driving him to distraction. The fact that she could become so utterly other that he really wasn't sure who he was looking at when he gazed into the familiar yet strange eyes of a Momoko no longer his, but someone else—the fact that the mask came *naturally* to her. She wore it, he concluded, with the ease of a woman accustomed to the many masks that ritual and play permitted.

Now, at last, she spoke. And, once again, it was not his Momoko. He stared at her, marvelling at the transforming powers of paint, make-up and coloured silk. Had she altered her voice? Or had the spectacle itself so changed things that he, the observer, had altered it for her? Whatever, when she finally spoke, it was with a voice he had never heard before. And the formality with which she addressed him was that of a woman speaking to someone she had never met before. Had he had a busy day…? A difficult day…? Yes, she could see…it had been one of those days. But, it was over. Didn't he know that at the end of every difficult day a man should relax and let the trials of the day fall from him? Had he never watched a cat in the sun after the rain, drawing in all the sun's warmth? No? Or, after a territorial dispute with another cat, how the cat stretches afterwards, immediately shuffling off the incident; how it smoothes itself with tongue and paw and quickly becomes indifferent to the world that has just ruffled it? Had he never stopped to observe this? No? Well, there is much to learn from cats. Then she paused, smiling the smile of a human doll practised in the art of the smile. Surely, Spin thought, she would soon ask him his name, and what he did. But perhaps not. Perhaps that would be prying.

She suggested tea, and Spin noticed for the first time that a pot and cup were sitting on a small tray on the floor between them. He had not as yet said a word and this, he felt, was what was expected of him: to sit, relax, be pampered and let the cares of the day fall from him. Besides, he had no desire to speak, for from the moment she began talking, he felt himself slipping into a dreamlike state. And happy to do so.

It was then that she reached across to lift the small teapot and an entirely unexpected and puzzling sensation ran through him. For, as she reached for the teapot, she slowly pulled her sleeve back to reveal her wrist and the bare skin of her arm. And while she poured the tea, chatting quietly about heaven only knows what, Spin sat, utterly entranced by her small, slender fingers, her perfect palm and the brazen expanse of her forearm exposed to him with the unself-consciousness of someone performing a task that necessitates the sleeve being rolled back. And, suddenly, he was asking himself why he had never before noticed her hand and wrist so particularly, and why the sight of her arm (and not all of her arm, but a small part of it) had never stirred him so until now. For he *was* stirred, and in a way he had never experienced. And while he contemplated the nature of the puzzling sensation passing through him with such force and strength, a sensation both disturbing and exciting, he realised, with a shock, that this was one of those deeply erotic moments that adolescent boys feel when they see, on a tram or upon a giant screen, a sudden glimpse of a woman's bare thigh above the line of her stockings. And, for a moment, he was reclaiming one of those lost sensations, those feelings that not only belong to distant youth, but to another age altogether. And all of it evoked by this other woman, this other Momoko, now so transformed that he was not sure just who or what had so suddenly stirred him. Nor could he help asking himself who else she might have affected the way she was affecting him—or how often—so well did she do it, this other Momoko.

Suddenly, the simple grace of Momoko's hands revealed a capacity for infinite suggestion, a poise that was breathtaking. He watched every movement of that hand, turning this way and that as she spoke, the pale fingers unfolding from the palm like origami dipped in water and suddenly sprouting shape at one moment, upturned the next, like some fabulous tropical flower blooming for his eyes only.

She replaced the pot on the tray and he sipped the tea, his eyes blank, indifferent to the pale green liquid she had so meticulously prepared. And, as he replaced the cup without even looking at the tray, she stared at him, her eyes appealing for a response to her efforts. I prepared that simple tea, her eyes said, with all the care of my mother, and all the care of my grandmother, in the days when they had all the time in the world to make things the way they should be made. I ground the leaves, I made the paste, as I saw my mother do and as she saw her mother do, her mother who wore this kimono and who served her husband tea at the end of tiring days. So, Spin, don't simply drink it and put it down. Here, her eyes said as she poured another cup, here, drink more. Taste it, savour it, give it the time that acknowledges the time it took to create, for I give you, Spin, my world in a cup. And her eyes lifted to him as she gave him the tea, imploring him to taste the soothing elixir as if she were offering herself. Seeing all this, Spin sipped slowly, now savouring the tea, and he nodded to her in genuine appreciation. As he did so, Momoko's face relaxed into a smile. *His* Momoko, still there, beneath the paint and the cream and the powder.

She then reached for a three-stringed instrument beside her, and while he sipped the tea, feeling its warmth flow through him, dissolving his anxieties, banishing his fears, she played to him. She played, and she sang, softly, a haunting, simple folk song about the passing of winter and the flower that blooms too soon to escape the rough winds of spring. Like the Momoko before him, this tune was both strange and familiar, and as she finished he realised he'd heard it before. Or, rather, he'd heard ten seconds of it before.

It was only when she placed the samisen back on the floor that she dropped the act.

'Well, poor, hard-working man, relaxed now?'

Momoko may have put the act down with the instrument, but Spin was still that lost traveller. Both thrilled and thrown. To break the spell she suddenly leaned forward, kissing him with her full, painted lips and Spin woke from his trance, protesting, and wiping the red from his lips.

'How long did it take to put all of that on?'

'Ages.' She was laughing, now wiping his lips for him.

'How does it feel?'

'Awful. I don't know how they can stand it.'

'But this—' And here he touched the kimono for the first time. 'So intricate, so delicate. Light…'

'It's as heavy as lead. It was my grandmother's, barely worn. My grandmother courted my grandfather in this. His favourite moment was when she poured his tea, when she would pull her sleeve back and he would glimpse her wrist and arm. And, do you know, before they married, that was all he ever saw of her. Of her body, I mean. But it was enough. In fact, he once told me there were times when it was more than enough. Can you imagine that?'

She was smiling, and Spin wasn't sure just how knowledgeable that smile was or who was smiling: his Momoko or the painted doll, for she still wore the mask and he felt that she might slip from him, back into that role again, at any moment.

When she returned from sponging the paint from her face, the colour from her lips, she knelt by the floor where the tea set had been left, and quietly, in the dutiful voice of the geisha she had just played, instructed Spin in the intricacies of untying the obi that held the front of the kimono together. The kimono may have been her grandmother's, and may have carried with it the sensibilities of another age, when a glimpse of wrist and arm were sometimes more than enough for the eyes of a suitor to feast upon, but when the obi was finally untied, and the front of the kimono fell open, it was a *modan garu*, a modern girl, who fell out, who emerged from the thing like Venus from a silk shell. *His* Momoko was back, and the feeling of being received into her arms not unlike returning to a place you thought you knew, but were seeing for the first time.

Chapter Eleven

She hardly dared admit it to herself, but somewhere along the way these visits to Yoshi had ceased to be a pleasure and become a duty. Besides, for some time now Momoko had been aware of an absurd element of subterfuge to her actions. As soon as she finished work she rushed for the tram to Yoshi's because she didn't want to be late for Spin. She could have been rushing to see an illicit lover, but she wasn't. From the start there had never been any suggestion of picking things up where they'd been left, or of attempting to forge something new. She loved Yoshi now as anybody would love an old friend—an old friend in trouble. She even felt responsible for him, though she knew he would be appalled to think that. Yet the situation was awkward.

Excitement led her into Spin's world and the promise it held. Duty took her back to Yoshi. Already that duty was weighing on her like a burden from a past she wanted now to be free of. But she couldn't walk away from that past any more than she could walk away from Yoshi. She would have to be granted her freedom. Only then, when she had provided whatever it was that was required of her—comfort, absolution, or her blessing for Yoshi to simply go on when the effort of going on seemed beyond everyone around them—would that freedom be hers. She glanced about the tram and saw exhaustion everywhere, written in deep lines across the faces of everybody she looked at. The man in front of her was in a deep sleep, his head slumped forward and his chin resting on his chest. Behind him a woman suddenly lifted her head from sleep, looked to the window and registered where she was, then fell straight back into an oblivious doze. And those who weren't sleeping were sleepwalking.

She understood she was needed, even if Yoshi could never bring himself to say it. But the secrecy made everything difficult. It occurred to her that if Yoshi were Spin she would simply have told him to cough up by now. Spill it. Just say whatever he needed to say and get it over with. But he was Yoshi, and, being Yoshi, she knew the shame that he felt made that sort of talk impossible. For all his art, for all his pinstripe suits, his laughter and his irony, Yoshi was the child of his country. He would spill his shame, if at all, when he was ready. She would just have to wait.

She stayed longer than she meant to at Yoshi's. She sometimes wondered if he was aware of his silences, or even aware of her hand holding his throughout them. But she stayed, hoping that that silence would be broken by confession and she would be free to go. But it never was and time dragged on.

By the time she reached her tram stop she had already overstayed, and, to make matters worse, the tram was late. Spin would be in her room waiting, and all she could do was stand in the bitter cold, urging the tram to materialise from the darkness.

* * *

Spin had hoped to surprise Momoko. On impulse, he'd gone straight to Broadcasting House when he finished his day's work, but she had already left. It was disappointing, but Spin had never been good with surprise visits. He was always turning up too soon, on the wrong day or on a bad day. A pity, he thought, strolling away. He'd liked the thought of meeting her there. He imagined Momoko breaking off from her work and greeting him. It would have been—and it hadn't occurred to him till then—a public display of affection. Natural and easy. Like a married couple.

Never mind, he thought, lifting his coat collar against a chilly wind. It was a nice idea. Another time. She would be at her place now and soon he would be, too. That was all that mattered.

When he arrived she wasn't there and the room was dark. 'Odd,' he said to nobody in particular as he stood in the doorway. He went in, slipped his shoes off, turned on the lamp and settled down on the futon. He sat in the dim light for over an hour, watching the shadows on the wall and jangling his keys. A tram occasionally passed below, its wheels grinding the rails, but otherwise he sat in silence.

When the door finally slid open, Momoko threw her shoes off and ran to Spin.

'I'm sorry, Spin. Have you been waiting long?' Her hands and face were cold and her eyes were bright as if from wine.

'Let me warm you,' he said, taking both her hands and breathing over her fingers.

'Have you been here long?'

'Not long,' he said, now nibbling one of her fingers. 'Where were you?'

'At work. I stayed late.'

Spin looked at her, saying nothing, completely still. Please, please, not again, not again, not again, he repeated to himself. And before he had time to repeat the mantra he heard a calm, deliberate voice saying to Momoko, 'No, you weren't. I went there to meet you. It was a surprise. But you'd gone.'

Momoko stared back into Spin's eyes, and for the first time in her life she cursed Yoshi and the whole, crushing weight of the world they'd lost, but hadn't yet left behind or been able to cast off. She knew straight away it was a stupid thing to say and that she should have prepared a better lie. But she hadn't, and it was the first thing she'd blurted out. Besides, that wasn't Momoko. Momoko did not tell lies. She'd never told lies before. But here she was, lying to Spin and staring into his eyes while formulating another lie. And at that moment she just wanted to just tell him everything, but that would mean telling him about Yoshi and she'd given her word. For if something ever happened to Yoshi, and it was her fault, she knew she would never forgive herself.

'I went back. I left, but I went back.'

'Why?' Spin's lips were still resting on Momoko's fingers.

'There's a speech that has to be translated and ready tomorrow. Rather than rush it tomorrow, I did it today. I must have just missed you.'

'What rotten luck.' His voice was flat.

'I wasn't away long.'

'I didn't stay long.'

She smiled. 'What rotten luck.'

And so it was. So simple. She'd gone back. Spin suddenly wanted to hug Momoko. It was one of those occasions when one's faith in someone is both shattered and restored in a moment. His nightmare seemed to be upon him again, then it was gone. All over, and he mentally snapped his fingers, 'Gone!' Momoko was smiling at him with the same bright eyes as when she had entered the room and everything—everything she said—made perfect sense.

It was only as he was leaving and during the drive back, his hands freezing at the wheel of the Jeep, that the devil shook itself and woke. The fools we turn ourselves into. The lies we swallow in make-believe trust. There was no particular reason, nothing he could put his finger on with any certainty, but by the time he reached the barracks every nerve in his body told him she was lying. The memory of Momoko's smiling face came back to taunt him, his blubbering words of love were humiliating to recall. His mind had betrayed him, but not his instincts. They stayed true and didn't waver when Spin countered his own doubts about her simple explanation. But the more he drove and the more distance he put between himself and Momoko's place, the more hollow her explanation became. She had lied to him, and he had lied to himself.

He sat in the Jeep, idly watching the guard at the checkpoint who was looking over his papers, and silently chanting, please, please, not again. But it was already too late.

Spin sat on his bunk with his head in his hands, not knowing what to believe any more. He lay back on the bunk, but couldn't sleep, and when he looked back on the fraud of the last few weeks he sneered at his own happiness.

The next evening they returned to the press club for the first time since they'd met. As they made their way to a spare table Spin remembered them as they had been that night. He remembered the excited conversation, the apprehension and the delirious sense of embarking on an extraordinary journey. But his memories were mingled with sadness, as if he were looking back on an old lover. Not that he'd ever had other lovers, but he imagined that this was what it must feel like to look back on old loves.

A makeshift band was playing fast music and the club was crowded. Tables had been shifted to make room for the dancers, who were moving frantically—still living, it seemed to Spin, with all the accumulated nervous energy of the war. Men leaned on the bar and eyed the women on the dance floor.

Popular music made Spin uneasy, especially fast music. It attracted the wrong types. He'd always believed that, and a quick look at the predatory lot crowding the bar confirmed his belief. There were people who felt at ease with it, to whom movement came naturally, but he was not one of them. Nothing could make a person look more ridiculous than this kind of music. Momoko, on the other hand, was eager to dance, and when a slow song started she coaxed Spin up from their table.

It seemed to him that everyone was watching her graceful, fluid movements as she drifted on to the floor. In a sudden panic he realised he had never danced with her before, and when he placed his arm around her waist it was with the timidity of a boy at a church social, not with the assurance of a lover.

The song finished and another fast one began. Momoko watched the dancers around her, eyes alight, before reluctantly following Spin off the floor. No sooner had they sat down than an American officer approached. He bowed, cap in hand.

'Excuse me, sir,' he said with excessive formality. 'May I dance with the lady?'

Spin didn't know the man, but he knew the type—handsome, tall, exuding social confidence. He reminded Spin of an officer at the barracks who had recently demonstrated the speed and efficiency

of the American zipper. Spin looked at Momoko, who touched his
hand reassuringly. Spin could see she desperately wanted to dance.

'Do you mind?' she asked.

'Mind? No, not at all.'

'Just the one,' Momoko said, kissing Spin and playing with his
curls. 'Why don't you dance?'

'It's not my style.'

She could tell Spin was uneasy, that he was still uneasy from the
previous night, and she was almost inclined to refuse the officer's
invitation—but the lure of the dance floor was irresistible. She hadn't
danced to American music since before the war when she was a teenager in London. Momoko learnt to jitterbug in the music room at
school with some of the more worldly students, those who had actually danced with strange men in real dance halls to real bands. The
lunch hour would pass in a blink. She would lose herself when she
was dancing, dissolve into delirious forgetfulness. Now, just for five
minutes, she wanted that harmless oblivion again.

'You're sure?' she added, while the American shuffled from side
to side next to the table.

'Of course.' Spin smiled. 'Dance.'

Momoko then rose and Spin watched as the American took her
hand and led her away. Within seconds they were just another
couple on the dance floor. The officer could dance, of course. He
was immediately at ease with the music, moving to its rhythms as
if it were just another Saturday night and Momoko just another girl.
Spin noticed that Momoko could dance, too. She knew all the steps
and she spun on the floor as the American twirled her and returned
her to him. The band went straight into another fast number and
Momoko was about to leave, but Spin waved to her, indicating he
wanted her to stay. And so she did. And as they danced Spin real-

ised that the American was showing him another Momoko, one that he had never seen because he had never shared that physical world of dance with her.

Then he saw her giggle. He couldn't hear above the music, but the brief smile, the sudden movement of her hand to her lips and the quick lowering of her gaze made it obvious. Momoko wasn't a woman to giggle. In the whole time he'd known her she'd never done so. But there she was, in plain view of the whole club, giggling with a handsome, rhythmic Yank who was well practised, no doubt, in the use of his zipper. Did she play the samisen for him, too, and did she also tell him that there was much to be learnt from cats?

When the band stopped, the two of them remained on the floor chatting. Momoko, it seemed to Spin, looked clearly reluctant to leave and when she finally gestured to Spin's table it was in a manner that suggested to him she was returning to a dull husband.

'You seemed to be enjoying yourself,' he remarked coolly as she sat down. 'You dance well.'

'Do I?' Her face was flushed and she didn't notice Spin's tone. 'One of the girls at school in London taught me. Celia Stokes had a wicked gramophone. We'd dance at lunchtimes to the American bands. I'm surprised I remembered,' she said, still beaming. 'You didn't mind?'

'No,' he said, recalling the American's slick movements and the way he twirled Momoko in his fingers like a flower stalk. 'Of course not.'

'Good. I thought perhaps you might,' she said, reassuringly taking his hand and telling him how she'd teach him to dance before the winter was out.

In her room Momoko undid Spin's belt and unbuttoned his shirt, quickly and decisively. 'So many buttons.' She grinned.

Spin tensed as he watched her. He suddenly felt as if he were not simply being undressed by his lover, but being stripped of his uniform, his rank and all the outward signs of power his garments carried. Still clothed, Momoko stepped back and smiled at his nakedness.

Soon they were moving like naked wrestlers on the floor. One second they would be poised in an equal embrace, the next moment one would have the advantage, then surrender it to the other, who eventually surrendered it back again. And so it went, each gaining and losing the advantage as they rolled across the floor. Momoko ran the palms of her hands down his face, darting her fingers in and out of his mouth, her lips falling to his neck, his collarbone, leaving a red stain where they had been. Spin held her head between both hands and kissed her, running his tongue in fluttering movements across her eyes. He brushed her hair with his fingers.

'So black,' he murmured solemnly. 'I've never seen such a deep black. And you know what they say.'

'No, what do they say?'

'Nothing shines like black.'

Slowly she pushed him backwards, his eyes closing as he came to rest on the mat. She looked down upon him as she stroked his neck and shoulders, smoothing the knotted sinews. He felt his muscles begin to relax. Moments later she moved upon him in a slow, circular motion.

Afterwards, shivering slightly in the chill, she picked his coat up from the floor and put it on, running her fingers lightly over the lieutenant's markings on the shoulders before buttoning it. She didn't know Spin was awake, but he watched her move about her room as though she were still dancing, humming a tune that he recognised from the club. He wondered who she was humming it for.

'You look sad,' he commented in the semi-darkness.

She spun round, surprised. 'Do I?'

'What about?'

She shivered by the window, standing on tiptoes and looking out over the city. 'Everything.'

He laughed, and for a moment she joined him.

'You can't be sad at everything,' he said, the laughter gone and a more inquisitorial tone entering his speech, sounding almost official. 'Is something the matter? Is there anything you'd like to tell me?'

She looked up sharply, annoyed at his tone. 'Like what?'

'Whatever you want.'

'Why do you ask? Am I being questioned?'

'You just looked like you wanted to say something.'

She pushed both hands into her coat pockets in a gesture of annoyance. 'Stop it, Spin.'

'Nothing to say?'

She suddenly looked at him, alarmed at detecting a sign of that Spin she hadn't seen since the incident with her dress. She stood by the window, shaking her head.

'No,' she said, a hard edge to her voice he was sure he'd never heard before. Then she swung round while he still sat on the futon. 'Now will you drop it? Please, no games. Okay, Joe?'

Until now jealousy had only been a word. And all the novels and plays he'd read in the past about jealous lovers were just stories. They never touched him. But he hadn't met Momoko then. He hadn't fallen in love in a foreign country and lost himself in ardent ways, hadn't known what it was to lie in her room and feel the hours pass like minutes, or lie in his bunk feeling the minutes pass like hours until the next day ticked round and he could see her again. He had never listened, like he had lately, to a devil's voice inside his head, and he hadn't watched Momoko coming in late and always, it now seemed, tired at the very thought of seeing him.

If only he'd never come to this country he would have been happy enough. Walking back into the barracks that night, it occurred to Spin that being happy enough might even be desirable. But he'd no sooner entertained the thought than he realised it was now impossible. Something remarkable had begun and he would experience it fully. All of it. He was ready to be led to wherever events would take him, whatever the end. And it wasn't choice. Love had taken all choice with it.

He had even fallen into making mistakes at work. The previous day Adler had called him into his office and told him to sit down, holding Spin's draft of a radio announcement. There were five factual errors and a paragraph that another translator could make no sense of at all.

Spin remembered the morning he wrote it, remembered the previous evening meeting Momoko and greeting her smiling face with his own fixed grin. Momoko's smile occupied his mind now. Whenever he closed his eyes it was there; he saw her smiling at him as she had yesterday, he saw her smiling at him as she had when they first started seeing each other. He recalled, in particular, one morning in the studio just after everything had started between them. He was seated and Momoko was standing beside him. An actor was completing a speech that Spin had translated for broadcast and the booth was silent. As the speech neared its end Momoko had leaned against him, very lightly, so that her thigh touched his arm. She looked straight ahead into the studio, leaving the weight of her body pressed against him. When the speech was finished she transferred her weight to the other foot, without looking down, as if completely unaware of the contact. It was only as she left the booth that she smiled briefly at Spin, leaving him to marvel at the poise with which she acknowledged their secret alliance.

But he wasn't marvelling now. If she could be so practised at hiding herself from everybody else, why not from him, too? Something was wrong. Her silences, her excuses, her lateness, a gesture here and there, and that smile that he loved so well and which troubled him so much.

The novels, the books, the plays, all made perfect sense now. The fallen handkerchief; the actions of the Moor; the sleepless nights; the obsessive lovers; the hired detectives and the stolen diaries; the lies and accusations. The sheer pettiness of it all now had a logic and inevitability that was both convincing and compelling, and every step on the twisted path to that final scene seemed inexorable.

Chapter Twelve

He watched her move among the crowds, her hair falling over the back of her coat collar, shiny and black like the feathers of a crow. She paid no attention to anybody around her, kept her eyes on the footpath, or glanced vaguely at the odd pockets of display windows, whose clothes and shoes only the Americans or those who profited from the black market could afford.

She was easy to follow in the dull light of the early evening and by now he knew where she was going, anyway. She would board a tram for what he knew had always been one of the poorer districts of the city and alight at a street with a cherry tree on the corner. From there she would walk briskly along the winding, damaged streets, keeping her eyes on the footpath. He knew all this because he had followed her before.

Hadn't he asked her the night after all that dancing if she had something to tell him? Hadn't he given her the opportunity to come clean? But she hadn't told him anything. Not that night, not the day after, or the day after that—and then he had followed her. She had left him no choice: he had given her every chance; he had shown more patience than anybody else in his situation would have done. If she would not tell him where she went, he would have to find out for himself. It was regrettable, but necessary.

He knew that she would open the door of a rambling, two-storey building that looked as though it might once have been an inn. He also knew she would remain inside for an hour or even more. Sometimes a young Japanese man would appear in the doorway, look nervously up and down the street, then disappear inside with her.

It was an easy house to observe. It was on the corner of a side street, facing back towards the main roads of Shinagawa. Spin could park his Jeep on the main street, and from a convenient doorway observe all the comings and goings of the house. Several families seemed to live there, and towards evening he would often notice young women in nylons and summer dresses, their lips bright red, leaving for the various parks, undergrounds or thoroughfares of the city where they would make their liaisons.

But these comings and goings were incidental. It was Momoko and this young man whom he watched. Sometimes they would bow; sometimes they would kiss briefly like friends do. But they rarely lingered long in the street. Other observers might regard their behaviour as merely that of friends, but Spin knew better than to trust appearances. They weren't merely friends, he was convinced of that. Convinced, but he needed to be certain. He would be prepared so that there could be no avoiding the truth when it was finally revealed. He would confront her with it in such a way that there would be no slipping out of it. There would be no games, no smiling denials, no tricks. He'd been on too many dead-end inspections to the country and knew the price of being insufficiently prepared. He was tired of being toyed with, tired of these people, tired of their knowing, superficial smiles. His anger was deep, but his patience was deeper. He could wait. There was no need to bungle in too soon like the innocent foreigner and ruin everything.

And so Spin stood and waited, a small camera in his hand, in the doorway of a gutted building opposite this questionable old house to which Momoko came. It was the violet hour. Evening was falling and the light was beginning to thicken, making it easier to remain an unseen figure in the doorway. Besides, Momoko and this young man were always entirely absorbed in themselves. The young man was edgy, but Momoko never looked back or about her.

They had just slipped into the doorway and entered the house. Spin could almost count the steps by now. Soon, a dull, yellow gleam lit the glass of the window he knew to be theirs, and from time to time thereafter shadows passed across it. She was inside the room now and he could imagine the rest. Her hair, shining as only black can shine, would be falling across her shoulders or tossed back as she laughed. Although she never smoked, Spin imagined her doing so now, while she unbuttoned her dress and the man watched her from the futon upon which he would be lying. He, too, would be smoking—one of the long American cigarettes his black-market dealings had enabled him to buy. She would shake her dress free for his amusement.

A silhouette against the window of the room roused him from his fantasy. Momoko's fingers touched the glass as if she were writing something on it. A name? Perhaps the name she had mumbled in her sleep. The name she, no doubt, secretly recited to herself when she closed her eyes during their lovemaking.

She stayed at the window for a considerable time and at one point seemed to be staring directly at Spin through the top, clear panel of glass. It seemed unlikely, but he stepped farther back into the doorway just in case. She continued standing by the window and looking down on the street as if she knew he were there. As if she knew about the spying, the tailing, the whole, pathetic flatfoot charade, and found it amusing; as if she were openly teasing this watcher in the street before climbing back into the arms of her lover.

Momoko breathed on to Yoshi's window and wrote Spin's name in the condensation. Underneath that she started to write her own, but paused for a moment, idly studying the letters. Behind her, Yoshi was talking about the isolated jungle camp in which he had spent the latter part of the war. It was a simple situation. Yoshi was telling her a story and she was listening. He was a good storyteller and she was a good listener. The story itself was unpleasant and the people in it were undeniably bad, but it was a story, that was all, and when the word *I* was spoken it was only the first person singular of the storyteller, not the young man sitting on the futon behind her whom she had known since she was nineteen. He was relating a story about other people he knew, had heard of, or invented.

Yoshi was an artist, after all, and many of his paintings contained quite intricate narratives. He was, she chose to reason, a storyteller by trade and this was another of his fictions. She noted the professional way he established the scene. The isolation of the camp, the prisoners—mostly British and Australian—the rain, the snakes, the diseases, the death and the road they had been ordered to build. She listened to Yoshi as if he were reading from a novel, its characters the camp commander, the soldiers, the village rice farmer caught feeding the escaped prisoners, the prisoners themselves. They each had their individual qualities, and each was doomed to do the things they did because the moments in the story were structured that way.

She knew all this, and so when Yoshi used the word *I* again she knew enough not to mistake it for the person telling the story. The 'I' and the storyteller were quite separate.

But when he had finally finished speaking, she became aware that her cheeks were wet with tears and that her nose was running. The story had moved her like good stories should.

In the silence that followed she remained by the window, sniffing, looking at the two names on the frosted glass, now surrounded by a heart. She had read of rooms that were filled with silence and had always been amused by the image, seeing silence as an absence, a negative rather than a positive quality. But the room she now stood in was shrill with the absence of sound, the ringing silence that follows when something unspeakable has at last been spoken.

When she was ready she turned from the window and looked at the young man whose face was now buried in his hands.

Spin was the invisible figure hidden in the shadows of the doorway when Momoko finally stepped back on to the footpath. He saw the young man's face disappear as the door slid shut, watched Momoko plunge her hands deep into her coat pockets as she walked up the street to the tram stop. There was no danger of him being seen. Her head was down, she was utterly absorbed in her own thoughts, enclosed in her own world. He could have waved to her and she wouldn't have noticed. Besides, it was dark now. He waited until the tram carried her away before he stepped from the doorway and walked quickly to the army Jeep parked around the corner.

That night at the barracks Spin tried to read, but gave up and threw the book aside. He watched it land upside down in the corner. Outside, two GIs on guard were throwing dice up against a wall, like Roman soldiers tossing bones in some shivering colonial outpost, he thought. He could make out odd words, but the sentences were muttered and the tone flat. They were looking forward to going home, driving open cars through warm nights and going to the movies.

Again and again, Momoko had stood framed by the window. Again and again, she had written something on the frosted glass, and may even have been speaking to the young man in the soft, confessional tones that lovers use. But Spin would never know the intimate details of the moment—and he would never know what it was that she had written on the window.

Momoko's eyes suddenly snapped open in the early hours of the morning. It was dark, and for a moment she could have been waking in any of the houses of her life. Gradually, her room came into focus. The dream she'd woken from was still fresh and Spin's image stayed before her. A collapsed wall is silhouetted against the evening sky like jagged rocks on a desert landscape. No wind passes through the land, nothing stirs. Then she sees it. There is the slightest flicker of movement and she instantly knows someone is out there. The moonlight suddenly catches his cheeks and his eyes, staring up at the window from a doorway. The mouth, the lips, the cheeks and the eyes, staring back at her from the gutted doorway opposite Yoshi's room.

She turned the lamp on, threw on her dressing gown and sat, still dazed, cross-legged on the edge of her futon. It was guilt, she told herself. She conjured Spin's face up and placed it in that dreamy, gutted doorway out of guilt and guilt alone. It was extraordinary that she hadn't had such dreams before. Deception wasn't part of her nature and secrets filled her with dread. It was with a deep, exhausted relief that she remembered Yoshi would be gone within days and the whole, awful business would be finished.

It was guilt, nothing more. But as she pulled her hair back and walked to the window a nagging thought found expression. What if it were true? What if Spin had been there? What if her brain had photographed Spin in that doorway but it hadn't registered with her until she recalled the image in dreams? It was fantastic. Or was it? Suppose her eyes had passed over that doorway and glimpsed Spin's face, but the conscious mind had been too engrossed in Yoshi's tale to take it in? If this were true, it would mean that she saw him and he saw her. And if he saw her, he knew everything.

For a moment the proposition seemed horribly true. All the reason in the world about the sheer absurdity of the idea meant nothing. Sense, logic, reason, were all empty catch cries when a flash of intuition, of animal instinct, came like this and took over.

But it was only a moment. As she paced about the room, feeling the solidity of everything it contained, she knew the real world had returned, and the whole idea was revealed as one of those silly thoughts that come to you at three in morning. She'd simply dreamed Spin into that doorway, and soon—very soon—she would never have to look upon that doorway again.

Her room looked tidy in the dull afternoon light, apart from a few clothes on the chair. As Spin slid the door shut behind him, the hammering began in the room above. He quickly moved to the large oak chest against the wall beneath the paintings, knelt beside it and flipped the lid back.

The chest had a musty smell; in opening it, Spin had the sensation of entering a forbidden room that had been locked for a long time. His hands were moist and unsteady as he sifted through Momoko's belongings. He had reasoned his way to this act again and again and he was now convinced he wasn't prying. He had not been reduced to snooping on his lover, he had not become pathetic. He knew all that well enough and would make no apologies if she were to suddenly walk in. He simply had to know the truth of the matter. For there was a truth to be discovered, and if he looked hard enough he would find it in Momoko's room.

Two photograph albums were stacked against one side of the chest, along with exercise books, articles of clothing, her silk kimono, a jewellery box and, folded neatly at the bottom, the navy-blue blazer of a girls'-school uniform. He touched the material of the blazer and examined the Latin insignia on the breast pocket, keenly aware of the vanished world it evoked. Suddenly, he was standing on a white boundary line tossing a cricket ball up and down, but the oval seemed impossibly far away, and the sound of the batsmen hitting the ball nothing more than the distant echo of another age.

It began to snow outside and Spin shivered. He lifted the collar of his greatcoat.

The photographs of Momoko's family in London he had already seen and he put that album back. The second was new to him and he flicked through snaps of the family just back in Japan, Momoko's father looking tired behind his spectacles and resigned to the course that events were certain to take. Spin stopped at a double page showing a younger, surprisingly plump Momoko with a young man who always seemed to have a sketchpad under his arm. The photographs had been taken over a number of occasions, in a garden, a park, outside a bar in what appeared to be Tokyo before the war. One of them he recognised as the photograph Momoko had taken down from the wall when they first became lovers. In all the shots they were standing or sitting together, holding hands, and underneath one a caption had been pasted. It read, 'Yoshi and Momoko, Kyoto, summer, 1941'. Spin studied the young man's face closely before closing the album.

Next, he picked up a bundle of letters postmarked from various places across Manchuria and Burma. They were in date order and were, he quickly realised, love letters, often containing intimate references that would mean nothing to anyone other than the lovers themselves. He shuffled through them, stopping every now and then to read, noting that as the years continued the mood of the writer became darker. The correspondence stopped in early 1944.

The final letter was one of Momoko's that had been returned undelivered. The envelope bore Yoshi's full name, his rank and regiment. Spin took out his notebook and wrote down the particulars.

At the bottom of the bundle he found what was obviously a recent envelope with no stamp, no postmark, simply Momoko's name scribbled across the front. He opened it and stared at the message inside; a small map, the address he already knew, and the name *Yoshi* scrawled across the bottom.

When he had finished he put the letters back in their correct order and carefully replaced the contents of the chest. Satisfied there were no signs of his intrusion, he stood up and found himself staring at the painting of the naked girl, at the curve of her neck and waist, the plumpness of her thighs and stomach, the bracelet around the wrist of the arm upon which she supported herself. The solidity of the subject had been conveyed with remarkably few lines and completed, he guessed, very quickly. Then, his chest tightening, he looked at the signature, at Momoko's bracelet, and wondered why he had never recognised it before.

He turned, his uniform suddenly that of the burlesque clown, and walked towards the door with the young man's details crushed in his fist.

Spin's camera clicked as she opened the door and turned briefly, looking back at the street as if she were worried that somebody was watching. The shutter opened and closed, drawing her image in with the flood of late afternoon light. Then she stepped inside and was gone. Spin waited for her to reappear at the window. When she didn't, he left and walked back to his Jeep.

His collection of photographs was mounting. If he wanted to, he could fill a notice board with snapshots and enlargements, all labelled and dated. Back in the barracks he arranged them chronologically and stared at them in the subdued glow of the lamplight. In some the Japanese man, still wearing the private's coat of the Imperial Army, stood in the doorway with Momoko. In the drawer beside his bed was the young man's name. He gathered the photographs into a bundle and put them away, then lay on the bed, smoking and staring at the piece of paper upon which he had written the young man's name and particulars.

But it was the same image of Momoko that he saw all the time now. She was smiling, a secretive, tantalising smile, giggling as she had on the dance floor, laughing to herself over and again, as she doodled on to the frosted glass in the young Japanese man's room.

Momoko wasn't laughing, nor was she smiling. As Spin walked back to his Jeep Momoko leaned against the wall of Yoshi's room, eyeing the titles on his makeshift bookshelf. Visit by visit she had watched the collection grow: works on Buddhism, a mixture of Eastern and Western philosophies, a large hardback history of Burma.

She knew he had gathered them from stalls and second-hand book-shops, often going without food to pay for them.

'Is this what you do all day?'

He nodded from the middle of the room where he sat cross-legged.

'Don't you get a little tired of it all?' she pressed, growing impatient with him.

'Not really.' A faint smile appeared on his lips and she thought he resembled a school teacher listening to an amusing question. Her impatience grew.

'You seem annoyed,' he said with a detached calm. 'Are you?'

'No. Not really.' She shrugged.

'Good.'

'But you can't stay here, in this room, all your life. Can you?'

Yoshi maintained a long silence while he watched her fingers play with her bracelet, remembering the day he had bought it for her.

'No,' he said finally.

'What are you going to do? If you won't paint again…'

'No, I won't paint again. It was a pointless egotism.'

His deliberately calm tone fed her impatience, and she toyed with the idea of suggesting that he had simply exchanged one pointless egotism for another.

'Have you decided on anything else, then?'

'Yes.' He did not continue, merely looked coolly at her as though he had already explained everything.

'Yoshi,' Momoko implored at last, exasperated, 'what have you decided?'

'I'm leaving.'

She started, both sad and relieved. 'Leaving Tokyo?'

He nodded. 'Yes.'

Momoko felt her sense of annoyance give way to loss. She was losing him a second time, although it was a different Yoshi and a different kind of loss.

'When did you decide this?' she said, coming to kneel beside him.

'I think I decided it even before I came back. And, Momo, all the time I've spent here has only made things clearer.'

'Where will you go?' she said, aware that now it was she who assumed a note of detached calm.

'Everywhere. Place to place. All over the country.'

'What on earth for?'

'Because that's what I've decided.'

'But what will you do?' Her tone was a mixture of pleading and incomprehension.

The smile returned to his lips as if the oddness of the answer he was about to give pleased him. 'Walk.'

'What do you mean, walk?'

'Exactly that. I intend to walk throughout the country. And don't ask me why.'

'Like a monk?'

'Possibly.' He was staring straight past her, noncommittal.

'Begging?'

'Yes, begging, if necessary.' He turned to face her. 'Is that so unthinkable?'

'But you've got nothing for a journey like that,' Momoko said, shaking her head. 'It's winter outside. Haven't you noticed that? You'll have to walk through a whole winter.'

Yoshi sat Buddha-like on the floor. 'I don't want anything.'

She looked at his feet. 'You'll need proper shoes.'

'I have shoes.'

'Good ones, to keep out the cold.'

'I don't intend to notice the cold.'

Momoko got up and paced about the room. 'How will you eat?'

'People will feed me.'

'Will they? What with?'

'Whatever they have. Momo, my mind is made up.'

'But you don't have to do this.' She moved towards him. 'It wasn't your fault. You didn't declare war. You didn't even want to go. Remember how we planned to hide until it was over?' Her voice was unsteady as she slid down the floor to her knees. 'You've already paid. You don't have to pay any more.' She shook her head slowly from side to side, barely containing her tears. 'This is childish.'

Yoshi sat staring at the floor, a smile on his face. Momoko knew the look. It was the silly smile that schoolboys wore when they didn't want their feelings known, the silly smile they wore like a mask, and Yoshi was wearing it now. For a moment she wanted to slap it from his face.

Outside, the light faded and the room darkened. Momoko lit a candle and stood staring at her reflection in the glass. Her eyes looked dark and tired. The early winter darkness was falling on the city and the idea of spring seemed to belong more to another age than another season.

'What will you do with your things?' she asked at last.

He gave an ironic smile. 'What things?'

She looked around the room. 'Your books.'

'I've read them. I don't need them any more. You have them.'

'Yoshi, I don't want them.' She looked at his hair, in need of cutting now. 'Sometimes I can't believe all this has happened.' She sighed. 'That it's all gone, that world we lived in. I pass places that aren't there any more and I make them up again, as I remember them. Then I catch myself slipping into the past and I stop. Do you do that?'

He shook his head. She knelt beside him and held his hand. 'I know there's no point in going back. But one day, Yoshi, maybe fifty years from now when everything's been rebuilt, I imagine we're all going to stop and look up from our toil. The whole country. Stop where we are, hammers and pens in hand, and look back. Just once.' She glanced down and shook her head, dismissing the idea. 'But we won't. Because if we ever did, we'd die of nostalgia.'

A breeze blew in under the door and the candle wavered in the semi-darkness. Momoko squeezed his hand. 'I'll come back tomorrow.'

'You don't have to.'

'But I want to. I'll bring you something. For the old days,' she insisted. 'Imagine. Here I am saying things like "the old days".' She let go of his hand and ran her fingers lightly through his hair. 'You'll need to get this cut.'

He smiled and nodded, lifting himself from the floor and walking her to the door.

'Tomorrow,' she said quickly.

Before he could reply she silenced his lips with the palm of her hand, then turned and disappeared down the stairs and into the night, leaving him on the landing.

Chapter Thirteen

Major Johnny Martin, former Boston detective, sat at his desk, which was overflowing with papers that had been shuffled from one part of the office to another, and toyed with his wooden name plaque while he listened to Spin. He was puzzled. Martin had met Spin on a number of occasions at the officers' mess and the press club, but he had never spoken to him officially until now.

'What exactly is it you want me to do?' he asked Spin when he had finished.

'Pick him up.'

Martin put down the plaque. His eyebrows rose slightly.

'And what do I pick him up for?'

'He's suspicious.'

The major leaned back in his chair. 'Spin, the whole city's suspicious.' His voice was weary. 'I need something more than that.'

'No, you don't. Trust me.'

Leaning forward, elbows on his desk, Martin looked at Spin quizzically. 'Why should I do that?'

'If he's got nothing to hide, well and good.' Spin stepped back, lowering his voice. 'No harm done.'

'Except,' said Martin drily, 'I've wasted my time.'

'Johnny, this man is hiding something. He's dodgy. He hardly ever comes out into the street and when he does he's shifty.'

'So?'

'Check it out. He's hiding something, believe me.'

'And how did you come to observe all this?'

'That's personal.'

Martin suddenly rolled his eyes.

'But what I've observed is business,' Spin said, holding Martin's gaze.

Martin eventually sighed and wiped his hand across his forehead. He rubbed his eyes, which were red from lack of sleep. Spin, sensing the argument had turned in his favour, pushed a crumpled piece of notepaper across the desk as if he were offering a bribe.

'Look into it. Hmm?'

Spin and Momoko lay on the futon, but there had been no loveplay that evening. Spin, she noted, had been distant and edgy since arriving. He was chainsmoking, staring at the wall, occasionally breaking into monosyllabic conversation. He had been edgy before, Momoko thought, but not like this. It seemed to her as if he were deliberately making himself unreachable, drawing away from her. Like a lover does, she mused, when the love is gone and he wants only to leave. And the only way he can find to do it is to make himself unreachable so as to emphasise the gulf between them. She tried all night to bridge that gap, but the more she tried, the more unreachable he became.

After an hour of grunts and hums he stubbed a cigarette on an ashtray beside him and spoke without looking at her.

'I get nervous when people talk a lot for no particular reason.'

Momoko looked at him, puzzled.

'It's called small talk, Spin.'

'So I believe. But whenever people make this small talk I always get the feeling there's something else they'd rather be saying, but haven't got the nerve, or the pluck or the honesty. Or whatever. Like they'd rather be making big talk instead. Do you know what I mean?'

Spin's eyes were cold, his face was hard. He was more tense than she'd ever seen him, and as he stared at her his tension became hers and she was suddenly aware of being jittery.

'Why are you telling me this? I'm just telling you about my work today. If that's dull…'

'Tell me about something else.'

Momoko sighed without bothering to finish what she was going to say. Then her eyes lit up. 'My first trip to the mountains,' she suggested, attempting humour. 'I was six. I still remember it vividly.'

'Not that.'

'My father's study.'

'No.'

'It was fascinating.'

'I'm sure it was.'

She suddenly folded her arms. 'You're impossible to please.'

'No, I'm not,' Spin said, in the faraway voice of the melancholic. 'I'd like to know what's going on in my Momoko's mind.'

'And I'd just love to know what's in Spin's.'

He watched the thin trail of smoke rising from his cigarette, then turned to Momoko, stared directly into her eyes and spoke slowly and carefully as if he were addressing a child.

'If you had something to tell me, something that was very, very important—you'd tell me, wouldn't you?'

Her nightmare came back to her and she stared back into Spin's eyes, wondering if such things could really be. She took a deep breath, her fingers playing with the floral sash of her dress. 'Of course I would, Spin. But there's nothing to tell. Please, don't go on like this. You've made me happy, happier than I ever thought I could be again. And I love you for that, Spin. I love you like first love. Like first and last love. Believe me, and never, never forget it. That…' and here she paused, nodding her head slightly '…is all I have to tell you. Is that big enough? It is for me. Big enough for a whole lifetime. Big enough to make life look too short. That's how I measure my love, Spin. By the certain knowledge that there simply aren't enough days left to exhaust it.'

Her eyes were bright with that love as she stared back at Spin, pleading for a response. But he only drew on his cigarette and did not answer. She turned away and faced the window.

'You're a strange one tonight.' She sighed.

In the doorway Spin ran his fingers down the back of her neck, then rested them fleetingly on her shoulder. He lifted his collar against the draught on the stairs, and turned back to her briefly before going. For a moment he seemed on the verge of responding to her at last and she waited on that moment in perfect stillness as if her life hung in the balance. But he simply nodded, spun on his boots, and his footsteps faded as he neared the street and disappeared into the night.

From the moment Momoko lifted the lid of the chest she had the distinct feeling that the aspic world inside it had been disturbed since the last time she peeped in. Her school blazer, her letters, photograph albums and jewellery were all exactly where she had left them. But something was wrong. Whenever she looked into the chest there was always a moment of breathtaking rapture when the jumble of nights and days contained in it arrested all movement, suspended all time, and everything would be before her as it always was—for a brief, explosive moment. She would smell the tobacco issuing from her father's silver cigarette case, hear individual voices rising above the clatter of school corridors, see the shiny black door of their house in Knightsbridge and hear Yoshi's young laughter. But it wasn't there this time. This time, when she lifted the lid she knew someone had been there before her, and as she pushed the lid back against the wall she suddenly felt like a Crusoe stepping ashore to find footprints in the sand.

Yet everything was exactly where she had left it. Nothing had been moved. Perhaps it wasn't the contents of the chest that had been disturbed. She carefully lifted the blazer and placed it on the floor. Then the photograph albums, the letters, the cigarette case and the knick-knacks—the restaurant menus and theatre tickets—of the world that had been blown away. When she was almost finished, when nearly all the contents of the chest had been carefully placed on the floor, Momoko reached down to the bottom of the chest and, with even more care than she had shown for everything else in the chest, she lifted the kimono and held it up to the light, her hands trembling.

The dazzling colours of the robe shimmered in the lamplight. The silk, smooth and soft, brushed her fingers, and she ran them gently over the garment, remembering the day she first touched it, and the fun, yes, fun, of wearing it for Spin. It had belonged to her grandmother, on her mother's side, and had been shipped to London when her grandmother had died. Even though it was what her grandmother would have called 'visiting wear', it still looked too elaborate and grand for most domestic occasions, and her grandmother had only worn it those few times when she was being courted by Momoko's grandfather. That was in a now distant age towards the end of the previous century, when the East and West of kimonos and pinstripe suits mingled freely on streets since blown away by the firestorm's winds. For all that her grandmother had called the kimono 'visiting wear', it was always the kind of garment that is looked at more than it is worn.

Momoko had worn it twice: once for her father in London when she served him tea, and once for Spin. She kept it for strong sentimental reasons. Like her blazer. City of London School for Girls. Another world. Now, she was painfully aware that this was an age that had little time for sentimentality. She carefully replaced the contents of the chest, but kept out the kimono. As she knelt on the floor she held it to her, closing her eyes and brushing her cheek against the collar, knowing that soon it would no longer be hers. When she had said her goodbyes she placed it inside brown paper and sealed the package with clear tape.

The Ueno black market was humming with trade in the afternoon light. The stalls were crowded and their owners were already drunk on the illicit concoctions they threw back all day. All around her men and women haggled over the value of gold watches, jewellery, suits and shoes. This was the place where those precious family items, emblematic of the private life, found their market price. That price was always too low, but the pots and pans the exchange bought would feed hungry mouths in a city where food was as popular a topic of conversation as the weather. This was where sentimental values gave way to practical ones. The street had a name for it, Momoko thought as she squeezed her way through the crowds. They called it the bamboo-shoot existence, and as she neared that section of the market known across the city as 'America Lane', Momoko was in no doubt that the street was right. For, all around her, people were shedding their possessions—coats, shirts, pullovers and dresses—like the layers of the bamboo shoot. It was a danger-ous existence to be adopting at the beginning of a nasty winter, for Tokyo would be a cold place to be when the layers ran out.

She edged her way along 'America Lane', clutching her parcel to her chest, and eyeing the greatcoats, the army-issue blankets and the stockings, lipsticks and make-up compacts that made their way into the markets via the prostitutes.

When she arrived at a table of army boots and shoes she stopped, picking them up one at a time, attempting to gauge Yoshi's size. She settled on a pair that she knew would be too large, reasoning to her-self that Yoshi could always wear two pairs of socks, for she would not be able to bring the shoes back. The young man behind the table still wore an airforce coat and Momoko wondered if the stories about ex-kamikaze pilots running black-market stalls were true after all.

She pointed to the boots she had chosen, then opened the pack-age, revealing the kimono inside. The man came over to her, breath-ing cheap alcohol, and snorted into laughter when he saw the kimono.

'What? These?' He laughed again, holding up the boots, then, pointing at the kimono, 'For this motheaten rag?'

'It is not,' Momoko replied, outraged. 'This is fine Chinese silk. Use your eyes. Is this a rag?' she said, holding it up.

She then watched, horrified, as the man snatched it from her and ran his rough, stubbled fingers over the cloth, a lascivious grin on his lips and an American cigarette sticking out from the corner of his mouth. It was almost as if he were running his fingers over her body, and he knew it. His eyes held hers for a moment and Momoko knew they were both contemplating the same thought. When he had satisfied himself, he suddenly turned to other sellers at the neighbouring stalls and laughed as he unfurled the garment for their general amusement. When he had finished he threw it back to her and it landed in front of her on top of the shoes. He snorted his price and puffed on the stub of his cigarette.

It had come to this, haggling with drunken stall owners in the black market, just like everybody else. Giving away precious, personal possessions for practically nothing, just like everybody else.

When he turned back to the small brazier burning on the ground beside him, Momoko took out her purse and paid the extra needed for the boots. He took the money, counted it and added it to a roll of notes in his pocket. He then wrapped the boots in the brown paper the kimono had come in and tied the package up with a piece of leftover string.

As she backed away, now clutching the boots to her, she watched as he picked up the kimono and casually dropped it without looking, its dazzling, swirling butterfly disappearing on to a wooden crate on the ground. But there was no time to dwell on it.

In the icy wind she began her walk to the tram that would take her to Yoshi for the last time. She would hand him the boots, they would embrace and they would part. Her strides were long as she pushed through the crowds to her stop. And although the wind was icy, she ceased to notice. She would hand him the boots, he would nod, they would embrace, he would bow and it would all be over. She hardly dared admit it to herself, but her burden was Yoshi, and she would soon shed it. For it occurred to her that if she had embraced the bamboo-shoot existence at all, if she were shedding layers at all, they were layers that places such as this neither understood nor had any use for. And as she strode to her stop, weaving her way through the market throng, she was impatient for it to be over and done with. Impatient to be free of a past that was pulling her backwards, dragging her down. Impatient to get on with the new life, wherever it might lead, wherever they might go. She pushed through the crowd and leapt on to her tram, like a woman who hadn't a minute to lose. A woman whose moment of final farewell and final release was waiting for her, an easy stroll from the last tram stop. A woman whose moment of liberation was just out there, less than an hour away, at the end of this one last, brief transaction in a bare room on the fringes of the city.

Chapter Fourteen

There was no answer to her knocking and she peered into the darkness of the stairs, hesitated, and tried the door. It was unlocked and she slid it slightly open. Craning her head around, she called softly into the unlit room.

'Yoshi?'

Silence. She pushed the door a little farther and called out once more.

'Yoshi? Are you there?'

It was dark inside the room, except for a faint glow coming from the window. She could distinguish very little as she stood in the doorway holding the package and letting her eyes adjust to the gloom.

'Yoshi?' she called, more urgently. 'Yoshi, are you here?'

His books were still arranged along the wall, and as she stepped forward she could see two teacups sitting on the low table in the centre of the room.

Suddenly a match flared behind her and she jumped. 'Yoshi, you frightened me.'

But the shiny brass buttons lit up by the match were not Yoshi's. Spin put the match to the candle he was holding and smiled.

'Surprised?'

Momoko tried to speak, but could say nothing. She stared at Spin, then swung around looking for signs of Yoshi's presence.

'Nobody else here,' Spin said, in a voice she'd never heard before. 'Just you and me, my little peach.' He put the candle on the floor and lit another. Gradually, the room lightened. 'There, that's nicer. I always like a little light, don't you?'

Still she could say nothing. She closed her eyes and increased her grip on the package, as if she were clutching a small child. Spin eyed it.

'Ah, I see you've brought me something.'

Momoko stepped back. When she finally spoke her voice was shaking.

'Where is he?'

'What can you possibly have bought me that I haven't already got?'

'Where is he?' she pleaded, her voice rising.

'Let me guess what it is.' Spin leaned nonchalantly against the wall, his tie loosened and his cap tipped slightly forward to rest on the upper bridge of his nose. He was chewing gum.

Momoko closed her eyes and dug her fingers into the package. 'Please don't play games. What have you done with him?'

Spin continued chewing. 'You mean lover boy?'

She ignored the remark and concentrated on controlling the anger and wretchedness that threatened to engulf her. 'Where is he?'

'Gone. Now let's see what's in the package.'

She closed her eyes, groaning softly. 'Oh, Spin. What have you done?'

'The package!' he snapped as he stepped towards her, his eyes fierce and his jaw set firmly.

Momoko started. This wasn't her Spin. This wasn't her poet with a happy knack for Oriental languages. This was no Spin she'd ever known before. For here, in front of her, was a soldier of the Occupation, performing a military inspection. He snatched the parcel from her and tore off the paper without bothering with the string. A black shoe tumbled to the floor. He held up its pair, examining it in the dull glow of the candle.

'Very impressive.' He smiled.

She stood before him saying nothing, head drooped, eyes closed.

'American, no less,' Spin said, turning the shoe slowly and appreciating it from different angles. 'Must have cost you a fortune.' He looked at her. 'They're beautifully made. But there's only one problem. They're not my size.' He spoke with the theatricality of the practised interrogator. 'How do you explain that?' he added, now deep in his anger and enjoying his own irony.

Momoko was staring at the shoe on the floor. 'What have you done with him, Spin?' she said flatly, not looking up.

'Never mind what I've done. Look what you've done! You've bought the wrong size.' He held the shoe up by the tongue as if it were a piece of courtroom evidence. 'Or could it be that these are for lover boy?'

She lifted her face, suddenly defiant.

'He's not my lover.'

'Really?'

'He's an old and dear friend.'

Spin smiled thinly. 'Forgive me,' he said, assuming an informal, chatty manner. 'I may come from simple Anglo-Saxon stock, but I would have thought all these secret liaisons smacked of something more than two dear old friends sipping green tea together.'

She stared at him in disbelief, wiping her eyes.

'Oh, Spin. You've got it all wrong. There were no lovers' liaisons. He is a dear friend and we did sip tea together.'

'Call me simple, but I'm not wrong. Am I, my little peach?'

He then grabbed her and wrenched her towards the table around which she and Yoshi had sat the previous day. With his hand on the back of her head he forced her to look down.

The photographs were arranged in no particular order and covered the entire table. Some were snapshots, others enlargements, and the shock of them initially worked on Momoko like an anaesthetic, dulling the pain of his grip and distancing his shouting.

'Look at them!' he screamed. 'Now tell me I'm wrong.'

There she was in one photograph staring back from the doorway in her English dress. In spite of her shock, she realised she could remember the day it was taken; the long wait in the cold wind for the tram to Yoshi's, the young GI who had ordered a man from his seat and ushered an old woman into it like a gracious courtier representing the new dispensation. In an enlarged photograph, Yoshi looked directly at the hidden camera from his doorway. He normally photographed badly and as she stared at it she almost allowed herself to be pleased with the product. Another blurred shot showed her in the act of bowing to Yoshi before leaving. In another, they kissed. And she remembered that kiss.

These were private moments that had been stolen from her, now made public. The worst she could imagine had come true. From the angle of the photographs she knew that they must have been taken from the doorway opposite and that he must have been there the whole time, waiting and watching. She hadn't dreamt him into that doorway out of guilt or anything like it. He had simply been there, and she had seen him. Once again the nightmare image returned to her: she saw Spin's eyes staring up from the gutted doorway as they had in her dream and waves of wretched nausea passed through her as nightmare became reality. In one photograph, only the week before, her coat collar around her ears, she remembered leaving Yoshi's and looking forward to seeing Spin that evening. And as she took in the whole table she realised that this photographic jigsaw must have taken weeks to assemble. Weeks of late afternoons standing in the doorway opposite before coming to her place to spend nights of lovemaking, followed by hours of lying in the dark.

She then heard Spin repeating himself, a desperate, pleading tone to his voice. 'For God's sake, please, please, please, tell me I'm wrong.'

He was pointing at a photograph and speaking to her. He turned the photo over, read out the date he had written neatly in pencil on the back, then recited her activities with himself that particular evening. He turned over another photograph and in scrupulously prepared detail did the same again. His lips were wet with spittle. And it was only when she looked into his eyes that she saw they were red and wide and moist the way eyes are just before restraint and pride give way and bow to the superior force of tears. And in that moment she knew he was still reachable, if only he would stop. If only he would just stop.

But he didn't, and everything he'd kept crammed inside him over the last weeks and months suddenly burst from him like a monstrous boil.

'I believed in you,' he spat through his tears, his chest heaving, his breath coming in desperate gasps and his whole body looking like a piece of machinery about to exceed its functioning capacity and shatter into a hundred parts. 'I did,' he cried, his hat falling to the floor as he frantically wiped his eyes. 'Poor, silly, stupid, bloody, piss-weak me. I truly believed we were better than all that muck out there.' And here he waved a dismissive arm, indicating the whole fallen city outside. 'We were the lucky ones. The chosen ones!' And here he paused, staring at the ceiling, wavering on his feet. 'But we were just like everybody else, after all. Weren't we? Weren't we? Tell me I'm wrong.'

But Momoko remained beyond him, contemptuous and silent, and he could no longer tolerate her silences.

She was faintly aware of his arm rising, of his hand opening and of the sudden rush of air as it descended and he slapped her hard across one cheek. Momoko had only ever heard a rifle shot once— a gamekeeper shooting a rabbit when she was visiting a school friend in Surrey—but the crack of the rifle discharging the bullet stayed with her. And when Spin's hand made sudden contact with Momoko's face it was with the sharp, sudden crack of a rifle shot.

She turned aside, her hair tossed with the blow, then stared back at him, a thin line of bright red blood running from the corner of her mouth, her tongue tasting the blood in silent defiance. Spin watched, horrified, as her tongue ran across her lips, staining them the colour of burgundy. In the dim light of Yoshi's room she stopped Spin dead in his tracks with a fixed stare. It wasn't a look of fear or of pain, for at that moment she felt neither. It was—and she fixed his eyes in such a way that there could be no mistaking it—a look of utter disillusion. And I believed in you, it said. I believed in what you brought with you, in what you offered. I expected better of you, she could have added. *Now, you join the rest.*

She watched him look down at his hand, at her, and back at his hand again, suddenly bewildered and lost, as if his hand were suddenly foreign to him or belonged to someone else. Or as if this very hand that he had always trusted had suddenly gone rotten like everything else, betrayed him, and he was now staring at it, demanding some sort of explanation.

Then his arms were around her, and he drew her to him, his lips covering her eyes with kisses, and his treacherous hand desperately wiping the blood from her chin. She tried to push him away, but he held her firm in what under other circumstances would have been a lover's embrace—his lips seeking to heal her wound as he whispered her name over and over again. On and on, his voice continued in the dimly lit room, as if he had suddenly convinced himself that it could all be made better and everything retrieved if he could just hold her to him for long enough, and she succumbed to his embrace. This, this would be his signal that all was mended and all was well again. And in her weariness, in her sheer exhaustion, she did precisely that. For a moment, she almost fainted and fell limp. And a moment was all it took. A moment of exhaustion that he read as forgiveness.

Then his body was moving upon her, and her eyes were blank in the way of a defeated people's who stand and watch their fallen city being taken. His hat lay beside her on the floor, the front of her dress was open, her breasts exposed. Yet his fingers stroked her face as tenderly as the gentlest lover, his lips brushed against her ears and neck and temples, then sought the oblivion of her perfumed hair. And somewhere in the room, in between the sobbing and the broken breathing, she could hear Spin's voice, whispering her name over and again, lost, disembodied, childlike, as if calling out to her through the dark mists of a bad dream.

She let her head fall to one side and waited for it to be over. Her nipples had contracted with the cold. Her whole body was chilled and motionless, her limbs prone and her arms flopped beside her, as she briefly acquiesced—the acquiescence of a corpse.

Momoko then wiped her eyes with one hand and thought of the young Yoshi with his sketch pad and his keen, quick eyes. She ran her tongue across the traces of her own blood, then tightened her fist, repeatedly telling herself that soon she would feel nothing, that nothing was easy to feel. You just closed your eyes.

When she opened them, Spin, his shirt hanging loose, his trousers still unbuckled, was whispering words of love. They were standing near the doorway. He was tender, his voice soft. His eyes filled with tears as he covered her cheeks and hands with kisses, while he whispered his words of undying love, over and over again. Over and again, as if he would saturate her with this love of his, weigh her down with it, till she was too weak to move. Too tired to leave.

But her arms flew out with more force and strength than she ever thought she possessed, and Spin tumbled backwards with a look of utterly uncomprehending shock in his eyes, his head cracking as he hit the wall, his body slumping to the floor like a drunk.

Then she was on the street.

Chapter Fifteen

The afternoon had turned dark and the wind was still icy when Spin opened his eyes, not sure for a moment where he was. His head ached and spun as a crazy slide-show played inside it. One mad image flashed before him after another. He sat slumped against the bookshelf, his trousers unbuttoned and his shirt out, desperately trying to piece them all together; to separate the real from the nightmare, the slide-show from the facts. But he couldn't. It was hopeless. And all the time Momoko stared, blank-eyed, back at him, as did his own face, rubbing up against the window of his memory, contorted and spitting words he barely recognised as his, but knew full well were. And as he sat slumped against the bookshelf, slowly returning to consciousness, Momoko's eyes never left him, her eyes and the silent pronouncement they carried. *Now, you join the rest.*

The door to Yoshi's room was open and a thin film of light fell across his legs. As he shook himself, he remembered falling backwards, remembered the force of Momoko's arms when she flung him from her. He remembered the back of his head hitting the wall. Had he fallen unconscious? Or had he simply hit the wall and blacked out for a moment? Had it been minutes or seconds? How long had the door been open, and how long had she been gone? He bent forward and began fastening the buttons of his trousers. Photographs lay strewn across the floor, and not far from them a pair of shiny, dark American shoes beside torn brown-paper wrappings. Spin closed his eyes, slowly counted to himself, then opened them again. But he was still propped up against the bookshelf, the room was still the same and it slowly dawned on him that the madness was real. Something had happened. His memory was good, it wasn't a nightmare from which he would soon awaken. Something had happened. The way it does in dreams, but the dream was real.

The door may have only just been flung open, Momoko could very well still be down in the street. Or she might be miles away. He sat frozen, unable to decide, unable to move, until the candles burned low and the room began to take on an illusory half-light. Then he shook himself again and rose from the floor, steadied himself for a moment, before closing the door behind him and clattering down the stairs, oblivious to the many eyes of the house.

He gave up knocking and used his key to open Momoko's door. The teapot was on the floor. The dresser had been cleared and the clothes were gone from the chair. He opened her drawers and found them empty and wheeled round, scanning the room. Many of her personal belongings were gone—dresses, underwear, shoes—but others remained. Her dressing gown hung from the door. Momoko had clearly only had enough time to snatch a few things before going.

Circles of dust had been left on the dresser, but her watercolours still hung on the walls. The oak chest had been emptied, the letters were all gone. He let himself sink into the chair, examining different possibilities as to where she might be, and then saw that she had left the doll. Wedged between the chest and the wall, its painted face stared back at him impassively.

He looked around at the bookshelf beside him, noting that a few of the titles had been taken, but most remained. His eyes fell on the pocket Donne. It was a common edition, one that Momoko had brought from London, and he took it down from the shelf and lightly touched the cover with the tips of his fingers. As he held the volume he silently mouthed the lines he had committed to memory in another, simpler life, and he yearned for the Spin, the Momoko and the world he knew he'd thrown away. He closed his eyes tightly to shut out the images the poetry excited. The words had been his, he had been Donne.

Suddenly, he threw the book across the floor, watched it hit the wall and listened to the sound of the impact echo in the emptiness of the room. He then stood up, retrieved the doll and left, sliding the door shut behind him. She was out there, she was out there somewhere.

In the street a convoy passed in the dark. Troops, their helmets caught in the moonlight, sat in the backs of trucks, rifles in their hands. An icy wind blew, carrying the laughter of GIs on leave from the provinces. Spin walked along the street, barely noticing the cold or where he was going. Eventually he took a tram, intending to go back to the barracks, but jumped off at Shinjuku Park. As he crossed into the park, as he walked past the pond and the indifferent lilies that sat on the water in moonlit silence, Japanese girls, shivering in floral, cotton dresses, approached him out of the darkness.

'Very good, Joe. Very cheap.'

He shook his head and watched two GIs take a girl each by the arm, offering gum and cigarettes. One of the girls laughed, and for a moment it seemed that Spin knew that laugh and that body. The group of four paused and the young woman stood blowing cigarette smoke into the night, the line of her knee and thigh just visible under her dress as she rocked back and forth from one foot to the other. Impulsively, absurdly, the doll still in his hand, he walked up to her, only to be met by the unfamiliar face of a stranger. She stared at him insolently, dropped the cigarette and left it smouldering on the ground. He turned away with the laughter of the young women, and the GIs telling him to be on his way.

But his way didn't take him back to the base, and like a drunk he wandered the city for hours, often not sure of where he was or how he had even got there. Beside the waters of the Imperial Palace moat he watched the same bloated fish that he and Momoko had smiled upon a lifetime ago, still automatically opening and closing their mouths to passers-by. He stopped outside the old insurance building that was now MacArthur's headquarters, remembering his first day in the city and the bus trip with the young private from Montana. Across the front of the building a brilliant sign wished everybody a Merry Christmas. Spin stood, momentarily dazzled by the brightness of the letters, which cast their glow across the waters of the moat behind him.

He told himself over and over again that it wasn't the end of the world. They would both eventually put the incident down to that peculiar intensity that lovers invest in each other's lives and resolve it all in a flood of passion, for what had taken place was an act of love. The twisted, hopeless love that sprang from a mind that might have loved too well, but loved all the same. A love as true as the jealousy that had twisted it, as total as surrender. And he consoled himself that there would be no more silences, no more darkness between them. Not now. They could begin again. Like the whole country.

But even as he silently mouthed the words, he knew the words were meaningless, as all his words would be now. The air was clear and cold, the wind sharp, and as he stood staring at the Christmas decorations his accumulated impressions and memories swirled and formed in front of his eyes as if the contents, the random scraps of his mind, were suddenly unravelling before him like rolls of freed celluloid. The predatory GIs on the streets, the shivering girls, the writhing parks of the city, the burnt-out blocks, the lunar suburbs, the ragged army of a shattered empire squabbling over cigarette butts discarded by the guardians of the New Order, the grubby children, the sweet, sickly gum, the dust, the dirt and the death. The images played on and on in the deserted cinema of his mind. And all the time Momoko stared back at him blank-eyed. *Now, you join the rest.* He could even smell her, wafts of her scent coming to him through the wintry air, until he was convinced that she was standing right beside him, and he spun round in circles, scanning the street. It was only when he stopped spinning that he looked down at his uniform, put the lapel of his coat to his nose and took in her perfume, still there, where she had rested her cheek so often that it was now drenched with her scent.

A Klaxon droned in the night, a rickshaw, carrying a drunken GI and pulled by a man still wearing his army hat, padded slowly by along the street. Exhausted faces, puffed, blank eyes, broken by war and bewildered by peace, came and went. Beyond, in the distant corners of the night, strip shows would be playing and American movies showing, while in the station undergrounds across the city families would be bedding down in the warmest and most sheltered places they knew.

Here a story had ended. And what was gone was no less than everything. And there had been no invisible hand at his sleeve, leading him on to a grubby ending in a suitably grubby room. No one to whom he could turn and ask, 'Why?' Only himself—whoever he was now.... For at that moment the arms, legs, trunk, head, heart, eyes and nerves, as well as the jumbled collection of appetites, fears, desires and random impulses that called itself Spin, was just as much a mystery to him as this ghostly place he had come to. He might have found himself here; instead, he'd lost himself here.

He swayed from side to side on a deserted corner, a junction of empty streets, with his collar up and the wind whistling in his ears, Momoko's scent in his nostrils and the dull ache in his head returning in random waves. One hand was in his greatcoat pocket, the other, he was surprised to note, was still wrapped around the doll, clutching it to his chest. Slowly, carefully, he turned the doll upside down and gently wound the lever at the bottom until it would wind no more. Then he breathed deep of the cold, perfumed air, put the doll to his chest, and let the lever go. For ten seconds a sparse, single-string folk tune played in the darkness and filled the empty silence as if he were holding an entire orchestra in his hands.

Chapter Sixteen

While Spin rummaged through Momoko's room for the last time, eyeing and touching the things that were hers, and later while the doll played in his hand, Momoko was sitting on one of the crowded platforms in the labyrinth of Tokyo Station. She couldn't remember running from Yoshi's room, but she must have done. Yet she had no memory of doors opening or closing or her feet on the stairs of that rambling old house as she left it. She remembered only the rush of cold air as she fell on to the street and started running in the dark.

And the streets that she ran through were clogged with convoys of American troops. All of them. Truck upon passing truck calling out to her in the dark streets. The country was already bursting with them. Where could they all go? They whistled and laughed and jeered at the lone woman, for nobody else was about. Nobody but a certain kind of woman was on the streets at that hour, and every truck that passed assumed she was that kind of woman. She couldn't see their faces, only the occasional glint of a helmet or a rifle in the moonlight. They were shadowy figures, leaning out of their trucks like dogs straining at the leash, jostling with each other for the best position from which to fling their invitations and blow their kisses. Others simply howled into the night and stamped their feet.

And it was she, Momoko, who was the object of their urges. The flattened landscape, the potholed streets, normally silent, resounded with truck horns, wolf-whistles and catcalls for her. And engines, everywhere engines. When the convoy had passed its thunder faded and the streets assumed their customary, lunar stillness. Then a tram appeared and she rushed to its welcoming lights and the warmth of the carriage that glowed with the faces of her kind.

It was only inside, as she looked into the window, that she noticed her face was smeared with tears. Passengers were staring at her. She was a spectacle. Her coat was open, her dress was torn. And as she looked back to her reflection in the window and tried to smooth her hair and wipe the smudged make-up from her cheeks and eyes, she realised that she did, indeed, look the part of the whore. As she glanced back at the faces mutely staring at her in the tram, she silently mouthed the words that were welling up inside her, but lay dammed up in her throat. What were they staring at? Didn't they know? They were all whores now. Everybody. Every last one. The kamikaze pilot who buys and sells on the black market, once a bright angel, the master of glorious death, was now a whore. The women who snatched at Hershey bars flung from the backs of passing trucks, the families who accepted the sacks of rice and corn flour flown in from other lands, the children who scrambled for discarded cigarettes and gum and played *panpan* on the steps of sacred temples, the once proud soldiers who now carted their conquerors about the city in rickshaws, bowed and pathetic. All whores.

At the same time the image of Spin falling backwards into Yoshi's wall and crumpling to the floor returned to her. And in that moment, with the eyes of the tram upon her and the dark rings of her eyes staring back from the window, she wished Spin dead. Spin and all of them. All their fine words, their pressed uniforms, their open, friendly smiles, their wandering hands, had led to this.

She had run from the tram to her flat and grabbed what she could, constantly looking out for Spin, imagining he would crash through her door. But he didn't come. Perhaps he really was dead. It didn't matter. They'd all died a death this day.

At the station she found a place on the platform that wasn't taken up by the crowds waiting for trains that were already days late. She sat, her hands clasped on her knees, her coat wrapped around her shoulders, either staring into the distance or studying the scene around her with the miserable, detached fascination of a botanist. Occasionally, American and British soldiers pushed their way across the platforms and boarded their special trains. They were indifferent to the crowd, of which Momoko had now become a part.

A man in a broad-check suit that looked more like a vaudeville costume than business clothes played a harmonica to a circle of people beside Momoko. He was, she heard him say, a picture-show man. He was travelling throughout the countryside with his portable screen and his projector, and a suitcase full of forbidden films. 'Why shouldn't we see them?' he said again and again throughout the night. 'They are ours, aren't they?'

She listened to the stories that emerged from that small circle. A family of four was taking the ashes of their son back home, the box containing them held by a white sash suspended from the small shoulders of the eldest child. They shared their food and tea with the others; noticing Momoko sitting alone without food or drink, they offered her what they had. She shook her head and politely refused. The wife urged Momoko again to take a small rice cake, but Momoko again refused and they gave up. Two soldiers, still in uniform, watched the scene impassively, and broke the cake in half when it was offered to them.

Just when their attempts to drag Momoko into their circle seemed to flag, a man who wore the sharp clothes of a black-market spiv turned to her with a tobacco laugh that a voice inside her automatically pronounced as common. A street voice. A voice that belonged to a species of life that she rarely brushed with—if ever.

'Perhaps the lady would like something a little harder.' And he winked at the soldiers to let the joke sink in as he produced a bottle of local whisky. He popped the cork and waved it under her nose, and Momoko recoiled reflexively. 'Cigarettes, then?' he said. 'American.' But she ignored him and he turned back to the circle, shrugging his shoulders and taking a gulp of the whisky as he did so.

'Proud, eh?' He was eyeing Momoko. 'We've all fallen from the nest, beautiful. You're not the only one. But let me give you some advice.' And here he touched her knee with the casualness of a man used to handling women as if they were his own personal property and she suddenly wondered as she swung away from him if he were something more than simply a black-marketeer. 'Don't stay proud for too long.' He waved his yellowed finger. 'Don't stay proud, my pet, or you won't survive.'

He then turned back to the circle and passed the bottle of whisky about. She looked around for somewhere else to sit, but the platform was full. Beside her, the circle closed again, and she was left to herself once more. The harmonica returned. An American dance tune she knew only too well and wished she'd never heard blended with the smoky laughter, the hard-luck stories and the travellers' tales. She was thirsty and hungry, but she would sit through the night till her train came—to Nara and the family cottage that might still be theirs. Soon, she told herself, soon she would be gone.

Until this night she'd skated over the whole writhing, twisting mess, untouched by it, cocooned and safe inside her room—the room that had become their room. Now, she was on the outside, sitting on a cold platform surrounded by all the flotsam and jetsam of the times, her coat wrapped tight around her shoulders as she wondered where it had vanished to: that cocooned world in which they'd lived and loved and played.

Chapter Seventeen

Momoko did not return. Spin waited, but she did not return. Nor did she write or leave any sign of where she might have gone. She had simply disappeared. And in a city which thousands left daily to live in the provinces while the reconstruction was completed, one more disappearance was nothing new.

The morning after the scene in Yoshi's room Spin had rushed to the radio studios and burst into the production booth. There were no scheduled recordings and the booth was empty. He went from office to office, asking after Momoko, but nobody had seen or heard from her. He sat down on the steps outside the building, desperately trying to unravel the mess. How often had she emerged through those doors at the end of the day? It didn't seem possible that she would never walk through them again, never meet him in the street and take his arm the way she liked to. Never catch his eye on a tram, make tea in her room or smile back at him from under her duck-feather quilt.

And when Spin moved through crowds to board the patched-up carriages that took him to the ports and inland towns, he searched the faces that sat on the platforms. On trams he examined the commuters, and one day even tapped a young woman on the shoulder, only to back away, apologising for his mistake before alighting at the nearest stop. On footpaths he stared openly at the passers-by, but he was always met with a stranger's gaze.

One weekend he travelled to the house just outside Nara where Momoko's parents had gone after the heaviest of the bombings. He introduced himself to her mother as a colleague of her daughter's, and sat on the bench her father had built, gazing at the rock garden he had created. He asked casually after Momoko's whereabouts, but her mother said little, only offering more tea and inquiring in broken English if Knightsbridge had been badly bombed, then sighing and allowing her silences to grow as the afternoon shadows lengthened across the ground.

Towards the end of that first winter after the war, Yoshi—whom Martin had arrested before Momoko had even left the market with the boots—was awaiting trial on minor charges as a war criminal. And as much as Spin had tried to intervene, as much as he'd tried to explain to Martin that it was all a dreadful mistake, that the young man was no more a war criminal than he himself was, Martin insisted that it was out of his hands, that a process had begun and could not be halted. It would see itself through, and if the young man were as innocent as Spin said, then no great harm would come to him. That was no consolation, for Spin had convinced himself that if only he could free the young man, then perhaps he could salvage something from the mess. But it was out of his hands. Everything seemed to be out of his hands. And the young woman with the hair as black as a crow's feather had taken wing and disappeared into the ferment.

* * *

Five months later, one bright spring morning, Spin rode in a US Army Jeep to Atsugi airport, where a gutted B29 waited to take him to Guam, Singapore, then on to Darwin, Sydney and finally Melbourne.

As he alighted from the Jeep he saw them, two geisha standing by the side of the runway, waving to an American bomber that had just landed. They wore elaborate kimonos, their hair was meticulously arranged and their hands fluttered in welcome. Spin gazed at the women, mesmerised by the spectacle. The bomber dwarfed them as it passed along the runway and the geisha turned as it did, smiling and waving, in perfectly choreographed movements.

They drew it into them, this defeat. They drew it deep into them and held it close and fast, this event so vast that the only way to comprehend it was to love it and merge with it the way lovers merge with each other and die. The very word 'love' tolled in his mind like an insistent bell and made him suddenly turn his head away and close his eyes. But Momoko was still there, triumphantly, inescapably before him as she would be for the rest of his days: her head turned, her hair tossed, a thin trickle of blood coming from the corner of her mouth, and her eyes fixed defiantly upon him in silent rebuke.

Surely, surely, he told himself as he opened his eyes to the airfield once more, surely, time would eventually do its healing work and these months would recede into a distant phase of his life—what he would come to think of as that strange winter and spring he had spent in Occupied Tokyo, interpreting for homesick GIs, raiding schools for arms and illegal literature, participating in the great, liberal restructuring of the country so that the only empires they would seek after that would be those of light. Just as, surely, Momoko herself would one day become a memory. He would be standing in a bookstore, idly flicking through a novel, when a word, a phrase, an expression, would stir the past, almost pleasantly, and the image of Momoko would briefly return.

Part Two

Chapter Eighteen

June & July 1973

What was it? What was it that held his gaze so, and stirred him once again, as she had done a few days before? Even before he reached his office, he felt the faulty muscle of his heart frantically pumping blood to the margins of his body as it did before some half-dreaded, half-longed-for rendezvous when he was young. It was precisely the kind of excitement that his body could do without. It was almost as though he were the student, and she were scrutinising him. He had kept their appointment, he told himself, as he would any other meeting with a student, but he knew this was different. Besides, few students these days sought him out, mostly because over the years Spin had perfected the art of giving them the slip. In time word went round the faculty—don't bother. For this reason he rarely had the inconvenience of meeting with a student face to face.

For all this, though, he wanted to be here. He knew this as he saw her sitting opposite him, her hair, black as a crow, falling to her shoulders, and she at ease with the 'oldies' in a way that his generation never was. She was speaking, but he was only vaguely listening. He had come today because, sometime over the last few days, a sense of what he could only describe as being 'called' had slipped under the guard of a mind proudly trained and drenched in the art of close textual analysis. A mind that had spent a lifetime judging prose, sorting out the flabby from the muscular, was now succumbing to the all-too-flabby notion that something in this young woman had called him, and he had responded. And so, flabby or not, here he was.

She was casually outlining her ideas. Whether it was the words themselves or the confidence with which she spoke, he couldn't tell. But he quickly concluded that she was clever. Her reading, he observed, was wider than that of most of the students he'd taught over the years. She was, no doubt, worth the listening; her ideas were both original and well thought-out. But he couldn't throw off the feeling that if a third party were to enter the room they would wonder who on earth he was listening to. For, as she had done before, she seemed just to have materialised. You looked up, and she was suddenly there—no footsteps in the corridor—and on both occasions he could tell from listening that the corridor outside his room, often so busy, was empty. Did anybody ever see her come or go? Or was it only him? Did she, preposterous to contemplate, exist only for him? It was while he was contemplating the preposterous idea, that this young woman raised her arm and pulled back the sleeve of the woollen turtle-neck sweater she was wearing.

It was clearly her way, when she was animated as she now was, to speak with her hands. One of those who lose half their vocabulary and the ability to articulate even the most simple of ideas if their hands are suddenly tied. She was expanding on theories she had outlined in their first meeting. And they were bright, new ideas. As exciting to young women such as the one in front of him, as the lectures of Mr Leavis had been to him when he himself was young and felt the force of powerful ideas. And he recognised in her talk the first glimmer of the new dispensation that would soon consign his kind to the ranks of the quaint and dusty, just as Spin and his kind had bundled the old fogies who preceded them into a basket labelled 'gentlemen scholars'. He didn't so much mind, as feel a creeping indifference to the whole business. Besides, didn't they all do it? There was even something oddly comforting about the whole thing, a confirmation that the songs might change, but the dance remains the same.

But as much as he may have been faintly registering what she was saying, and as much as he may have been contemplating all this, from the moment she raised her arm and slid back the sleeve of her sweater, he was gone, lost to the world. Lost to this world, at least, and inhabiting another, more distant one. She was talking to him, yes, even perhaps posing questions, but it was of no consequence to him. All his attention was focused on the movement of her hand and the shapes that it took on: one moment, upturned like a fabulous tropical flower blooming for his eyes only, the next, her fingers slowly unfolding, popping into shape like origami responding to the touch of water. And throughout the next few minutes her hand moved, folding and unfolding with infinite grace.

He became aware of her voice. A question, she was asking a question, but what was it? He responded as if in a dream, lifting whole paragraphs from lectures he'd long since committed to memory, reciting them with the faintly distracted air of someone whose mind is elsewhere.

Then silence. The paragraphs ran out. He may even have stopped in mid-sentence, for she was now leaning forward slightly, waiting for him to go on. But he couldn't. He had nothing left to go on with. The paragraphs had run out and he was off the page, in the no-man's land of the mental blank. Then he was staring into her eyes, eyes that stared directly back at him in a silence that demanded that one of them say something—anything—so that they might recover whatever lies had sustained them until then and given them the kind of composure that the day-to-day world required. And, for a moment, it seemed that she would be the one to break it, leaning forward almost conspiratorially, her lips quivering on the verge of speech, but nothing came. And Spin, who could only bear so much of those eyes, blurted out something about the time. He rose, barely finishing the sentence, complimented her on her work with words such as 'fresh', 'fascinating' and 'promise' as he suddenly bounced about the room as if on springs. He gathered his briefcase, drawn to the door, and muttered something about the time again with what, to the young woman, must have seemed a puzzling urgency. But when he looked at her, still seated at his desk, there was nothing puzzled in her eyes at all. And, again, as before, he detected in those eyes a distinct hint of knowing, of a young woman perfectly aware of the jumble of stirred emotions tumbling about inside him. He had the distinct feeling that she was about to say something, but she simply rose with a curt, albeit polite, thank you.

When she was gone, leaving with a backward glance that seemed to speak for all the world of things unsaid, he was deeply relieved. For he knew that whatever it was that she might or might not have been about to say, he hadn't wanted to hear it. She had faded into the corridor, a figure from an odd, disturbing dream; faded, on the sounding of the horn, a figure from an insistent line of poetry, gone for the moment, but always just waiting to return and knock at the closed door of memory with all the insistence of the real thing. Suddenly the corridor was empty, and silent. Nobody else about. No one had seen her come, and no one had seen her go. He locked the door, unnerved by the shiny, still silence of the corridor, unnaturally uninhabited.

And so, Allen 'Spin' Bowler, Emeritus Professor of English Literature, appointed judge of the difference between the muscular and the flabby, proclaimer of ideas that stood upright and traversed the real world, made his way from the department at which he had taught all of this for most of his academic life, with the nagging, insistent feeling that he had been 'called' and that the flabbiness within him had answered.

Eventually he stepped out into the brilliant midwinter sunshine, fedora over his forehead, coat open, and fled the university into the unexpected distraction of a sunny afternoon. The air was sharp, and he strode along the wide, leafy street, like a man in need of a vigorous walk.

After dinner that evening, he was back as usual in his study, his sanctuary—until lately. He slumped rather than sat at his desk. The books around him seemed suddenly to have acquired the look of books that are looked at rather than read, and he had no desire to open any of them, even to browse. Once again, the young woman's hand rose, pulling the woollen sleeve of her sweater back; once again he was utterly entranced by the glimpse of wrist and arm that the gesture afforded him. And then she suddenly stopped in midgesture—as she had not that afternoon—and stared at him. Silence fell upon them, and in reproach, or pity or anger, she finally uttered those words that she had not uttered that afternoon: *Now, you join the rest.*

The silence had been filled. *Now, you join the rest.* The very words he'd been so relieved not to hear. The lies that had sustained them until that moment now quietly left the room, and, in the wake of their withdrawal, he was left with the muscular fact of those five words that had returned to him, as they were always going to: words that were never going to go away, which would always be there to knock insistently upon the closed door of his memory.

Chapter Nineteen

The light was mellow in the square opposite. Shadows stretched long over the deep, green lawns. The smartly dressed woman in her early fifties, sitting at a large desk in her London office, said to herself, 'Goodness, is that the time?' How long had she been staring out her office window on to the square? How long had she been lost in those luminous shades of green, thinking green thoughts. Then the old mantle clock she'd inherited from Charlie Boy chimed in and she noticed the time.

The windows were broad, the office was wide and the walls were almost entirely lined with books. On the desk were ordered piles of manuscripts and correspondence, the reading glasses she'd put down a few minutes ago and a couple of framed family snaps, some in black and white, others in colour. On a rare patch of wall was a framed photograph of a wintry tree branch, possibly apple. It was one of the few items she'd taken with her when they left Japan not long after the war. Momoko had as few friends then as she has now.

One of them is Eiko, the woman who took that photograph. She'd always loved her pictures; her solitary trees and wide, sparse skies, except for the odd watchful falcon, were strangely comforting. In them she felt the camaraderie of those who go alone. Then her eyes shifted from the wintry image to the clock on the mantel.

Within minutes she was strolling through the green park opposite, dressed in blue jeans and a summer shirt. She crossed the park, eyeing the groups of young people lounging on the lawns. Behind her, set in a corner of the square, her office receded and disappeared behind the overhanging branches and drooping leaves. The famous brass plaque, too, faded from view. The building might be small, but this was where the best writers of the age had come, before and after the war, and it was Charlie Boy who'd found them. Then Charlie passed the keys to her and she sat in his old seat as though she had been born for it.

At the end of the park she crossed to her tube stop, taking in the trees, the street, the shop windows and the blue and amber sky of a late summer's day; the whole city was vibrant with colour. The young, it seemed to her, brought the colour with them. They were sick of the past, the whole, grey past, and Momoko, strolling through the park, gave silent thanks for the way they had coloured her world. For there was energy in all that colour. It was as if the natural world were responding to the new dispensation of the young, with flowers bursting into bloom and trees shimmering with green leaves. And, as she left the park and strolled down to the tube, she was once again thinking in green.

The city as she knew it just after the war had been another world. There didn't seem to be a place on earth that hadn't been damaged then, or a person, and for a time it felt as if it would go on that way for ever. Stained, unpainted and damaged by the years like everywhere else, it was a weary, edgy place. The very air was grimy and smelly, like that of a new dark age, and the world so weary, spent and exhausted that victory and defeat blurred to the point that nobody could tell the difference any more or nobody cared.

No one looked particularly victorious then. Except the Americans. They always did, wherever they went. In Tokyo they had looked every inch the victors. With their pressed uniforms and their full, well-fed faces, their gifts of chocolate and cigarettes and the easy, loping strides with which they got around the town, they had exuded victory. They weren't shy about it, nor did they try to be discreet about the enormous power they so clearly possessed. They were crass and loud and overbearing the way victors should be, and, looking back, she could now see that there was something wonderful in their crassness that might make you want to join in. Empires rose and fell, of course. She knew all that. But it was important then that nobody told the Americans. Momoko felt almost privileged to have seen them at the height of their power, and she realised that in those drab and jittery years she'd drawn on the hope they brought with them far more than she had admitted.

If there were any victories to be plucked out of the past, they were the little day-to-day ones of wounded people gradually mending their wounds and learning to live again. And it was at times such as these that she allowed herself a sense of triumph, of having come through it after all, and the world sparkled just that bit more for having taken a brief look back.

In the tube subway she merged with the throng; just another bright summer shirt in a crowd of bright summer shirts.

Chapter Twenty

Was it all for this? All around him the walls of the city, the new Tokyo risen from the ashes, shimmered and blinked like the open pages of vast, luminous comic books. Once, the skyline had been ablaze with Molotov flower baskets, incendiaries, bombs and fire. Now wherever he looked the city was ablaze with neon. Entire walls exploded again and again and again, blue turning to green, yellow, red, pink and orange. All around him the pages of the city flickered and blinked, their insistent signs written in a jumble of languages, and all of them alien to Spin, who turned in slow circles at the traffic lights of an expansive intersection.

Towering Japanese characters shimmered in the night, shivering from one colour to another, while beside, above and around them, giant signs transmitted their messages in English and French to all those who gazed at the electric sky. Cartoon figures skated across the night, their grins illuminating the intersection. It was, he mused, a comic-book world, its never-ending pages turning, again and again and again, without ever leaving the surface of things.

Spin left the intersection, the noise of the traffic and the hum of life, and disappeared into the labyrinth of lanes and streets that radiated from it. But everywhere loudspeakers, shrill and harsh, broke on his ears like shattering glass. Continuous loops of advertising jingles played their messages, Japanese turning into English, English into Japanese, on and on, all through the night. And somewhere, floating through it all, through the still and heavy summer air, the recorded voice of a solitary child. *Twinkle, twinkle, little star…* The notes fell softly in the darkness from invisible speakers. Wherever he wandered, through booming lanes and side streets, the fairytale chorus fell softly upon him as if sprinkled on the evening air by one of the neon cartoon figures whose eyes gazed upon the city below with manic indifference.

Was it all for this? The question returned as Spin ambled about the city. He stood, his short-sleeved holiday shirt sticking to his body from the perspiration that poured continually from him, his arms limp by his sides, unable to find the answer. Was this comic-book world the lasting gift of that distant victory that nobody now remembered? The lasting gift of the Occupation that nobody spoke of? Was this the light, the sweetness that Spin imagined he'd brought with him all those years ago?

He passed along the footpath, a ghost from another era, pausing to look for the way to the underground that would take him back to Tsukiji and the oasis of the tiny rectangle that was his hotel room. A careless youth passed him on a small scooter, nearly knocking him over, but made no apology. Spin raised an ineffectual arm in protest, but the youth was gone and nobody noticed. All around him the fast-food shops, the record stores and the windows filled with brightly coloured telephones or heaped with jogging shoes throbbed with trade, while delivery vans came and went and one sticky pop song gave way to another.

So this was Shibuya. Somewhere near here was the street he had walked along a few days after arriving at the end of the war. Back then, his feet had rung out in the eerie silence of the cool night air, and he longed now for the silence that he always thought of whenever the city came to mind. Somewhere near here, long ago, he had seen a door without a house on a vacant lot, and close by he had found a restaurant that served fresh fish when fish was a luxury. This was the first time Spin had seen Tokyo since the end of the war and his memories were slowly returning. He looked about, desperate to convince himself that, under the glitter and the noise, the world he had known was still there—and ready to welcome him back.

But the fancy had no sooner occurred to him than he felt a great weight pressing down on his chest. He lurched forward, suddenly faint and short of breath. He scoured the vast, concrete plain of the intersection and realised there were no benches or seats to sit upon. The horizontal traffic lights changed from green to amber to red and back again. Spin knew that he must either sit on the footpath where he stood or fall down. So he sat, and let the comic-book world go on around him.

As he took a pill from his pocket he could have kidded himself and chosen to believe that it was just the congested city, the heat and the noise. But he knew now it wasn't. 'It's like having a time-bomb inside you, Mr Bowler,' his doctor had told him a year before. 'Only no one knows when it's set for. It could go off next month, next year, or in ten years' time. To an extent, it's up to you. Be careful, and you just might outlive us all. And take these when you need to,' he'd said, writing out a prescription as he spoke. 'How long have you been aware of the problem?'

'Some time,' Spin had answered vaguely. 'I can't be sure.'

'Months?'

'Yes.'

'A year?'

'Possibly.'

'More?'

'Possibly. Is it important?'

'Yes.' His doctor nodded his head slowly, looking down at the new carpet on his surgery floor. 'It never struck you as odd?'

'I managed to live with it.' Spin had paused, looking at the various medical posters on the wall, now aware that he might not simply have been referring to his medical condition. 'Until lately.'

To his surprise his doctor nodded in complete understanding, implying that he had long since ceased to be amazed at what people managed to live with. It had been a short consultation, but he had strolled back to the university under a bright winter sun, looking at familiar streets with a rare intensity. His doctor had, of course, only told him what he already knew in his bones—even if the news had been more dramatic than he thought. Still, he felt strangely calm, even serene, as if something within him had been finally released and he was experiencing a kind of freedom he hadn't felt for a long time.

That night he sat in his study, staring at his illuminated garden and slowly absorbing the implications of that ten, possibly fifteen, minutes he'd spent in his doctor's consulting rooms. He wasn't to exert himself or go rushing about. And he wasn't to treat it like a death sentence. Some people went on for years and years. He could outlive them all. Once the few, simple facts of the situation had been outlined, there seemed little point in staying.

Not long before leaving he'd changed his travel plans, and had touched down in a Tokyo that was as foreign to him as, he imagined, the moon would be. Things that once would have seemed reckless were now quite plausible. Time might be infinite, but not one's share of it. With the memory of the young Japanese woman still more vivid than he'd have wished, he'd absent-mindedly taken down the doll from the bookshelf. He'd wound the lever at the bottom, and its music had sounded in the room for the second time in as many weeks, bringing with it the sights, the silences and the smells of that world he'd once known.

Spin was sitting on the footpath, slowly regaining his breath when a man he guessed to be his own age stood beside him and urged him to follow—there was, he said, a bench at the station, which was not far away. Nodding acceptance of the suggestion, Spin rose and moved forward on unsteady legs and, supported by the stranger, took those few, endless steps to a cool, marble bench where he slumped and waved his thanks. It was then that the man suddenly bowed and spoke to him in English.

'Thank you, awfully!' he said, smiling and bowing.

Spin smiled and nodded back, saying in English that he was the one who should be saying thank you. But the man only repeated himself. Spin watched as he bowed again, turned, and disappeared into the constantly moving crowd. It was quite possibly the only English that the man knew, dredged up from the lost pages of an old phrasebook. The words weren't important, it was the gesture. Just before he'd gone the man had caught Spin's eye with a look that said, 'We understand each other, you and I. My words may not matter now, but we both come from a time when they did.' And with that, the man had departed. Vanished, it fancifully occurred to Spin, on the fading of a thousand car horns.

Earlier that day Spin had gone back to Kojimachi. He found a modern suburb, anonymous like all modern suburbs. He'd been happy to wander while he found his bearings, looking for old landmarks—if any still existed. The place was quiet and secluded in a way that expensive suburbs always are. The aromas from French-style bakeries and restaurants followed him about. There was virtually no traffic, no noise and no cheap advertising.

He had strolled along those narrow, tree-lined streets for over an hour and was quietly admiring the trimmed hedges along the street he was in when he stopped. The flats were modernised, but there was something familiar about the doorway, the windows and the round stairwell that told him the building dated back to before the war.

He looked up, shielding his eyes from the sun. If this were the block, then Momoko's room would have been—where? He studied one flat, then another, until his eyes came to rest on a second-floor window. Was that it? Was that where they found each other, and lost each other? Where Momoko for ever receded from him and Spin for ever lost his way? He could call that Momoko's room if he wished, and he could imagine his younger self staring out through the top panel of clear glass on to the Tokyo he knew all those years before, but he would never be sure. And he wondered if it would be like this everywhere: never knowing, never sure.

In a small bar near his hotel the ever-present baseball was on the television. He sat up at the counter, the only Westerner, while the rest of the place watched and squabbled over the game. Once they might have squabbled over their Go boards or their newspapers. Spin rose to the cheers of a home run, slid the door of the air-conditioned bar open and stepped back once more into heavy, summer air.

Back in his room he checked his train ticket to Kyoto. It was a late-morning departure and he would be there by mid-afternoon. From Kyoto, as he well knew, it was only a short hop to Nara.

He leaned back on the bed and idly scanned the room. His breathing was easy now, and the pain had passed. The blind was drawn but there was no view, anyway. A small television had been fixed to the far corner of the room and coloured brochures on the table detailed the pornographic movies available.

Again, that cacophony of eager voices that had plagued him before he left home rose in his ears, telling him only fools and those with nowhere else to go went back. Soon the voices were silenced by a group of businessmen in the hallway, back late after a night of carousing at strip clubs and bars.

He sat up and fingered the cellophane wrapping of a packet of rice crackers, and contemplated the jar containing his prescribed pills. He had known a Tokyo that had only existed for a brief moment, and in that moment he had met Momoko. And just as the city was no longer the place he knew, Momoko, if he ever found her again, would not be the Momoko he'd known. She would be a stranger to him, as the city itself was. There was no past to go back to. Nobody was there any more. If the past was anything at all, it was an empty room that had been cleared of its furniture and stripped of its chattels.

He rose from the bed then and almost threw his train ticket into the bin. Damn the rotten luck of that young woman coming to him just when she did. Damn her bright young ideas and the infinite, bloody grace of her hand. And damn you, Spin Bowler, for the stupid, bloody things you do. He hesitated then, staring at the ticket as if he just might rip it up. In the end he placed it carefully in his document case along with his plane ticket and his passport; the passport that contained a photograph of a sixty-year-old professor of English Literature, whose curls were now grey at the sides—the passport that told him he was Allen Douglas Bowler, born Melbourne, 1913. No mention of anybody called Spin. But Spin was back all right, and Allen Douglas Bowler cursed him once more as he lay back on the single bed and closed his eyes.

Chapter Twenty-One

While Spin slept, Momoko spilled out of the tube and strolled through narrow streets down into the market of Covent Garden. Punch and Judy were going through their motions for an ever-changing audience milling round them. Momoko was at home in the crowd. It gave her anonymity and it gave her comfort, allowed her to be by herself, and with her thoughts. Slowly, happily, she eased through the throng under the afternoon sun, eventually drawn irresistibly to a table of old books.

Books always did that to her, always had the power to change her course. Like meeting Charlie Boy. Well, she quite naturally called him Charlie Boy now, but it wasn't always like that. She'd heard of him, of course. Everybody knew C. E. Morris. But she'd never thought she'd meet him until Eiko wrote her a letter of introduction before they left Japan. Momoko never really knew how her friend came to know him, or even how well she knew him. And, what with Charlie Boy's reputation, she wasn't about to ask. Especially as Eiko was old now and her memory prone to sudden lapses. As she sifted through the volumes on the stall, the sensation of smelling the aroma of Charlie's pipe tobacco, and the shock of first encountering his unpleasant breath, came back to her. That, and his springy eyebrows, and the eyes themselves bright as if from wine. Which perhaps they were. He was one of those writers who, supposedly, catch the mood of a generation. He didn't look like his photographs, but his voice didn't surprise her. There was even something oddly familiar about their first conversation, as though reading him were tantamount to talking with him. She knew his voice would be fast and busy, barely pausing for breath, for his writing was like that and she'd always imagined that he wrote the way he spoke. He was short, but robust, and she could see the ladykiller in him as he chatted to her, his hair falling across his forehead like that whole generation of pre-war British intellectuals; that generation which, when asked how old so-and-so was, would reply either 'our age' or not, as the case might be.

She'd left that first meeting with a job. A lowly job, but a job. She didn't know just what Charlie did to clear the way, nor did she ask. Not even now that he was retired and she had his chair. It was still a cause of wonder to her that she'd gone from reading her favourite writers to publishing them; gone from imagining what it might be like to talk to them, to meeting and working with them. She discovered right from the start that she had a nose for the real thing, and Charlie came to trust her judgement.

By that time he'd begun to feel that he was losing touch, that he could no longer pick the young ones, and he leaned on her increasingly. And the more she felt the weight of his trust, the more certain she became about where it was all leading. So, it was no surprise when he finally passed the keys of his office over to her. By then, he'd long ceased to be C. E. Morris and had become—as he was to all his friends—Charlie Boy. Good-time Charlie, but with a razor tongue for anyone who took his generosity for granted. For, beneath all the charm, he had a memory like a steel trap and eyes like the shutters of a camera. You didn't have to spend too much time in Charlie's company to see how it was done. He was a good teacher, and she enjoyed watching him go to work: all charm, the razor well hidden in the warmth of his smile, but always at the ready. She had been tired and scared—tired beyond her years—when Eiko's letter led her to Charlie. Now she sat in his chair, and passed that famous nose of hers across the manuscripts that came her way, sniffing out the vintage from the plonk.

Suddenly dropping a paperback on to the stall table, she remembered why she'd rushed to the market in the first place. Naomi's shirt. It didn't seem like much of a birthday present, but it was all she wanted and you could only get them here. Besides, they'd never, either of them, ever made a big fuss about birthdays. And perhaps, she mused, it was because in those early years when her daughter was small, there was little energy or money to make a fuss.

Naomi was just back from Japan. She'd never seen it before because Momoko had never gone back. Well before the Occupation officially ended, she'd leaned on her father's old diplomatic friends and was one of the first out. No backward glance, no looking back—escaping from the stain of being one of the Occupation's whores who had the front to bring up her little bastard openly. Luckily, Naomi didn't remember any of it. Her trip had been a happy one, evident from her chatty postcards.

By the time Momoko had found the shirt and left, the walls of the square were turning dark. Crowds were spilling out of the pubs and on to the footpaths, and broken choruses of vaguely familiar songs came and went on the breeze. A young man at the centre of a noisy group caught her eye and she was puzzling as to why he should, when he hastily expelled cigarette smoke into the air in the manner of the young intellectual he no doubt was—she instantly knew the type.

The tube swallowed her once again and on the train she dwelt on the young man, the puff of smoke, the smiling quip, and the name Spin passed through her mind for the first time in weeks. And, as she did at such moments, she wondered what he might be up to. She counted the years and calculated his age, then wondered if she would even recognise him if she saw him now.

Then her stop came and the sliding doors of the train parted. Minutes later she stepped out into the warm air of Camden Town. They happened, these sudden flashes. Suddenly, a red lantern would swing before her or an ancient pine blown away by war would sway once again in the breezes of her memory. This happened. Then the everyday world of her life would return in all its solidity and she would get on with things, cool and calm, Charlie Boy's anointed.

Chapter Twenty-Two

Once he accustomed himself to the shop signs, the occasional, discreet neon displays, the cafés with odd, English names that made no sense, and the ubiquitous piped music in the modern shopping mall, the town of Nara wasn't really that much different. The town centre was still quite small, and it hadn't taken him long to get his bearings.

The evening was still hot, but the darkness made the air seem cooler. The red and orange lanterns that lined the circular pond in front of him glowed on the still water. The deer reclined against the trees or slept under the benches. Lone men and groups of friends either sat in contemplative silence or engaged in quiet conversation so as not to disturb the night. Every so often a match flared and cigarette smoke rose from one of the benches. Apart from the crickets and the occasional low laughter, there was little other sound.

Spin was counting the years since he'd last sat by the pond, a young soldier raiding the local school for arms, interpreting for GIs and missing his girl. He counted forward, he counted back. Each time he arrived at the same figure. It didn't seem possible that it had been twenty-seven years between then and now. Twenty-seven years of carefully written lectures, classes, corrections and long Christmas vacations. Twenty-seven years of dinners, end-of-term drinks, book launches and recitals; of talking, laughing, listening, drifting off—of breathing in and breathing out without ever really paying any attention to what he was doing. It was easy enough to lose track of twenty-seven years, he thought, you just did all that.

And now there was this other thing that he barely knew what to make of. He'd come back to this country simply to make his own peace with the past, but everything had changed in one afternoon. No, not an afternoon. A moment. A look of sudden understanding, a widening of the eyes, an unspoken exclamation—and his whole world had flipped. It wasn't just the past that preoccupied him now.

Earlier that morning he'd stood in front of the cottage that Momoko's parents had lived in through the last months of the war and after. It wasn't that difficult to find. An easy walk from the main street. In fact, once he was past the shops and into the quiet, residential part of town it was surprising, even alarming, how little things had changed. The same moss-layered high walls along the streets, the same trees in the gardens, probably.

When he turned a corner and passed the governor's official residence he knew for sure he was standing at the top end of Momoko's street, and that her parents' cottage was only a few paces away. Here, everything seemed eerily unchanged. He slowed his pace and stepped quietly along the street as if it were the pathway to a shrine. And in a way it was. Yet, when he reached the spot, he suddenly became confused and couldn't be sure which house had been theirs.

There were two small cottages next to each other that must have been built about the same time and looked very similar. Behind him, in the vast gardens of the house across the street, giant crows called to each other and swooped from pine to pine. He couldn't remember noticing them when he first entered the street, but now they seemed to be everywhere, and he couldn't help but wonder if his arrival had stirred them up, as if they instinctively knew he was a stranger whose very presence threatened to upset the order of things.

It was difficult to see over the walls and into the houses. In front of the two cottages, he stood on tiptoes, and tried to peer into the small front gardens, looking for something that might jolt his memory. Nothing did. He moved closer and, as he did so, a man passed by on a bicycle and eyed him warily. A motorist turned the corner and slowed, scrutinising Spin before moving on. He was arousing people's suspicions; of course, it must have looked odd, peering over people's walls like this, but he had to know, and moved even closer to one of the cottages.

Suddenly an elderly woman seemed to materialise from nowhere and was standing beside him with a shopping bag under her arm. He was disconcerted, not only by the suddenness of her presence, but by her appearance itself. Aside from looking not quite Japanese, she didn't look quite human. Rather, she looked like a fantasy figure from one of those escapist novels that his students read all too frequently for his liking: a benevolent gnome, a guardian goblin that spoke, or some such nonsense. Although initially keen to be rid of her, it occurred to Spin that she might know something, might even be useful. He brightened.

'Good morning.'

Spin's Japanese had been rusty at first, but now the fluency was returning. The woman heard the greeting, but remained silent and unmoved. She even looked briefly about the street in search of the speaker, giving every impression that she thought it impossible that the greeting could have come from the European gentleman standing in front her. But there was nobody else around and Spin repeated his greeting.

'Good morning,' he said, smiling and bowing. 'May I trouble you a moment?'

The woman bowed and nodded, but still looked confused. Perhaps it wasn't the fact that Spin was speaking Japanese that puzzled her, for the small number of Western tourists who visited the town sometimes spoke an amusing smattering of the language. It was, quite possibly, his fluency that surprised her.

'I was here a long, long time ago.' Spin looked about, taking in the old walls and the green trees, trying to affect a comforting, relaxed demeanour. 'It is a lovely street.'

'It is,' the woman agreed, a little vaguely.

'Have you lived here long?'

The woman was still uneasy. 'I have always lived here.'

'Ah.' Spin sighed, expressing his pleasure. 'Indeed. Why would anybody leave?'

Again the woman nodded without speaking, only this time her silence clearly implied that if Spin had something more to say then he'd better get on with it.

'I knew a woman,' he began. 'Miss Yamada Momoko. She lived here, I believe. She was the daughter of…'

But he didn't need to go on, for the woman was already nodding and pointing to the house next door.

'You knew her?' Spin said, keeping his tone casual.

'I knew them all. Momoko. Her mother. A fine woman.'

'Kyoko?'

'Yes,' the woman said, studying Spin closely, his grey curls, his pale skin, his sun hat like the hats the men in her youth wore. 'Kyoko.'

'You might say I'm an old friend of the family,' Spin said, hoping to relax her. And it seemed to be working. 'Momoko, Toshihiko and Kyoko.'

The names rolled off his tongue with a reassuring familiarity and the woman nodded again, this time, it seemed to Spin, a little sadly.

'A nice family,' she said.

'Yes, a nice family.' Spin smiled, then added, 'It's been a long time. I couldn't quite remember the house. This one, you say?'

'Yes, it was this one.'

'Was?'

'Kyoko died. They haven't lived here for years.'

'Oh, that's a pity,' said Spin, squinting into the sun, still troubled by the absurdly uneasy feeling that he just might be talking to an apparition. There was a faraway sound to the woman's voice and for some reason—perhaps her awkwardness and vagueness—she gave Spin the impression that she hadn't spoken to anybody for hundreds of years. 'You don't know where they went?' he added, as casually as possible, hoping not to disturb the fragile trust he seemed to have established.

But she was distracted, as though quietly remembering the times, and hadn't heard the question. Perhaps that distance in her eyes was simply the distance that comes to old people's eyes when they suddenly drift off. Spin judged her to be somewhere in her eighties, perhaps more. But she was oddly timeless, as well.

'The daughter was here not long ago. Oh, I forget the dear child's name,' she said, clearly troubled by the lapse in her memory.

Spin thought that that was an odd way of referring to Momoko and was puzzled, since her name had already been mentioned twice. He was even beginning to doubt the reliability of anything the woman said, taking into account her age and memory. But he repeated his question.

'Kyoko died here. Right here,' she said, pointing to the house.

'And Momoko?'

'It was the winter the Americans left.' And, staring up at the sky, she added, 'Whenever that was.'

Spin let the moment of reflection pass before repeating himself.

'And Momoko?'

The woman slowly turned back to him and Spin had the uneasy feeling that she'd completely forgotten he was still there.

'Momoko? Oh, she went away.'

Spin waited a moment before continuing.

'Forgive me…'

'Eiko,' the old woman suddenly offered without being asked, smiling and bowing her head.

'Forgive me,' Spin continued, recognising that he was indeed talking to someone who had lived alone for many years. 'I'm an old family friend and it's been so long. You don't know where Momoko went?'

'Oh, yes. England. Everybody knew.' The woman was nodding, suddenly alert, even pleased, confirming the truth of the statement to herself. 'Kyoko received letters from England. The postman made a big show of it. Every time one arrived.' The woman stood in the narrow road shaking her head. 'Most annoying.'

Spin was preoccupied, and a little impatient with the old woman by now. 'Annoying?'

'For the life of me, I can't remember that child's name. It's gone.' The woman was once again deeply troubled by this and Spin decided to leave her alone. It was only after they'd said their farewells and the woman was walking away that it hit him like an oncoming tank and spun him round on the spot. He ran after her.

'A child, you said?'

The woman turned. 'Yes, there was a little girl.'

'Momoko's?' Spin gasped, his voice suddenly rising.

'Of course,' the woman said, oblivious of Spin's reaction. 'Think of her, poor woman. A little foreign girl in a little town.' Her eyes suddenly shone and she clasped her hands. 'Naomi.' Then she looked directly at him, her expression now quite lucid, suddenly doubting his credentials as a family friend. 'You don't know this?'

But Spin simply stared at her and said nothing. He was perfectly still, barely seeming to breathe. And although he was staring at the woman, he wasn't taking her in. And somewhere, lost in one of the interminable hallways of his consciousness, there was a question that he should have been answering, but couldn't bring himself to. His whole being had come to a standstill, and nothing—head, heart, voice—seemed to be functioning. It was only as she edged away from him that he became vaguely aware of her again, of the alarm in her eyes and the look on her face, that sudden thunderbolt of insight in which he knew without doubt that she had summed up the situation with devastating accuracy. A look that clearly said, 'Oh. You!'

As Spin lifted his weight from the bench and strolled around the edges of the lantern-lit pond, he also carried the knowledge that the neighbour had so casually passed on to him. A child… His steps were sluggish, his feet barely left the ground. Had he always walked this slowly? Why had he never noticed the weight of his bones before, the dead weight of his arms hanging by his sides, the droop of his head? A foreign child. The woman had then looked at him and, like Spin, had wasted no time in putting two and two together. Throughout those twenty-seven years that had so easily slipped from him, a little girl had been growing up. He couldn't even begin to comprehend what he had missed because he had never watched a child grow. He had no idea of when she had been born, where, and how. What she said, what she did. She had lived half a lifetime of which he knew absolutely nothing. He only knew that she was out there somewhere, flesh of his flesh, a life that was drawn from him. A deer raised its head as he passed a bench occupied by two old men conversing over a chessboard, but he barely noticed either the animal or the men. Why had he been left to live his life in the dark? Had he never come back to Tokyo, he would never have known.

But it wasn't anger he felt. The loss was too great, the hurt too overwhelming, the simple facts of the situation so vast, it couldn't be reduced to anger. He stopped, deep in thought, near the chess players. Perhaps she had tried, had no luck and given up. It was possible. He had been very quick to leave the army and take up an academic post. And even though he'd left his address with the army he knew the trouble they had, just keeping their heads above water with thousands upon thousands of soldiers, all wanting to be demobilised, to get out at once and just go home. A letter, vaguely addressed, could so easily go missing and, with it, a whole other life. The simplicity of it all was excruciating to contemplate, but it was its very simplicity that made it quite possible.

Then again, he thought, perhaps Momoko had never tried to contact him. While part of him acknowledged that he couldn't blame her if she hadn't, another part of him refused to believe that she would ever do such a thing. Not *his* Momoko. He slowly shook his head, aware that he was now sighing. He wasn't someone to sigh often, but it seemed that every time he exhaled he sighed and he was incapable of stopping it. The air was close, it was still hot. If only there were a breeze, he thought, looking about the park. But the lanterns were motionless, the water of the pond a mirror reflection of everything around it, except when a carp broke the surface in pursuit of a moth.

It didn't seem possible that the same lanterns would glow on those still waters when Spin was no longer part of things or that the same carp would break the surface of the pond when he was gone—as indifferent to his departure as it was to its own brilliance. Now desperately tired, he left the park and walked slowly back into the town and to his inn. He took his shoes off in the foyer and chose a pair of slippers from the range left out for the guests.

In his room he sat on the floor and drank the cool water that had been left for him. He rested his head against the wall, the look on the neighbour's face still vivid in his memory as he closed his eyes and silently vowed that he would find Momoko. Whatever it took in time, money and effort, he would find her. And once he had found her he would also find that part of his life he had not known existed until a few hours before.

But London—he assumed she had returned there—was so vast. Still, there couldn't be too many Yamadas in the telephone directory. He had allowed the thought to pass when he remembered what a common name it was, like tracking down a Smith or a Brown— and that was only if she still went by that name. In all likelihood she had married and might now be called anything, for God's sake! And that was if she even lived there.

Suddenly the whole business seemed so ridiculous that he considered calling the airport there and then and booking his ticket home. Yet he knew he had no choice.

And so he sat in his room, drinking iced water and staring into the blank, white space of the opposite wall as the old hurt made room for the new, and the two assumed their places in the spinning chambers of his sixty-year-old heart.

Oh. You! That simple, two-word exclamation played over and over again in Spin's head on the fast-rail trip back to Tokyo the next day. He looked around the plush, first-class carriage and remembered the battered, overheated trains that had carried him all over the country half a lifetime ago, trailing soot and steam wherever they went. There was an unnatural hush in the carriage. His fellow travellers were mostly silent or spoke only in whispers. Most disorientating of all, he couldn't hear the rails. Spin was a sentimental traveller and missed the steady clickety-clack of the tracks. The silence of the carriage only accentuated the power of the old woman's two-word exclamation, which continued to haunt him throughout the afternoon.

At first he took it to be an accusation. That he, like all the other vandals that had plundered the country in the name of 'democratisation' or whatever the fancy phrase was, had left the poor woman behind, knocked up and stuck with his baby, and gone back to the comforts of home as if nothing had happened. Now, after all these years, the look said, you dare to come back posing as a family friend. And why? To gaze upon your youthful handiwork? To bring stockings and lipstick and false words of love and friendship once again? It was all undeniably there in her look, and the moral censure stung him deeply. He had come to Japan all those years before certain that he carried with him the gift of light and convinced of the righteousness of his mission. Though he would never have publicly claimed to be one of the elect, or believed himself to be so vain, it was what he thought, all right.

Then again, perhaps it was a knowing *Oh. You?* It occurred to Spin that Momoko may have conferred with her neighbour. That during those difficult years in the town, bringing up a child whom everybody would have regarded as a half-caste brat, an untouchable or worse, her neighbour would possibly have been a source of support in whom Momoko could have confided. That woman might very well have been told things that Spin himself had never confessed to anybody, for he had never told anyone about the madness of those last few weeks. Now, his neck and cheeks flushed as he speculated on what she might have known.

Stations and towns passed in a blur of colour outside the window, and he suddenly felt as if he were riding the express model of time's arrow, being shot into an uncertain future without the option of getting off.

Perhaps it was a pitying *Oh. You?* Perhaps… That Momoko, as part of a lasting and final punishment, had resolutely refused to contact him. But what if she had confided her intention in her neighbour, or in her mother, who in turn told her neighbour, who had now expressed her pity as diplomatically as possible with a polite and simple *Oh. You?* He thought again of what might have been, and he stared at the passing rails as if searching for traces of a parallel life that he could now only speculate about.

Spin took a book from his travel bag, tapped his jiggling knee with it while he continued looking out the window, then stuffed it back into the bag. It was absurd, the old girl didn't know anything. And it wasn't just because she was old that she looked silly. Momoko would never have said anything to such a woman, would never have divulged the details of their life together to *anybody*, just as she would never have been petty enough to seek his punishment. That was the heartbreaking truth. She wouldn't have, not *his* Momoko.

But why did he have to learn a momentous truth this way? As the outskirts of Yokohama came into view, an entirely different thought struck him: What if the child wasn't his after all? It suddenly occurred to him that, in the rush of his thoughts, he hadn't even stopped to consider this possibility. What if there were other affairs after him; other indiscretions. Why not? Momoko was a beautiful woman. And at that he saw her face, clear and immediate, as if she were sitting in front of him and he was gazing once again into the singular blue-green of her eyes. No sooner had he recalled those eyes than he ached with the old desire. It was a dull, sweet ache, but he knew it straight away, and the thought of his Momoko in the arms of some gum-chewing Yank, who promised her no less than an all-American future and left her knocked-up in some gook town, left him miserably seething with a jealousy he'd long since lost the right to feel.

Yet he allowed the jealousy to flow through his veins now, almost welcoming its familiarity. Besides, perhaps he did have the right to feel it: after all, he and Momoko might yet be connected, might they not? The possibility of a child had entered his world less than twenty-four hours ago, and as he stared at the endless concrete and glass of Yokohama, he silently prayed he was right. For, already, he felt that there was a living part of him out there that would still be there when he was gone. A continuation of himself, living independently of him, but a reminder to future generations that he had, in fact, existed and that his life hadn't been a complete waste. That, Spin felt, on the fast train from one foreign city to another, was something. And so he silently prayed he was right and that he had been Fortune's fool long enough. The old hurt and the new jostled for space, and he embraced these painful twins as he settled back into the plush, air-conditioned silence of the long, silver arrow in which he sat.

Inside the train passengers reclined in their seats, sipped fruit juice and wine, read, belched, farted and waited to be fed. Outside, the endless, blue firmament waited for them all, indifferent to everything: love, loss, birth and death. And what, Spin silently asked himself, did he have to pit against the incomprehensible vastness of it all? Only this absurd hope, that somewhere out there was a past that might yet be soothed and a brief future yet to be embraced. And if these two things could be accomplished, then he might walk into that endless blue horizon with a lighter heart.

Chapter Twenty-Three

Momoko sat in her lounge, the shirt for Naomi on the sofa where she'd dropped it and an unread manuscript on the table beside her. The picture of the affected young man in the pub was still clear in her mind, his affectation both reassuring and annoying. *You meet someone a dozen times…* Odd how the small things stay with you. Odd how we forget how hard it was *to* forget.

There'd been days, in those early years here after the war, when she'd felt as if she were truly going mad. Times when waves of anxiety broke over her again and again as if they would never end. She hadn't known then that life was long and all things passed, and she quietly recalled once more, in the deceptive comfort of her lounge, how we forget how hard forgetting was.

Somewhere, stuffed away in one of the many drawers and hiding places in the house, was a folder she hadn't looked into for years. The manuscript she had had to write simply to get it all out of her; to get the whole thing off her chest and out of her life. And it hadn't been difficult in the end. Not really. She'd gone away to the country for a week, left Naomi with Charlie Boy, and written her memories out day by day—until the week was gone and there was nothing left to say and no more memories to record. In the end it had only amounted to forty or fifty pages, and these days she barely remembered the process of writing or any of the words—only the effect. Like telling a story, or making one up. The 'I', the 'me', the 'they', the 'us' all became somebody else. Familiar strangers. When she came to those parts in the tale when the girl cried and the young man went mad, she was moved the way stories should move you. She sympathised, and felt better able to understand what made the young woman weep and what made the young man mad—understood better than the young people themselves had done.

For, when she came to write it all down, she found that she was telling a story about someone named Momoko, the 'I' of the tale. It was she who ran up those stairs at Yoshi's old room; someone named Momoko who approached the door breathlessly with the gift of new shoes for the long walk her old friend contemplated; someone named Momoko who had pushed the door open and stepped into that dark space illuminated only by the eventual flare of the match of someone named Spin. And it was someone called Momoko who had endured what followed.

The victors may write history, and the world may only ever listen to them, see only the smiling, happy faces the victors want them to see, but when she'd finally finished writing it all down that long-ago summer, a voice had cried out triumphantly inside her saying, 'No, *this* is how it was.' This is the contorted double head of victory and defeat, defeat and victory, each as dark and distorted as the other. In the end there was no triumph of right, no empire of light.

In the end, the only thing that shone was a private light, the sweet light of a love that defied the weight of that long-ago world for a few precious weeks before succumbing to it. And this, finally, was what she carried with her when she left that country retreat with the manuscript in her travel bag. This was all that mattered, the knowledge that for a few precious weeks they had won. By the time she put the folder away in her bedroom drawer, by the time the 'I', the 'he', the 'she', the 'they' and the 'us' had done their work and the young woman called Momoko had rushed up her old friend's stairs for the last time, she knew what it was to see her tears wept by someone else. And it was only then that she knew she'd come through, and she began to see the colours around her and knew that the world wasn't going to stay grey for ever.

She picked up a magazine from the table and strolled through into the kitchen as the phone rang. She recognised the voice instantly, pulled a stool across to the telephone and settled in for what she knew from experience would be a long conversation with her daughter, who would be full of traveller's tales and eager to share them all.

Chapter Twenty-Four

It was very simple really. Extraordinarily simple, although at first his fingers had fumbled with the pages of the telephone directory. He had even dropped the book at one stage, picked it up and began flicking through the pages once again under the watchful gaze of the young woman at hotel reception. He looked up from the directory. Did she mind if he took the book into the lounge? It might take some time, he suggested. And she nodded, slightly amused.

In the empty lounge he sat down and slowly worked his way through the pages until he eventually found what he was looking for. There were seven listings under the name of Yamada. Three K. Yamadas, two under S, one under T and one under M. His index finger circled the name again and again. Only one. It seemed miraculous, even portentous, that there was only one. But whether this M. Yamada of Camden Town was Momoko was, of course, another matter.

His first impulse was to rush straight off, but wiser counsel prevailed and he sat quietly for a time, looking out the window. He was wearing the same trousers and shirt and coat that he worked in, and he calculated that if he were still at home he would be just getting up for breakfast. All through the last week a recurring but insistent voice had been telling him that that was where he really ought to be, back home rather than sitting in a hotel on the other side of the world, where now he gazed out at the evening crowds spilling from the pubs and cafés.

Since he'd left Melbourne, the days had passed like weeks, and seemed to belong to another life. Spin sat, the telephone book still open on the low table in front of him, continuing to stare at the passing crowds on the busy street while absorbing the thought that, at this moment, she just might be out there after all. No more than a short tube ride away. Within reach. In fact—and this would not have surprised him at that moment—an hour before, Momoko had been strolling through the Covent Garden Market, just a short walk from his hotel, browsing for the shirts she would buy for her daughter's twenty-sixth birthday—before going home and thinking of Spin. He checked his watch. It was half past five and he wondered what she normally did at half past five. Was she leaving work, or having an after-work drink? Perhaps she didn't work and was at home, doing something simple like preparing an evening meal for her family, or lounging in a chair reading while waiting for her family—her daughter. Or, perhaps, nobody?

And while he was lost in speculation, Spin recalled how, in another life, at this hour of the day, he would have been waiting for her in the foyer of Japan Broadcasting, counting the seconds until she appeared. And he would note that when she did she would give him a pleased smile because he was prompt. Punctual. She liked it, and it amused her. He never kept her waiting because he treasured every second with her, and she knew it. Just as he thanked her for all the days she gave him, until everything went wrong and their days together ran out. Momoko was as vivid before him now as she had ever been, and he closed his eyes, marvelling how this could be. He saw every detail: the fall of her hair across her forehead, her eyes creased in amusement, the long steps that carried her towards him, the last of her English dresses that she so loved to wear, her lips, poised to kiss. It was a shock to open his eyes and hear a young woman's voice.

'Are you all right, sir?'

It was the hotel receptionist, clearly concerned about him. The crowds filed past the window or paused at the glass, looking in, like so many passing schools of fish. He looked at the receptionist, summoning up all his concentration so that he might reply.

'Yes. Yes, thank you. I'm quite all right.'

'Can I get you something? A glass of water? Some tea?'

'No, no. I'm perfectly fine,' he added, puzzled by her continued concern. Puzzled, that is, until something made him pass his fingers across his eyes and he realised there were tears in them and he had no idea how long they'd been there.

'Oh, dear,' he said, quickly brushing the tears from his eyes, closing the telephone book and passing it back to the young woman. 'Thank you, I'm perfectly all right.' He smiled.

Still concerned, she took the book and slowly returned to her desk.

He muttered to himself as he ambled along the street. Fancy going on that way, crying in public. There was nothing more pathetic than looking ridiculous in public. Spin had always despised that sort of thing, public shows of emotion and the like. He'd al-

ways considered it nothing more than a sort of emotional inconti-
nence. Embarrassing in others, intolerable in oneself because it
made you ridiculous.

Then there was the sound of bells, and heavy-bellied pigeons were
lumbering skyward. It was six o'clock and he had no memory of the
last half-hour. His light summer sports coat flapped in the breeze,
his curly hair and forehead were damp from the exertion of walking. A young man was performing acrobatic feats in the open square.
Spin stopped for a moment and watched the young man somersault
and turn in the air as if he were a creature of flight, unaffected by
the usual pull of gravity. If he was honest with himself, he'd believed
in his heart of hearts that he would go where he had to and do what
he could, but he had always secretly assumed that the trail was only
ever going to lead to a dead end.

Yet there was an unnerving sense of Momoko's presence all
around him, an alarming feeling that any minute he could easily
bump into her. And had he arrived an hour earlier he might have
done. His whole body trembled with the thought of actually staring into those singular blue-green eyes again and hearing that soft,
melodious voice once more. He didn't really know if he could bear
it, wasn't convinced that he mightn't just die, suddenly cease to exist
out of sheer—what? Joy? Can the heart just explode and the body
die of joy? It suddenly seemed like the sweetest of deaths, and one
that was entirely within the realms of possibility. Spin manoeuvred
his way through the crowds. His shirt began to dry and turn stiff in
the breeze, his forehead to cool. The walk would clear his head.

Later that evening, as the twilight thickened, Spin sat looking
from his hotel window at London streets he'd known since his
youth, when he'd made the first of his many visits to the city. The

lights in the pubs, cafés and restaurants were blinking into life. The hazy, violet streets were filled with expectancy. An almost alcoholic thrill coursed through his veins. She was out there, doing something. At that very minute.

Chapter Twenty-Five

Eiko's telegram lay on the table behind her. Momoko was gazing through the window out on to the street. She'd lived in the house, which had been large enough for the two of them yet now felt too small for Momoko alone, for the last ten years. It was a nice house in a convenient part of the city, and she had enjoyed a pleasant life here. The sale of her parents' home and the other odds and ends that came with the inheritance had bought her a pleasant place and she had grown attached to it. Naomi now lived with friends in Islington and was doing postgraduate studies at London University. She liked her life. She wasn't far and they saw each other every weekend or when they needed to. Charlie Boy dropped in regularly and they all went out together, whatever excuse there was.

Naomi had only ever known that her father was a soldier in the Occupation. When his tour had finished he had gone home as they all had, ignorant of Momoko's condition. That was the line. That was all she knew. She didn't need to know any more. There had only been that one time. Naomi was ten? Eleven? It was midnight or later and Momoko had all the old photographs spread out on the kitchen table of one of the wretched rented places they'd lived at first—the 'Japs' on the third floor. Shots of Momoko, East Gate, Imperial Palace, Spin on a bridge somewhere. Shots of her, shots of him, shots of them. And suddenly, somebody had taken her hand. Naomi hadn't spoken. And she said nothing when Momoko gathered the photographs and letters and put them back in an old chocolate box. Later that same night, while her daughter had slept, Momoko had slipped down on to the street and stuffed the tin box into the rubbish bin. When she heard the rattle of bins early in the morning, she rose from her bed and watched a stout man in overalls casually pick up her bin and throw the contents into the back of the rubbish truck. There, she'd thought. Gone.

What Momoko didn't know was that Naomi had already discovered that old tin chocolate box, had often stared long and hard at the young soldier with the curly hair after school while her mother was at work. She had looked at the letters with the young soldier's name, at one unopened envelope in particular that had gone all the way to, and come all the way back from, an impossibly distant place called Australia. That was Naomi's secret, the only one she'd ever kept from her mother. And so when her mother told her the story about her father going home at the end of the war like all the soldiers did, she nodded as if she need know no more. A nod convincing enough to satisfy Momoko that the past was distant enough not to claim her.

But why now? Why seek the past out after all these years? Spin would now know that he had a child. Perhaps he had always known. Perhaps he really got the pitiful letter she sent all those years ago when she realised what was happening to her. Perhaps he'd skilfully opened it—he was an intelligence officer, after all—read it, resealed it and sent it back. Perhaps by the time he got the letter, and who knows how long it would have taken to reach him—if it ever did— perhaps he had already found another life and it was easier all round simply to return her envelope as if it had never been received and their affair had never happened.

For a moment she silently cursed her friend's big mouth, then took the curse back, remembering that she was an old friend whose mind wasn't what it was, who had helped her through the hard years in the town and coaxed the laughs from her when all laughter seemed to have vanished. Would he simply come to the house? she wondered. It wouldn't be that difficult to find her, now that he was here. Would she open her door one morning, afternoon or evening, and find herself staring at the foreign and familiar features of the Spin that he had become and the Spin she remembered? A face that she could very well now pass on the street and not even recognise— or would she?

When the phone rang she jumped, then walked towards it slowly, her hand hovering over the receiver, convinced it was him. Her voice was tense.

'Are you all right?' Charlie was worried.

'Yes.'

'You don't sound it.'

'I am, dear Charlie. I am.'

'You're still on for lunch tomorrow, then?'

'When did I last miss lunch?'

He was seventy-three, as stringy and fit as ever, and still came into the office two mornings a week. Lunch was a ritual that had begun soon after she'd started work, and, as Charlie was a creature of rituals, they kept up the practice even after he'd officially gone.

She put the phone down, then took Eiko's telegram and placed it in the drawer of her writing desk. Then she telephoned her daughter and suggested she drop in. Her tone was casual, but Naomi's 'yes' was quizzical. It was always the case—the moment you tried to pull the wool over her eyes she just pulled it right back again.

The street that she had lived in all these years was changed by the knowledge that the early morning post had brought. She looked round as if seeing its doorways and the small lanes that ran off it for the first time. And as she made her way to the tube she looked over her shoulder, unable to shake off the uneasy feeling that something wasn't right.

Chapter Twenty-Six

He watched her move along the footpath, her hair shiny and black like the feathers of a crow. How easily these things return, blotting out the passage of years. The street, quiet and tree-lined, was dotted with the latest cars and, beyond it, the billboards of the city peddled the latest clothes, gadgets and magazines. The doorways of the street shone with fresh, bright paint, and even the flowers in the gardens bloomed as if they had never bloomed so brilliantly before. But all that fell away and dissolved into insignificance. All Spin saw was the fall of her hair. One glimpse, and the neat divisions we call time—all the yesterdays, todays and tomorrows of the everyday world—became totally meaningless. There was only the fall of that hair as she moved along the street, her head bowed as she foraged in her bag for something or other. He was watching her here, today. But it might just as well have been on the other side of the globe in another time. Some things the years can't touch.

Then she looked up briefly to examine the day and Spin saw her eyes—her singular blue-green eyes—turn skyward, and, in the same instant, her lips moved. She passed out of the street without looking at the dark hire car parked on the other side. He watched her turn at the corner, the same liquid steps he'd loved all those years ago, the same grace that left the street looking shabby when she'd gone.

Spin sat staring blankly at the dashboard, unable to move. For a moment everything had stopped, his breathing, his heartbeat, his thoughts. It was as though all the constituent parts of his being had realised that he could not live through that moment without breaking and had shut down for those few seconds it took Momoko to leave her front gate, walk to the corner of her street and disappear from view. Only now, as he idly fingered the dust on the speedometer, was he aware of the air passing in and out of his lungs and the unsteady thump of his heart, pounding inside his chest like a bass drum played by a drunk.

That evening, with the unrelenting buzz of the movie and theatre crowds swimming all round him, Spin stood gazing at the spectacle of the wide square. All cities were the same at night, the same tired, glossy surfaces, the same clogged streets full of crowds looking for something more. The same blinking neons. And there, above a theatre and looking down onto the milling square, was the dazzling spectacle that had held him fast and fixed him to the spot from the moment he saw it.

At first he thought he must surely have imagined it. But he hadn't. An illuminated billboard dominated one corner of the square. A motor car, possibly a Jaguar or a Humber—Spin didn't know cars—with the subdued colours and curved lines of a more elegant age stood in front of a country manor. But it wasn't the car that so caught

Spin's attention, it was the slogan, written in bold, elegant letters beneath it: *Time future contained in time past.*

Everything Spin loathed about the age was there. All things were grist to its mill. If ever there was any doubt in his mind, the billboard banished it. This world could no longer be taken seriously, and those who tried to do so were ultimately defeated by its unrelenting lightness, its ubiquitous surfaces. Soon his kind would all be gone. Nobody had any use for the Spins of this world any more and he had no time for them. He drifted back to his hotel in a daze, at one point stepping back hurriedly from a kerb to avoid being run over by a bus with the name of some pop band emblazoned on its side. It would, Spin reflected when he'd recovered himself, have been a fittingly symbolic death.

Momoko's jet-black hair, her blue-green eyes, had been with him all day, all evening. Again and again, whether his eyes were closed or open, he saw her hair tumbling over her coat collar, saw those eyes once more, and was lifted above the tackiness of the world around him by the same thought that had uplifted him all those years ago—there really was someone out there, after all. They shared this world of electric light and flickering thought. That, and that alone, made it bearable once more.

In his hotel room he sipped on a third whisky and looked down on the street. Where had she gone? When she turned the corner, leaving the street and the insignificant parked car behind her, where did she go? And what was on her mind as she went? What thoughts preoccupied her? Once he would have been privy to those thoughts, the big and the small. For she would have told him freely in the days when he had a right to know, and have delighted in doing so.

But who was she now? She'd lived another lifetime since then and was another woman. Or perhaps not. He emptied his glass, breathing in deeply, and for the first time in decades his nostrils filled with the recalled scent of her perfume. Once, night after blessed night, he had reclined in her room, gazing at her garments strewn across the floor—her clothes were always strewn across the floor and furniture, such was the abandon of those days—and had known for the first time in his life what a lover did. Then he thought of the child. He hesitated to use the word daughter for it rang strangely in his ears. She would be—what? Twenty-five? No, twenty-six. A fine age. The best age. Everything in front of her. The adventure of *life* waiting to be taken. About the same age, it occurred to him, that Momoko was when they'd first met. And suddenly it wasn't enough just to live in the same city as she—he had to know more. Where *had* she gone when she turned the corner that morning? It was absurd to come so far, and stop so short. He need only know, after all. And she need never know.

It was then that he determined on going back. Just one more time. Oh, it was degrading, but he had to know where she went. Somehow, just walking up to her front door, knocking on it and saying hello after all these years, seemed an utter impossibility. No. It was degrading, but he would sit in the anonymous car, which he would park at a discreet distance from Momoko's house, and wait. He *had* to know, and with every second that passed he became more and more convinced that he had every right to know. She had entered his life and never left it. They had been joined, and though separated, had remained bound for ever. This was his right: her scent on his lapel, her breath on his cheek one cold, clear evening, the raindrops that she had brushed off herself and on to him one rainy day long ago and which he had happily accepted. This, and the many other memories that would never go away. The sights and sounds and smells and sensations that had entered him years before and never, never left him; this was his right.

He lay back on his bed without bothering to undress, listening to the late carousers in the street, impatient for the morning to announce itself at his window.

Chapter Twenty-Seven

It still came as a surprise to Momoko that Naomi was now an adult. She was her own woman and went her own way, unfettered by the past because she was largely unconcerned by it. But the slight curls at the ends of her hair and that unmistakable cowlick at the front always served to remind Momoko that the past was there all right, and not that far away.

It was near midnight when Naomi dropped her bag in the hall. She was tired. She hadn't slept the night before because she was studying, she announced. Did Momoko mind if she just crashed? And Momoko had shaken her head as she watched her daughter straggle up the stairs to her old bedroom.

In the kitchen the next morning Momoko gave her her birthday package and watched as her daughter tore the wrapping off with the relish of a four-year-old and held the shirts up with delight.

'Happy birthday,' she said, embracing and kissing her daughter. 'Are they the ones?'

'Yes.'

'Good. I don't mind them, myself.'

'I'll get you one.'

Momoko laughed, pleased with her daughter's reaction, and thanked her for the offer while shaking her head at the thought of wearing shirts like those—young people's clothes.

It has been quick, it was quietly done. Birthdays mattered, but they never made a fuss. It was their way.

Momoko was suddenly silent and abstracted, and Naomi eyed her knowingly as she poured tea from an elegant, Oriental pot.

'What is it?'

Momoko looked up with feigned surprise, then lowered her eyes. 'I assume you're not asking about the tea.'

Naomi rolled her eyes.

'You didn't get me across town to talk tea.'

'Didn't I?'

'No. You can't fool me. What's up?'

It was true. Her daughter always knew when something was up. The kitchen was bright. There had always been a quality of light and joy about the room that had often led Momoko to ignore the rest of the house. It was unnerving then to be thinking of her old room in Kojimachi, when she'd been about the same age that Naomi was now and the thought of a daughter hadn't even entered her head.

It was a conversation she never really thought there'd be any need to have. And although there'd been times in the past when she'd contemplated how she would ever begin it if she had to, she still didn't know. Nor did it seem fair. She'd always thought of Naomi as being free of it all.

'When you think of your father,' Momoko began, still looking down at the cup, 'how do you think of him?'

Naomi started for a moment, her eyes widening, then, thankful Momoko wasn't looking at her, she stared at the bent head of her mother, leaned back in her seat and composed herself.

'Well,' she eventually answered, her voice just that bit brighter than she'd intended, 'I don't, actually.'

Momoko looked up sharply.

'Don't what?'

'Think of him. Not really. In fact,' she went on, almost chatty, 'I don't even think of him as a *him*. He's like this distant figure out of mythology. Why?'

Momoko loved the confident disregard of the past that her daughter and all her friends seemed to have; their determination not to become bogged down in what had been, but to press on to what might be. She'd even started to like their music. She envied Naomi these years and quietly congratulated herself on the name she had chosen for her child. She was the free spirit Momoko had always wanted her to be, just as her fictional namesake had been all those years before. With a trace of sadness Momoko realised her daughter was actually going to live the adventure that Momoko herself had been robbed of.

'Why?'

It was only as Naomi repeated her question that Momoko realised she'd drifted off. She smiled.

'My youth might have a misty, mythological look from where you sit, but it wasn't always like that. Besides,' she went on, 'myths can be a lot closer to home than you think.'

Naomi studied her mother coolly for a moment, drawing in the implications of this like smoke from one of her French cigarettes.

'Are you going to tell me my father's hiding in the next room with a bunch of flowers in one hand and a box of chocolates in the other? All for his long-lost little girl?'

'Not quite.'

'Not quite? Then, what are you saying, Mother?'

Naomi only ever called Momoko 'Mother' when she was teasing her or when she was annoyed with her, and although the title was always delivered with irony, Momoko couldn't at that moment tell if the irony was fuelled by anger or amusement or anxiety. There was certainly something unusually edgy about her daughter today.

Momoko rocked back and forth in her chair, weighing the possibilities, the different ways of saying what had to be said. In the end, there was only one way to get through it and that was just to say it. She smiled faintly at her daughter and bit her lip.

'You've never quite known all the circumstances of your birth because I didn't tell you all of them.'

Naomi was silent. Momoko went on, choosing her words carefully.

'It was complex. I was going to say messy. Perhaps I should have. But neither of them comes close, anyway. The truth is it was pretty bloody awful, actually.'

She then turned to a manila folder lying on the bench beside the sink.

'I wrote it all down. Years ago. It was just my way of turning it all into history, I suppose. You may like to read it. Not for the writing, heaven forbid. It was just something I did. But—'

'It's easier than telling me.'

Without looking up Momoko nodded.

'I never meant to keep things from you.' She looked up to the ceiling, sighing and wishing she was a smoker so she could suck on one of her daughter's French lung-busters. 'There were just certain things you didn't need to know.'

'What's changed?' This time there was clear anxiety in her daughter's voice.

'I may have this all terribly wrong. And I may not. But I've got pretty good reason to believe that your father is here. Except—and this wasn't his fault, it was nobody's—if he is, he's only just discovered he's got a daughter.'

Naomi was silent, contemplating the familiar objects of the house that had been her home for most of her life—the pine table, the nude watercolour in the lounge, apparently painted by an old friend of her mother's, the ceremonial sword in the hall—her grandfather's. She barely noticed when Momoko slipped the manila folder across the table.

'When things were difficult,' Momoko said, explaining the manuscript, 'when you were very young, I wrote it all down. As I remembered it.'

Naomi stared at the folder, suddenly looking—it seemed to Momoko—like an innocent hesitating on the brink of knowledge. Then, without a word, she swivelled off her chair, scooped up the manuscript, vanished into the hall and dropped it on top of her waiting bag.

Back in her student room later that morning, the short tale her mother had written years before now read, Naomi stared out her window, wondering over and again if she had summoned this man, her father. For, as much as she may have fooled Momoko and even tried to fool herself, the image of a smiling young soldier, on some long-ago afternoon before she was born, had haunted her from the very first time she'd secretly opened the tin box that contained the remnants of the past. For all her casual chat, those photographs never ceased to haunt her—even when the box mysteriously disappeared, the memory of its contents lingered on. Even now, she could conjure him up, as she had throughout her adolescence. It was a game, and he was her plaything. When she wanted him, she conjured him, and he materialised before her like magic. And, of course, she made him up in her own way. Always happy, always there whenever she called him.

Now, Naomi wondered if such things were possible; if she had conjured and called him so often that, somehow, finally, he had answered. Can we do such things? For, if she had, she was now wishing she hadn't. She now found herself wishing he'd just go away. And it wasn't simply that she'd now read in her mother's manuscript of another side to that smiling face of her teenage imagination. Playthings can be called into life, and packed up again at will when playtime is over. This was the role of playthings, to be picked up and put away—not to acquire a will of their own. But he had, and he was here, and mingled with the feeling that she wished he'd just go away was the fear that she had somehow conjured him into life just once too often, that her monster had finally come to her, looking for love. But she wasn't a girl any more. Her love had been spent on playthings, and playtime was over.

On the train, and throughout the morning in the office, Momoko thought of Naomi turning the pages of her manuscript, and found herself trying to remember what she'd said and what she hadn't said— suddenly not sure that she felt comfortable about anybody reading it, let alone her daughter. They were private observations, thoughts and confessions never really meant to see the light of day, and at one point in the afternoon she wished she'd left it that way. For the story wasn't hers any longer and the world she'd talked about—gone for ever now, except in memory and memoir—seemed suddenly cheapened by the act of being exposed to the prying eyes of those who were never there.

Chapter Twenty-Eight

A tube ride and a short walk after leaving his car, he stood in the shade of a green square. He had a good view from his corner. He had often made a point of coming to this square on past trips and knew the spot well. Many of the writers, with whom he had kept in distant contact by letter over the years, gathered at the modest-looking publishing house in the north-west corner of the square. Those poets who had given a generation its voice and defined an entire age, all came to and from here. It was almost, for Spin, a place of pilgrimage. And so he had come whenever he could, breathing in the same dense lunchtime air that those distant, admired figures would have done. Of course, he'd never been inside the place nor would he. The truth was he'd never been invited and he was never the sort to invite himself. Others were comfortable with that kind of thing, but not him. Instead, he'd waited patiently for a short post-script at the bottom of one of the many letters that passed between him and the many poets, academics and writers with whom he corresponded. A short note that might have said, Drop by whenever you're in town. A scribbled invitation. Nothing grand. But it never came. The replies were always cordial and signed with kind regards, but never anything more. And so Spin had never stepped inside that dark doorway, set in a fantail arch of white and blue stone. But Momoko had. He had just watched her.

An hour later she still hadn't emerged and Spin was becoming restless as the lunchtime crowds began to gather. It was a famous door that she had so nonchalantly entered. She was clearly no stranger to that door, had barely noticed it. She had, in fact, almost barged through, slapped it open with the palm of her hand without reverence and entered as one would one's place of…yes…work.

Why not? Why on earth not? And that thought had no sooner come to him than another followed. If this were her place of employment, and if—as her manner suggested—she'd been here for quite some time, then it was possible, just possible, that she may have handled the many letters he had sent care of this address to those authors with whom he corresponded. He turned his face to the warm July sun, screwing up his eyes and wincing at the idea. Then his heart leapt when he remembered that the stamp on the back of his correspondence only ever gave his address at the university, never his name. But it sank again when he thought of somebody mistakenly opening one of his letters and reading it out loud—derisively, as these people do. The thought of Momoko hearing such a thing, then hearing Spin's name—his real name—casually tossed off at the completion of the reading, twisted his heart, and his whole body contorted as he stood contemplating the doorway through which she had disappeared.

Of course, it wouldn't have happened. Then again, it was precisely the kind of coincidence that happens more in life than in fiction and it just damn well might have happened after all. He just might have been the butt of some silly office joke, on some cold, wet, miserable morning when everybody was in need of a lift. And as he stood, uncertain, on the warm grass, he grew convinced she had triumphantly read his letters after all. He could see Momoko coolly perusing his overly polite requests, his small entreaties. And in that instant he saw himself reduced to the level of the constantly deferring academic, the admiring small-town critic from the other side of the world; the side that didn't matter. A fan, for God's sake. Or worse still—what did they call it now?—a groupie.

He was about to leave when the door slowly opened and sunlight fell across the doorway. He'd never met the small, wiry-haired man in the dark suit who stood on the doorstep, but he knew him immediately. He knew him through his books of essays and criticism, his photographs, and through the limited correspondence they'd shared. He always signed off *Yrs etc*. No, he'd never met him, but everybody knew C. E. Morris. It was quite a jolt, then, to see him standing there on the doorstep, smiling in the sun, checking the sky. He was gesturing towards the street and Spin didn't notice whom he was speaking to at first. Then he saw Momoko turn, raise her head to the heavens, and even from the distance where he stood, across the babble of the crowds and the bellows of the buses and cars and taxis, he could have sworn he not only heard her laughter, but also instantly knew its music as if it had been only days rather than a lifetime since he'd last thrilled to it.

The great man took her hand and led her to the pavement, then guided her through the crowds on the footpath till they reached the corner and disappeared from view. And all the time Spin, in the light summer jacket and casual open-necked shirt of the carefree tourist, watched their departure from his corner of the park.

He could have been listening to the crack of dice outside against his wall at Yoyogi, the squabbling of the local children and the bored, tired talk of homesick GIs. Nothing had changed. Nothing would ever change. Spin would always be waiting for Momoko, always be waiting for the day to end.

The sounds of the street floated in through the hotel room window along with the occasional car horn. It was late. The traffic had thinned, the crowds had dwindled to vocal drunks stumbling home. But they were incidental noises. Spin lay on his bed, his mind elsewhere. Once again Momoko stepped forward from the fantail arch of the doorway, once again she looked up to her companion who was whispering something indistinct into her ear and once again Momoko's laughter filled the sky. Then he, the instantly recognisable C. E. Morris, had taken her arm. He had taken her arm like one accustomed to doing so, Spin mused, slowly twisting a wicked cigarette in his fingers. The man's other hand had rested briefly on her shoulder and he had guided her to the footpath. There was a clear element of proprietorship in the act. He was one who knew her body well and was used to handling it. For, and Spin knew this in his bones, it was an act performed with all the casual, confident assurance of a lover. Her body had responded to him easily. She had allowed herself to be handled like a small boat responding to hands expert with sail and oar. She bobbed on the water for him and allowed herself to be guided through the hazards of the crowded footpath.

And, of course, his hands were expert—but not with sail and oar. With buttons and blouses, fabric and flesh. His hands had been busy all his life. His affairs were folklore, and had been throughout his career. His lovers had ranged from kitchen maids to duchesses, the old and the young. He was an omnivorous lover, what society once called a womaniser. Spin jack-knifed out of bed and lit the cigarette while staring down at the winding street below, but remembering how, all the time Morris's hands had claimed her, she had giggled, like a silly little boat that had nothing better to do than bob up and down at his beck and call.

And no doubt he knew the daughter. Had known her for years. Had watched her grow. Naomi. Spin could still barely bring himself to pronounce the name, even to himself in the silence of his room. Yet it had become precious to him now. Even sacred. And he marvelled that its simple three syllables fell from his lips, however effortlessly, with the same neat divisions that Momoko's always had. Mo-mo-ko. Na-o-mi. Mo-mo-ko. And he'd no sooner spoken her name out loud than he suddenly saw himself playing games with the child as he *could* have—another Spin, in another life. And once again he felt the intolerable helplessness of only ever being able to stand and look upon the life he could have led, like an eternal understudy.

All the time, while he had been completely unaware of this life unfolding thousands of miles away from him, this gracious lover with the busy hands would have been playing the dutiful stepfather; giving Naomi advice, attending to her needs when her mother was indisposed, giving her the benefit of his opinions—of which there were many—moulding her nature like an ageing sculptor. And, no doubt, whenever the chance arose, throwing lascivious glances her way when he thought she wasn't looking. Or, worse still, when he thought she was—and Momoko wasn't. It was intolerable. The bright orange missile of his cigarette butt described a brief but perfect arc as he flicked it through the cool summer air.

Even as the butt disappeared into the darkness, he knew he was talking nonsense. Knew that they were the ravings of a young man who had once let the devil into his head and let the devil do his work. No, he'd been there once, and he hadn't come all this way to go to that dark place again. When Momoko had walked off with the great C. E. Morris clutching her arm, they'd gone to a small restaurant. He knew because he'd followed them. And it was a table that had the look of being *their* table. It had a Reserved plaque sitting on it and they were ushered to it as if there were no other table in the whole establishment. It was clearly theirs. And clearly, they lunched together regularly, probably every day.

It was a simple plan. One that might just work. A large city, an extraordinary coincidence. As he stood staring down into the dark street below the hotel room he could almost hear the casual surprise, the sudden, heartfelt greetings of long-lost friends. How extraordinary, they would suddenly be saying, reaching across the divide of the years, clasping hands, stuttering into speech. Did she realise that, mathematically, the chances of such a meeting must be infinitesimal, he'd go on—elated but composed. Just as well none of us is very good at mathematics, or we shouldn't all be here, he would say. There would be laughter then, and he would silently rejoice in being able to make her laugh the way he never could when he had her. And so it would go, one thing leading to another—light, amusing, convincing in its very preposterousness. Why not? Surely, they all at least deserved this much.

Spin was almost starting to believe in the coincidence himself, as if he were simply being treated to a sneak preview of what fate had in store for him. And tomorrow he would be as surprised as anybody else when he looked up from his table to find her there.

Chapter Twenty-Nine

Momoko looked out on to the dark street as Naomi's car drew into the kerb that evening. Her walk had the bounce of the young, of energy and impatience. A walk that implied that the bearer of those legs was all for getting on with whatever it was that had to be got on with, and right away. But, and Momoko had known this for years—from the moment her girl put on corduroys and sneakers—it was a walk that resonated with more than just her age and temperament. It was her father's walk: the bounce, the confidence, the carefree air—all those qualities that had caught her tired eye when he first came along. She watched her daughter coming up the path and it was as though Spin were in her shoes, guiding her steps up to the front door.

Naomi dropped her bag in the hall where it usually stayed till morning. In the sitting room, she turned to Momoko by the table and quietly announced, 'I read it.' She then embraced her mother and held her for more than the usual greeting time before stepping back.

'It was hard to read,' she said, affectionately stroking her mother's arm. 'I can't imagine how hard it was to do.'

Momoko held her breath a moment, then let go of it. 'It was a long time ago,' she said.

There was an awkward pause in which they stared at one another, each waiting for the other to go on.

'Spin?' Naomi's face finally flickered with half a smile, but her eyes weren't in it. 'It's a pretty ridiculous name. I'm not calling him that, for a start. If I ever have to call him anything.'

'I don't think you will.'

'Not "Dad," either.'

'It won't be necessary.'

'What do you know?'

'Nothing more than what Eiko said.'

Naomi stood still again, a slight hunch to her shoulders. Then she shrugged. 'I care about you. I don't want you hurt again.'

'I won't be. I'm a big girl with a big desk.'

Naomi eyed her mother closely, not quite convinced that she didn't need protecting any more, and went on. 'It is *you* I care about. You know that, don't you?'

Momoko nodded.

'Frankly, I don't give much of a toss about him,' Naomi continued breezily, but, Momoko thought, a little too breezily. 'Reading what you wrote was very moving, but it didn't change things. He's still far away. Unreal. Like some character in a book I've read. Like Magwitch or something.' She broke into a short guffaw, then quickly collected herself. 'But not my dad. I gave all that up years ago. When everybody had dads, I had you. You were my mum and my dad. My everything.' She grinned. 'Besides, there was always Charlie Boy, and still is. I'm used to all that now. It was hard enough bringing *you* up. Believe me, a father at this stage of my life is something I just don't need. Maybe when I was five, ten, fifteen, even. But not now.'

She fell into a chair. Momoko was nodding, perplexed, as if she were suddenly talking to someone other than her daughter. She pondered this new Naomi, this *modan garu* as she, too, sat down. She was light, on top of it all, untouchable as the young are, but something wasn't right.

'Suppose,' said Naomi, 'just suppose he *is* here. What does he want after all these years? What can come of it all now?'

Momoko was still eyeing this cool-headed daughter of hers, half-admiring, half-scared that the whole, sorry business and all those sorry, long-ago years hadn't done their damage after all. Worried that one day this girl of hers might wake and not believe anything she'd just been telling herself. She hoped not, but she feared for the day when it might happen and all her cool-headed talk would go up in a puff of French smoke. But why was she staring at her now? Oh, yes, there was a question.

'Well?' Naomi prodded her again. 'What's he want?'

'A little peace of mind, perhaps,' she answered vaguely. 'I made my peace years ago. But he hasn't, has he? Why else would he be rattling around the world like this? Poor Spin.'

'Poor him,' Naomi said flatly, staring at her mother, still not convinced that her mother didn't need looking after.

'Yes, poor him. But the last thing he'd want is my pity.'

When Momoko later left the room, Naomi sat staring out the window on to the dark street. She was as still as the scene upon which she looked, the only movement the fluttering trail of blue smoke rising from her fingers. Just a few miles away the vermilion missile of Spin's cigarette butt was describing its brief, perfect arc, before falling on to the night-time streets. Once again, she asked herself, 'Do these things happen?' Had she called him and, impossibly, had he answered? Had her monster come for love at last?

Her reverie was interrupted by Momoko, who entered the room with a sigh.

'You all right?' Naomi asked.

'Yes, yes,' Momoko answered, but with a strained urgency in her voice and eyes. 'Why shouldn't I be?'

'Mum.' Naomi looked directly at her, the hint of a rebuke in her eyes, her voice just that little bit louder than it needed to be, her manner just that little bit more forceful than was required. 'I know you. Remember, that was me standing beside you when you cried in the night all those years ago. When you cried in the night, again and again and again, and I never thought you'd damn well stop. That was me.'

'I know.' Momoko raised a hand to calm her. 'I just had this odd feeling.'

'That he's out there?'

Momoko nodded, then shrugged. 'I wish he were,' she said.

'I don't. Why do you?'

Momoko smiled faintly. 'You know me.' Naomi stared at her, waiting for the real answer. 'I don't like unfinished business. Who does?'

She watched as Naomi picked up her cigarette pack from the table and headed for the door. Momoko followed her.

'You're all right for lunch tomorrow? My treat, for the birthday girl.'

'Charlie Boy?'

'Not coming.'

'Pity.'

'Same place, same time. Okay?'

'Okay.'

The door closed and there was silence in the house.

Chapter Thirty

Spin arrived early. He'd spent the morning at the barber and although his curls still retained the silver threads befitting his age, the unruly grey scrub had been clipped from the sides and back of his hair, his eyebrows and ears had been trimmed, and even the spikes of bristle had been pruned from his nostrils. The conscientious young man with the scissors, clippers and razor, the aftershave and soothing lotions, had missed nothing. After more than an hour, light-headed from the pleasantly astringent scents that rose from his face and neck, Spin examined himself from different angles in the mirror. He nodded his approval, a reserved smile on his lips, but inwardly thrilled with the result, and left the barber's feeling almost young. His moment, the moment by which he would rise or fall, lay before him, and he was eager to meet it.

He had booked his table earlier that morning, at a discreet distance from where Momoko had sat the previous day. A waitress now led him to it, leaving him to contemplate the menu—and the street.

For he had chosen to sit facing the window so that he might appear casually engrossed in the passing show. On the other side of the room a Reserved sign sat next to a small vase like a No Trespassers notice. It was a little before one, and he smoothed his napkin over his knees. It was all in the manner, he told himself again and again. Stay calm. He was about to experience a most extraordinary coincidence, one that would blow open the door of the hitherto lost world of Momoko's room; blow away the years like so many cobwebs and bring him face to face once more with the only human being on earth who had ever made him feel that he wasn't alone after all. It would be a coincidence so extraordinary in its nature and so shattering in its repercussions that it might lead one seriously to contemplate the existence of some benevolent guiding hand in the seemingly random affairs of men and women.

With that in mind Spin adjusted his shirt collar, his tie, his cuffs. He thought of taking off the favoured corduroy jacket that made him feel relaxed and invested him with the casual air he sought, but, aware that it was not a warm day and that he would not normally remove it, he didn't. It was all in the manner, and his manner had to be as convincingly natural as the extraordinary event would seem.

He took a book from his jacket pocket, smoothed the napkin across his knees and opened the menu. But his eyes roved over the busy lunchtime street before him, observing the fleeting vignettes of life through the window. A conservatively dressed woman waited in a doorway with the demeanour of someone used to waiting in doorways; the extended line of a young family rippled through the crowd in search of fast food; a young couple emerged from the photographic shop opposite and looked at their snapshots where they stood. It was an intricately woven, constantly moving tapestry, and he sat rapt in its tales.

He didn't notice when they arrived. His peripheral vision alerted him to movement and shadow at her table, but his mind was still on the street. And when he finally looked around he saw a young woman in her early twenties, wearing jeans and a brightly coloured top, sitting with her back to the street. She was with another woman, her back to Spin. His first reaction was outrage. This wasn't it. This wasn't how things were supposed to go. He was expecting a man and a woman. Couldn't these people read? Didn't they see the Reserved sign on the table? He was about to rise from his seat and summon the girl when he was suddenly arrested by the hair falling over the shoulders of the woman with her back to him. For he knew that hair, black as the feathers of a crow, and instinctively turned his head away, putting his hand up to the side of his face to shield his eyes, even though she could not possibly see him. At the same time an invisible wave lifted his heart and bobbed it about inside his chest. On the surface everything stayed the same, the street still flowed with lunchtime crowds as it had a second before, the conservatively dressed young woman still waited in the doorway and his book remained unopened on his table. Only now he couldn't speak. He knew he couldn't because the waitress was standing beside him and asking him if he would care to order now. When she asked again he pointed to the first thing he saw and returned the menu without comment. When she was gone he lifted the book, opened it and pretended to read.

He wasn't sure how long it was before he had the courage to lift his eyes again. It could have been minutes or seconds. When he did it was the quickest of glances. The cheeks, the nose, the lips and the luminous white skin were her mother's, but the eyes and the cowlick falling over the middle of her forehead were his. He knew she was talking because her lips were moving, but he couldn't hear.

Their speech existed on another wave of sound to which his ears were not yet attuned.

While they were still deep in conversation Spin slowly eased his gaze to Momoko's back. He dared not look up, hardly dared breathe. His head turned fractionally, then came to a sudden stop. There, no more than ten or fifteen feet away, was Momoko's arm, resting on the table, its whiteness accentuated by the deep burgundy of the table cloth. Her hand—it was ringless—was palm down on the table, her fingers spread out, calm and still. He could imagine the fine, dark hairs of the forearm he had stroked a lifetime ago. Had he not been in such a state he might have noticed the little, short, nervy movements that would have told him that beneath the composed exterior she was not calm. But he didn't. She was near, that was all that mattered. His centre had returned, and she was calm and still as centres ought to be. What he also didn't know was that she did not, in fact, lunch every day at this place, only once a week with Charlie Boy. Today was an exception, a belated treat for Naomi's birthday, and thus, unbeknown to him, really was that extraordinary coincidence he'd so craved. In another life he would have reached out and enfolded that hand in his or entwined his fingers in hers.

At the risk of drawing attention to himself he held his gaze, lingering on the only part of Momoko he could see. The thrill of holding that hand and touching that skin returned to him. That, and the joy of simply having someone, of being admitted into a world beyond the tormenting confines of his own. It was then that he noticed the only piece of jewellery she was wearing, a dark bracelet that became more familiar the more he looked at it. At almost the same moment he closed his eyes, and a longing close to despair overcame him as he breathed deeply, convinced he could smell Momoko's perfume. It entered his bloodstream and was instantly pumped to the extremes of his body, leaving his fingertips tingling, his whole frame momentarily weightless. Whether it was the perfume of memory, or the scent she had carried into the air of the restaurant, he didn't know. It didn't matter. Suddenly, he could have been in any of the places they used to go when he had the right to touch her: under her old quilt in her room, sweat and perfume mingling in those endless nights of lovemaking and laughter; in the street at the close of day, meeting her as he loved to; standing dazed and uncomprehending on an unfamiliar street corner with a tin doll under his arm and the last of Momoko's perfume on the lapel of his coat.

'Excuse me.'

Spin looked up in sudden panic to see the waitress standing beside him, impatience in her voice, and he wondered how long she'd been there.

'Excuse me, sir.'

She was holding a plate and Spin put his book to one side, creating space for the dish and convinced that he had created a scene watched by everybody. But when he dared look up again he noted that the business of the restaurant had gone on oblivious of him.

He wasn't hungry, not even sure that he could eat, but knowing he must, he cut the food into small pieces and shoveled a few morsels into his mouth at odd intervals. But he was soon distracted by something else, a scent that carried him back even further than Momoko, and he glanced furtively about for the source of it. The girl—this daughter of his—had just lit a cigarette. French. He knew that pungent, heavy aroma instantly. She was the only one smoking in the restaurant and the smoke seemed to drift across the room towards Spin, as if seeking him out. And as his nostrils twitched he even remembered the brand. He, too, had smoked them in his youth. It was the favoured weed of the student of literature, radiating West Indian soil and sun and reeking of dead poets. When inhaled, one took in the very compost of literature—or so it had once seemed. He glanced briefly across at their table just in time to see her expel the smoke into the air with the impatient, argumentative air of the young intellectual. He smiled inwardly. Daddy's girl, he thought. Daddy's girl.

But how was he to begin the seemingly impossible task of introducing himself? If only, he thought, if only—just once more, even—he could gaze into the blue-green of Momoko's eyes.... The two women talked, it seemed to Spin, not so much like mother and daughter, but like old, close friends engrossed in each other's tales. Their meal was served. They ate, they drank a little wine, and as they ate and drank, they talked on, barely noticing anything around them. Plates came and went, desserts appeared. As the afternoon wore on it seemed to Spin that he would have to wave a banner to be noticed, and as he sat there, toying with a brandy that had somehow materialised, the same question returned again and again. How on earth was he to squeeze himself casually into this tight, exclusive world of theirs? How to introduce himself, with the relaxed air of, say, a stranger after street directions, so that they might all discover—courtesy of this most extraordinary coincidence—that they weren't strangers after all?

Act! A voice was bellowing in his ears. Act, you fool! The afternoon is disappearing and they'll be up and gone before you know it. And it suddenly occurred to Spin that this actually *was* a remarkable coincidence, for he hadn't anticipated his daughter being there. But she was. And so was Momoko and so was he. They were all there, a family for God's sake! And all he had to do was open his mouth and speak—but speech was beyond him.

Then, he saw Momoko raise her arm, and watched with something akin to horror as she summoned the waitress for her bill. The exchange was fast and efficient. He watched, helplessly, as she and Naomi rose and left, Momoko never once turning her face in his direction. In a panic, the day suddenly a disaster, Spin, too, called for his bill. Without even glancing at it, he dropped a number of notes on the table, grabbed his jacket and book and headed to the door.

Momoko had strolled with Naomi down to the corner, where they'd kissed and parted—the girl to return to her studies, her mother to go back to work. And so Momoko turned back in the direction of the restaurant, making for the green park on the other side of the street which she would cross on her way to her office. As she reached the restaurant, smiling to herself at her daughter's youthful confidence, the restaurant door flew open and a distraught man of late middle age, wearing the trademark corduroy jacket of academics, burst on to the footpath in front of her, almost knocking her over as he desperately scanned the street, this way and that, as if having lost someone. Then he turned his attention to the woman he had nearly knocked over, framing an apology, when he froze, unable to speak. Instead, his face drained of all colour, he simply stared. And Momoko, taking in the curls and the now grey but all-too-familiar cowlick falling over the man's forehead, was locked in to an answering stare.

Chapter Thirty-One

The small park just across from the restaurant was familiar to him, yet for ever altered now. All the times he'd strolled around it before, usually alone, seemed to belong to a life he had temporarily left in abeyance and to which he would inevitably return. But not just yet. Something breathtaking had taken place after all and the park would never be the same again. Momoko was beside him. He barely dared look at her. She barely dared look at him. In this hour before work finished, there was space enough in the square for two people to talk without attracting attention or being overheard, yet they had barely said a word. Their manner was stiff, their tone formal. She walked with her head inclined, watching the ground, occasionally looking up to observe the gardens. The day had warmed up and people were out. On an expansive patch of lawn, a brightly dressed group of young people lounged in the afternoon sun, their music rising from a small radio. Behind them, plump as the pigeons that surrounded him, a Victorian-looking gentleman sat on a bench, his chin resting on his walking stick. Momoko's hands were folded in front of her. Spin's were folded behind his back. For a moment they could simply have been a conservative, middle-aged couple taking their customary stroll through the gardens. A vacant park bench appeared before them.

'Shall we walk?' Momoko looked briefly at him and sighed, looking out across the trees and the lawns.

'Yes.' He looked down at his shoes. They weren't the first words she had spoken, but they were the first he'd been able to take in, the first he'd felt remotely capable of responding to. For the last few minutes he'd felt that he'd been walking beside an imaginary Momoko and was convinced that she could disappear at any moment and melt back into the crowd he had somehow conjured her from. 'There's a good bit of sun,' he added, ridiculously, as if they did this sort of thing every day.

They strolled on in silence: a silence that they needed, Spin thought—or, at least, he did. It was important just to walk beside each other for the moment, without talk. He wasn't even sure he *could* talk, so overwhelmed was he by her presence. Her eyes darted from rose bush to rose bush as they followed a narrow path, the roses in their second blooming glowing in the heat. Like a bird's, he thought, as he watched those eyes travel the square in a wide, sweeping arc until they finally finished at him. For the briefest of moments he dared to test their depth before quickly averting his gaze.

Then she stopped dead in her tracks and eyed him curiously.

'What are you doing, Spin?' She was slowly shaking her head from side to side, as if contemplating an unfathomable puzzle. 'What are you doing here?'

'I…' he stammered, looking up at the sky briefly as if summoning assistance, but went on noting that none was forthcoming. 'I hardly know myself.'

He noticed his tie was askew, as if someone had half-successfully attempted to wrench the thing from him. The top button of his shirt was undone and when he tried to refasten it he discovered that the button was gone altogether. When did this happen? Relieved that Momoko was staring into the distance, he hurriedly adjusted his clothing and desperately brushed his hair back with his fingers.

Beside him, Momoko wavered on the path, unsure whether to continue or stay put. Spin then attempted to continue, in that strained, conversational manner they had affected so far, and which had so far got them by.

'Are you…?'

She stared at him, waiting on his words.

'Are you well?' He sighed, looking out across the roses to the lawns and the casual, lounging figures on them. 'Are you happy?'

She gazed out across the gardens, slowly shaking her head again. 'I'm well enough. I'm happy enough. I came through.'

Spin nodded. 'I'm pleased to hear that.' He added, with greater emphasis, '*Very* pleased.'

'Did you come all this way to hear that?'

'I might have. I just might have. I realise that this must all be a bit of a shock after so long.'

Momoko said nothing. Spin continued. 'I'm here, I suppose, on the wild hunch that I just might find you and I might say certain things that need to be said before we're dead or too old to say them.'

He waited for some response, but there was none. Momoko remained impassive, looking across the square as if she were listening to the birds in the trees—and a part of Spin suspected that she actually was.

'I didn't like the feelings…I'd carried round with me all these years… My life is not…'

Momoko suddenly swung round, resentment in her eyes.

'How did you find me?'

Spin, preoccupied with the sentence he didn't finish, stared at her for a moment, desperately trying to recall how he did find her.

'A couple of minutes with the phone book. It was quite simple, really.'

'And before that a few days snooping around.' She looked sharply at him, daring him to lie. 'Eiko telegrammed me. She told me you'd been there. Well, she'd never met you, but she knew who you were.'

'Oh.' Spin nodded, as if this were a surprise. 'Is that her name?'

Momoko looked quickly at her watch. On the other side of the square she could see the last of the office staff leaving the building. The park was beginning to fill with commuters taking a short cut to the tube and workers idling an hour away in between work and play. She turned briefly towards him, gestured, 'This way,' and started walking at a brisk pace. They crossed the square in silence, Momoko always a few paces ahead of him.

The solid door beneath the fantail arch slowly—finally—opened for him as Momoko leaned against it with her shoulder and gave it a shove. The late afternoon light fell across the entrance hall and he was transfixed by the row of portraits that ran along it. For a moment it seemed that he wasn't going to enter the building at all, that he was on the point of running away, but Momoko hurried him on and he stepped across the threshold into the establishment that he had for so many years viewed from afar. Momoko had gone ahead and was calling him on along the hall, past cluttered rooms of books and manuscripts. Writers and poets, dead and alive, grinned or frowned down at him from the walls. He crept on, led by the sound of Momoko's voice, for she had disappeared into one of the distant rooms.

She pushed another door open and they entered a large, book-lined office, with a wide desk strewn with manuscripts, papers and trays and a window that looked out on to the square they had just walked across. Momoko was standing by a tea trolley; Spin stood frozen in her doorway. He was looking about, dazed, but fully understanding, all the same, that this was Momoko's office.

'Come in. Sit down.' She gestured to an armchair by the desk. He sat, uneasily. Her face gave nothing away.

'I'd offer you tea,' she began, 'but the urn's off, and, quite frankly, it's a bugger to get started again. Will whisky do?'

Spin nodded, his eyes vague, helpless, obliging, like a man who'd given up all pretence of any longer controlling the course of his life. Yes, whisky would do. He received the glass and drank automatically. It was only when he looked down that he realised he'd emptied it and Momoko refilled it without even asking, then sat on an office chair beside her desk.

'So…' Momoko was staring straight at him, the blue-green of her eyes as clear as ever. 'You didn't like these feelings you'd been carrying around all these years?'

'No.' Spin leant forward in his chair, the fumes from the glass mixing with the last of his aftershave and the faint, unmistakeable scent of Momoko's perfume, unchanged after all these years. 'No, I didn't.' He gulped from the glass.

'And you thought you'd bring them to me? Is that it?'

Spin was about to reply, but no reply was required and Momoko went on without taking her eyes off him and Spin was suddenly too afraid to look upon them.

'You thought you'd bring them to me and I'd tell you that it was really all right and that I was well. That it was such a long time ago and everyone's got on with their lives, anyway—and you could get a load off your chest and stop carrying all these feelings around with you.'

Momoko was now staring down upon her desk, twisting a brass paperweight of the three wise monkeys in her fingers, her head slowly moving from side to side. The smell of boiled rice, the cold air of Yoshi's room, the photographs scattered all across the floor, the spittle in the air from Spin's lips as he spattered her with questions, the single sharp slap to her face, the blood on her lips and the pitiful words of muttered love—*love*, for God's sake—that he weighed her down with afterwards all returned. The 'I', the 'she', the 'he', the 'us' belonged to them again. The distance was gone. It was all there again in front of her and she went on without even looking up at him.

'Well, Spin. It's not all right.' She looked up, the tears of half a lifetime ago stinging her eyes. 'It's not all right.'

Spin stared at the carpet. He dared not look up until Momoko suddenly slammed the paperweight down upon the desk and it was as if a shot had gone off in the room. Spin jumped; the whisky flew from his glass and splashed his shoes. He looked up into the judgement of her eyes.

'You come here with your *feelings*.' Her voice was raised, her fingers clenched tight around the paperweight. 'Do you have the slightest notion of the damage you did?' She wiped her eyes. Her hair, tied neatly behind her earlier in the day, had fallen across her face. 'I weigh it in years. Years that should have been wonderful and free and unforgettable. You took them all from me. It took all that time to get over the damage you did. When everybody else was laughing and joking and doing all the little, inconsequential things that people do without thinking, I willed my way from day to day in steps that small—' She stopped for a moment, the space between her thumb and forefinger measuring an inch. 'There was a whole life that could have been lived. Where, where do I look for it now?'

Silence fell across the room.

'You crushed it. You *crushed* it.' Again, she brought the paper-weight down upon the desk, and one rifle shot after another rang out in the silence of the office. When she'd finally exhausted herself and the violence had drained from her veins, she wiped her nose and eyes and stared directly at him. 'And we can't pick it up, and we can't put it back together and we can't go back. It's all gone.' She dropped the paperweight back on to the desk as if relinquishing a weapon and looked straight at him. 'Oh, I'm all right. I'm all right now. I came through. But you must know, and you must never for-get, that what you did, Spin, will never, ever go away. So don't bring your *feelings* to me. I've got enough of my own.'

She slumped back in her chair, drained of something so elemen-tal that it seemed to have been wrenched from her body, leaving it bruised and torn. But there, it was said. It was all finally said, and now, finally, perhaps, it could be put to rest. She was breathing deeply, her chest heaving from her enormous effort. In the long, ag-onising silence that followed it gradually returned to normal and she quietly nodded to herself. 'Oh, yes. I came through. But only just.' Her voice was soft now and he almost whispered in response to her.

'How you must hate me.'

She smiled faintly.

'I stopped hating you years ago, Spin. Just like I stopped loving you.'

She slowly twirled the whisky bottle, then held it up to Spin, who shook his head. 'So—' she smiled bitterly '—are you happy? Are you well? You don't look it.' She lowered her gaze and shook her head. 'Oh, Spin.'

The silence that followed went on and on, not seconds in duration but minutes—the type of silence that signifies an end to proceedings, not a pause. He waited for her to go on, but she didn't, and he wasn't sure if he shouldn't just leave. Just put his glass down, give a quick nod to the slumped figure before him, and navigate his way along the dark hall to the clatter of that alien world out there. But as he was about to rise he saw the muscles in her forearm tense as she compressed her fingers into a fist and released them, once, twice—and he suddenly felt as though it was Momoko who was waiting for him.

Spin began hesitantly, apologetically, not even sure if she were listening. None the less, he found himself reciting words that he had rehearsed over and over again for years, never seriously imagining that he would ever get the chance to say them. And like a speech that had never been tested it sounded all wrong from the moment he opened his mouth.

'It may not mean much now. No doubt nothing I have to say will mean anything to you.'

'It matters.' Momoko looked up sharply from the desk. 'It just won't change anything.'

He barely took in what she said. She spoke and Spin was relieved simply to hear her voice. He looked about the room, gathering the necessary strength to begin and waiting for the moment to start. Momoko was staring at him silently, with an intensity that rattled him, and he eventually stuttered into speech.

'You must believe me. Not…not a day has passed when I haven't thought of you. Of us,' he added, a wince in his eyes. 'And not a day has passed when I haven't wanted to obliterate that…that awful…' He looked about the room, the air thick with memories, and it seemed for a moment he wouldn't be able to finish the sentence. 'That awful business.'

A terrific, still silence hung in the air and Momoko drummed her fingers on the table as Spin stumbled on.

'Often, it occurs to me, and it's a dreadful, dreadful thought because the things we do—when we barely know ourselves—shouldn't be this irrevocable. But the thought occurs to me that if only, if only I could obliterate one—' he held up his forefinger and jabbed it into the air '—one hour of my life, so that it never happened, then the years that followed would be obliterated, too—and I, too, could live a different life; we could live a different life. One wretched hour. God, one hour was the difference between *living* and dying slowly.' He looked about the room, vaguely noting the teacups on the trolley, looking for the traces of lipstick that might tell him which one was hers. His breathing was heavy and before resuming he seemed to gulp the air, but speech remained an enormous effort. 'Not a day—that's not an exaggeration—not a day has passed when I haven't craved, dearly craved, the thing you can't give, and I don't mean your love. That's gone. As you so correctly say, I crushed it. I mean,' he went on, looking about the room, his lips quivering, 'I mean, your...what shall I say?...your forgiveness.'

'I can't.'

'No.' He shook his head as if it were tasteless even to mention such a thing. 'No, no, of course you can't.'

'And I don't mean because I won't. I can't. It's not mine to give. You have to settle that in yourself.'

'Of course. You're quite right. That's my job.'

Spin stared down at the empty glass—unaware until then that he'd emptied it again—the eyes of Momoko, and the eyes in the portraits that hung on the surrounding walls, all upon him. The weight of their collective judgement was unbearable and he was about to rise again and dismiss himself when he turned to Momoko.

'I suppose…I suppose you're very busy. And I won't keep you.'

'Don't be absurd, Spin.'

'*Oh*, but I am.' He put the glass on the floor and clasped his hands, resting them on his knees. 'If I may. One question.' Here he lifted his eyes to the ceiling and closed them for a moment before speaking. 'May I please, please know why you never told me?'

Momoko suddenly looked at him, defiance and sorrow in her eyes.

'You mean Naomi?'

Spin nodded, his lips moving without sound, unable to say her name because he was convinced he had no right to—and never would. 'Yes.'

'Oh, but I did, Spin,' she implored. 'You must believe me, I did. I wrote to you.'

'I never got it.'

'I know. It came back to me unopened.' A wretched tone entered her voice as she stared up to the ceiling, her chest heaving. 'I didn't know where you were. And I was so alone.'

Spin dug his nails into his knees and suddenly turned his head from her as if from a blinding light. He sharply rapped his knee with his knuckles.

'Dear God. How did this happen?'

He looked back to her to find the glare of rebuke in her eyes as clear and unmistakable as it had been all those years before. A glare that clearly said, You—Spin—you of all people should know how these things happen. He raised his hand to placate her.

'Yes, yes. You're quite right.'

He listened to her breathing return to normal, then turned back to her, a faint touch of wonder in his voice.

'Tell me. What…what is she like?'

Momoko looked about the room, noting for the first time the light thickening with the early evening. Spin's face was turned to her, waiting on her, the ache and the wonder still in his eyes.

'To know that, Spin…' She sighed. 'To *really* know that, you had to be there.'

When it happened, when Spin's head seemed to fall from his shoulders and land in his lap, when his body began to heave, Momoko almost rose and, for the first time that day, almost touched him. But she knew precisely where he was and she knew, for the moment, he was beyond her touch, or anybody else's for that matter.

And somewhere in that collapsed construction that was Spin he knew this was it. That their extraordinary coincidence had amounted to this and only this. That there could be nothing more and there was never going to be anything more. That when their time was up they would rise and part and that would be the end of it. He could never enter the tight, sealed world of those lives from which he had been absent: absent too soon to have known Naomi. And now, present too late to learn how to say the word *daughter* without stammering and stumbling all over it.

Momoko waited for the sobbing to subside. He finally looked up, glancing at the room, at the dull, cathedral light and wiped his eyes.

'Dear me,' he said, standing. 'Dear me. I've kept you.'

She shook her head. No, the gesture said, he hadn't kept her. And it was then that she rose slowly from her chair, and he looked up at her. You called, his eyes were pleading. You called. Now please, please, do something. She seemed to nod in acknowledgement of the unspoken plea, and the next moment, Spin felt Momoko's arms closing around him, encircling him and drawing him to her. They closed around him and for the briefest of moments the world was whole again. Then she slowly stepped back, and once more he was the fragment he'd always been.

The many rooms of the office were now dark. The portraits hung from the walls in shadow and he slipped past them as unobtrusively as possible, as if hoping not to be noticed. He had no idea of the time. How long had they been there? Hours? Days? As the door opened the twilight fanned the hallway and they stumbled out on to the front steps of the office, the streets a discordant babble of buses, taxis and cars. He gazed about at all the activity as if wondering where on earth he was. The world hadn't stopped spinning when Momoko's arms enfolded him, of course, although, for the briefest of moments, he felt it had. They stood facing each other in the fading light, then Momoko nodded a brief goodbye, turned and joined the crowded footpath. Her hand was in her coat pocket and in her hand was Spin's address and telephone number.

He stood on the footpath, watching her disappear, and had an absurd impulse to raise his arm and wave farewell. But it would be a pointless gesture. She never looked back. He'd followed her often enough.

He walked away and slowly began to melt into the warm, summer crowd. Just as she reached the corner, Momoko suddenly turned and looked for him, the rebuke gone from her eyes, as though a long-dormant capacity for forgiveness had finally won out.

Chapter Thirty-Two

Spin had no idea how long he'd been walking, but his trail had led him down into the crush of the market square near his hotel. It was early evening and the half-light cast an unreal glow across the walls and rooftops. A crowd, resembling a giant writhing beast in its death throes, had gathered around a young fool on a penny-farthing, who was wheeling himself backwards and forwards while shouting political slogans into the air. The jaws of fascinated faces jutted forward the better to observe the spectacle, open mouths gaped in wonder at the feats of the fool, and dull eyes rolled in delight at his antics.

He slumped on the steps of the church and observed it all as if he had stumbled into a Brueghel wedding scene. Her perfume was with him once again, as well as the sound of her voice, the paperweight hitting the table and the sweet oblivion of her arms enfolding him. He never saw the penny-farthing depart, but two youths with guitars strung round their necks were now the centre of attention. They shouted something. The crowd laughed. And then they started, and then he heard it—a simple, little pop song. The sort that Naomi quite possibly danced to, if, that is, she shared her mother's affinity with popular music and dance. How was it that two or three chords banged out on a cheap guitar could sound like the end of things, but they did. This music was alien, belonging to an age that no longer had a place for the Spins of this world, and in those two or three simple chords he heard his own requiem being screeched out and knew it was time to leave.

Slowly drifting away from the square, not caring where he wound up, Spin wandered aimlessly through streets and alleys until he came face to face with an old-fashioned second-hand bookshop. His eyes ached. The buildings around him had blocked out the light and he felt chilled by the evening air. Just then he craved the comfort of books, the warmth of words—words that mattered. And suddenly he longed for his home, so far, far away. He saw his house, his garden, his book-lined study and the chair that he sat in, and was briefly buoyed by the knowledge that they were all there, solid and weighty, ready for his return.

The air inside the shop was heavy with the smell of old books. For a moment he might have been a child again, standing in the local vicar's library. He browsed until he came to a leather-bound volume of verse; although it bore no publication date, he placed it somewhere in the middle of the nineteenth century. At least, that was where the poetry stopped. As he leafed through the coarse, thick pages that some long-dead fellow reader had once carefully cut, he came to a halt. Did he find the book or did the book find him? At that moment he was inclined to believe it was a little of both, but as he read the lines that he hadn't read in years he became convinced that the book had been waiting for him, for just this moment, just this day, when the solace of words had never been more dearly sought. Grasping the little volume eagerly, he paid for it and left.

Spin slept uneasily, in fits and starts, and left at first light, driving through near-deserted streets until he came to Momoko's house. The street lights were still on and the early sun had no warmth in it yet. He took the antique book, now carefully wrapped in plain gift paper, and quietly, stealthily, made his way along the footpath. He was the only figure on the street and when he reached her house he paused for a moment in front of it. The lights were out, the blinds were drawn, the house was sleeping and he had no fear of discovery. Strangely calm, he gazed for a moment upon her door. Without further delay he slowly pushed the metal gate open, took a few short steps and bent down to lay the book on Momoko's doorstep.

Chapter Thirty-Three

This is the way it happens. The street is bare, you think nobody is about, and suddenly the door opens. Spin might well have wished to have had the street, the house, the doorstep to himself—the whole universe, for that matter. But life intruded. Naomi was leaving early enough not to disturb Momoko, and early enough to disturb Spin, who was in the process of lowering the book on to the doorstep when the door opened.

'Oh! You!'

The exclamation burst from her. She had opened the door on to the empty street and found herself looking down on the greying curls of a stranger kneeling at her doorstep. But she was neither alarmed nor frightened. Nor was he a stranger. Shock and an odd sense of familiarity ran simultaneously through her. Then the exclamation, 'Oh, you!'—and, she might well have added, 'I waited for this, don't you know? I waited years for this. I got bored. I stopped waiting. I don't care any more. Just go away.'

But she'd summoned him once too often, and here he was, her plaything, and however much she wanted to stuff him back into the toy box from which she'd conjured him, she knew that the playtime years were over. Those furtive moments rifling through the tin chocolate box after school, the photograph of a smiling young soldier standing on some long-ago bridge before she was born, rushed back to her with extraordinary clarity. She'd often asked herself if she would recognise him if, by some extraordinary chance, they were to pass in the street, and had concluded that she would have. Some people change to the extent that they become unrecognisable. Assume another face altogether. But not him. As she mentally superimposed the face before her over the only image she had ever had of him until now, she saw clearly the boyish young man smiling beneath the older, alarmed man who had obviously been taken quite by surprise. And, as she looked down at him, the same fantastic proposition came back to haunt her: was this all her doing? Is this what you get for playing around with things you know nothing about?

Spin said nothing. They stared at one other without speaking, neither knowing for how long. At last Naomi quietly closed the front door behind her, then slid down on to the step, resting against the door in a trance. There was a vacant place beside her on the doorstep that Spin recognised as his, and, without asking, similarly entranced, he sat down beside her. In silence, they sat, father and daughter, staring out on to the blank street.

Naomi quickly turned her head to look at him, then returned her gaze to the street.

'Do you often creep about like this?' she said.

Spin didn't turn in acknowledgement of the question, nor did he reply for some time.

'You must realise, I knew nothing of—'

'I know you didn't.'

'If I had, believe me, if I had—'

Without letting him finish, Naomi turned and met him with a direct look.

'I know everything. I know it all.'

The look in her eyes, which he stared into, close up, for the first time, left Spin in no doubt as to what the 'all' meant. In her mother's eyes the look had once said, *Now, you join the rest*. In her daughter's eyes the look told him he'd never occupied a privileged place from which to fall. And while he was taking this in, he noticed her cowlick and the quickness of her eyes, and a silent voice inside him proclaimed 'mine'. For a moment he had to look away.

'What's in the package?'

Spin looked down at the little parcel in his hands.

'A book.'

'And what's in the book?'

'Poetry.'

She eyed him, nodded knowingly. 'Poetry,' she repeated.

Spin was turning the parcel round in his hands. 'It's an old book. Oldish. Not terribly expensive.'

'But it's *your* book?'

He nodded, understanding the plural nature of the 'your'.

'Yes, it's *our* book. Or, it was.'

'And you found it.'

Did he find the book, or did the book find him? The answer was still the same, a little of both. Not sure if it was a question or not, he left it there. They fell silent again. A car passed, disturbing the silence, and they both looked up, vaguely resentful.

He didn't have the gift for squeezing his life into a few words, although he was sure that was all it would take. Nor did she. And so they sat, slowly succumbing to this endless, awful silence until, unable to bear it any longer, Spin finally wrung something from the moment.

'Your mother,' he said, stumbling into speech, 'was—' he quickly corrected himself '—is the only woman I have ever loved. Unreservedly loved.'

And it was then that Naomi raised her head to the sky and laughed, a natural, breezy laugh that was all the more disturbing for its ease.

'Love?' she said, the laugh eventually dying down. 'Is that what you call it?'

There it was again, that laughter. Spin stared out across the street, until it ceased. And when he spoke the quiet, emphatic conviction in his voice surprised even him. And Naomi. She looked at him, this long-lost other side of the story she'd grown up with, this soldier who went home after the war like all the others, and suddenly he was not like all the others. He was the face in the photograph, breathing, speaking, and letting her know that he didn't like the tone of her laughter—the way fathers do.

'Yes.' He nodded, again and again, as if he were only just grasping the simple fact of the matter. 'Yes, I do. I do call it love.' He had uttered the word with the pride of one who had loved, not wisely, but too well. And then he was speaking again, and she was stunned by the power of his conviction. 'Your mother was about your age. I was a little older, but so much younger. The world had just blown itself up and all we surviving bits were just wandering around trying to imagine what came next, if anything at all. Then I met your mother, and for a while we managed to get above it all. And, believe me, it takes something bloody powerful to do that. I called that thing love then, and I call it love now.'

He stopped there, but the expression in his eyes told her unmistakably that, whatever may have happened afterwards, this love was no laughing matter, so spare me your breezy laughter, my girl. I'm here, aren't I? And what do you think brought me here? And it was then that his face contorted, his lips curled upwards at the corners and a low sound radiated from inside him as if something were about to burst. But it didn't. And Naomi saw that this grimace, this desperate attempt to hold back whatever it was that threatened to burst from him, or within him, had creased his lips, cheeks and face in such a way that it could be interpreted as a smile by any casual observer passing by—their whole conversation a breezy morning chat. Slowly, his rocking ceased and the agonised humming sound subsided.

He hugged his knees to his chest on her mother's doorstep in the early morning light, the street still blank. This was no Magwitch, no distant figure from the mists of her mother's youth, no cuddly plaything to be picked up and put away at will, but flesh-and-blood—her flesh and blood—unbearably here, now. He wasn't aware that she'd risen from the step, but when he looked up she was standing in front of him, a look on her face, it seemed to Spin, caught somewhere between loss and gain, dread and hope: the desire to believe in him and the wish to be rid of him.

'I have to go.'

The words were sudden, urgent. And Spin knew that this need to go had nothing to do with time or work or whatever. It was the simple fact of him that she had to go from.

He nodded. Naomi sighed, a sigh that carried the tremors of something larger, something that had to be taken away and seen through in private. She shook her head, staring out at the familiar houses and yards that had barely changed as she'd grown.

'I don't even know what to call you.'

Spin suddenly rose from the doorway and took a step towards her as if, absurdly, he were about to introduce himself. But she retreated a pace as he did, and he stopped, his eyes almost pleading.

'Call me Allen. Nobody calls me that.'

She hesitated, seemed to plant the name in her mind, but she said nothing. She strode off and he saw the bounce of his youth in her walk and once again this voice inside him cried out 'mine'. Within seconds she would be gone from him, and they would have passed like ants on the footpath. But as he watched her leave, she suddenly stopped and threw a last glance back at him from the street. And although there was neither welcome nor goodbye in that glance, she had, for whatever reason, made the effort, and Spin returned the look with the most minute of nods.

Behind them, unnoticed by either Naomi or Spin, the curtains of Momoko's bedroom parted. Her daughter, whom she noticed first, was standing on the street looking back towards the house. But at what? As she followed the line of her eyes she saw a man in front of her house. Her daughter had shot this man a backward glance, and he had received it with the most minute of nods. What? The initial alarm and outrage at the intrusion evaporated when she realised who it was. Even then her impulse was to rush downstairs immediately. To rush down and uncover what on earth was going on. But she stayed where she was, the curtains discreetly parted. She stayed where she was and let them be. It was only a matter of seconds, but they were long seconds. Then Naomi was gone.

The mind moves quickly, she noted. In certain circumstances the mind moves quickly. For although it was only a matter of seconds that her daughter had been on the street, and given that backward glance of hers, Momoko knew that it was *their* scene, their moment. She was not only not required, she was not wanted. And had she had time to rush downstairs, it would have been she, Momoko, who would have been the intruder. Naomi's glance was for Spin; a glance that almost suggested they'd somehow met before, that he was familiar to her. This was another daughter, one who was quite possibly only just coming to life. But although she couldn't read her action the way she could usually read her daughter's gestures and sudden looks, she knew without doubt that that quick glance shot back to the stationary Spin carried with it an acknowledgment. It was a glance that said, Yes, there is a you and I. And it might also have said, I don't know what to do with this you and I, but it is there. And we both know it, don't we— you and I?

Until now they'd looked after each other, mother and daughter, just the two of them. Now, for the first time in their life together, Momoko was the third presence looking upon the two of *them*. The outsider who was not required at this moment. And the miracle was that, somewhere inside her, she was registering the fact that the sensation was good, that she didn't mind this exclusion. She stood for a long time, unable to move, staring through the curtains at the suburban sky outside her window. It was a clear, blue sky, not a cloud, no sign of a breeze, and she knew that it would be a perfect summer's day.

When Naomi was gone Spin lingered on the empty street, heard her car door open and shut, then listened as its motor faded into the city, knowing that it was his daughter who was at the wheel. And as he listened, he was suddenly possessed by the unshakeable belief that she was fully formed. She was herself. She was complete. She would be all right. He might never see her again, but the picture that stayed with him when she was gone was of a young woman who wanted for nothing and who would be all right. Somehow this miracle had happened. She had grown and become what she was. He hadn't been there, true. But his spirits lifted when he thought of her, out there in the world, fully formed, as complete as a young fox putting its face to the wind for the first time. She would be all right. And, at that moment, he was suddenly happy. Impossibly happy. She was out there, she was doing something, and, for a second or two, he had been part of it. They'd brushed, they'd crossed, and a speck of happiness had been blown his way.

Then he swung round, as if suddenly realising where he was, why he'd come, and looked once more at Momoko's door. Again, in the nearness, in the proximity of her door, he felt Momoko's arms enfold him, heard the last of Naomi's car departing, and for a moment the world was whole. He approached the door, as he had some twenty minutes before, and this time deposited the parcel on Momoko's doorstep without being disturbed. Then the fragment turned and, for the second time in his life, stepped out into the unplumbed depths of a life without her. He closed the gate behind him as quietly as he had opened it and left the street with a quick, sideways glance at the sleeping house.

There was a leather marker in the book and when she unwrapped it she would see, underlined in ink, the words he had once committed to memory and casually whispered in her ear a lifetime ago in the sanctuary of her old room—as if that sort of thing happened all the time:

And now good morrow to our waking souls,
Which watch not one another out of fear;
For love all love of other sights controls,
And makes one little room an everywhere.

With the marker was a small piece of paper from a hotel note-pad. It contained his address, should it ever be needed.

Chapter Thirty-Four

She almost stepped right over it, almost missed the package altogether. Spin had long gone, and she'd let him leave at his own pace, let him leave by himself, for to stop him would have meant acknowledging that she had—even as an observer—intruded upon their scene. There was no stamp, no postmark, no address and no return address. She wasn't even sure if she should open it at first, concerned that it might be meant for one of her neighbours and had been mistakenly dropped on her doorstep.

But from the moment she opened the package she knew who it was from and she knew that there was no mistake. It was an old first edition and must have cost quite a bit. She ran her fingers across the brushed leather of the cover and shook her head, her eyes still tired from restless sleep. She had awoken from one haunting dream after another, all of them the same: the distant figure of Spin with his back to her, quietly slipping into the maelstrom of the crowd. And always this lunar silence all around them, a silence so vast that not even her cries could disturb it. Indeed, it was the restlessness of her sleep, not the voices downstairs, that had woken her. Now, hastily dressed, hair uncombed, eyes tired, she noted the bookmark and knew immediately that it wasn't randomly placed; knew that she was meant to open the book at precisely that page.

Her eyes fell on the marked lines. She dropped the brown paper wrapping, slumped on to her doorstep to read, and as she lingered over those four lines, she was shaken by the power of the words to summon up the past in such a way that she saw the scene again with aching clarity: her room, Spin reciting those words she was reading now, his boyish curls, her girlish grin as she lay on the futon listening and welcoming the fun back into her life. And, it seemed to her as she rested her head back against the door, that the lines were inseparable from the sound of Spin's voice all those years ago—as though he were Donne, and the words were his.

The book was, she knew, a farewell gift. One that sought peace with the past and revived an inextinguishable time when they had lived, laughed, loved and known the very best of each other. Yes, she nodded in silent agreement with the absent Spin, the memory of those precious few months when everything was still good must never be lost.

She looked about her at the small front path, the metal gate, and realised that he had left his gift without having had the heart to stay. She knew Spin; she knew *her* Spin. He would have come at a fugitive hour and left the package so as not to be disturbed by anybody. But he had been, hadn't he? Life had intruded on his plans. She knew, because she had watched it. She had watched as her daughter had shot a backward glance in his direction, and watched as he acknowledged the glance with a nod that told her that they were all now less lonely for Spin having received it.

It was then that she noted the small slip of paper that had fallen from the book when she'd opened it. Neatly printed, in Spin's writing—which hadn't changed—was his address and a brief note: 'For anything, anything at all.' She stared on to the street, a flicker of a smile on her lips, an old happiness, old but still good, passing briefly through her like an old melody. Then she folded the paper carefully and placed it in the book with the page marker. The time had long passed when she needed anything from him, but it was good to have the paper ready to hand and know that the invitation would always be there—for anything, anything at all.

Chapter Thirty-Five

He had little memory of the drive to Cambridge and less idea of what he was doing here. A canvas deck chair had appeared; he had slumped into it. A straw hat kept the afternoon sun off him. Out on the smooth, deep green of the playing fields a game of cricket was in progress.

The tiled roof of the clubhouse—where sandwiches, cakes and teacups were, no doubt, being laid out for the change of innings—glittered under a clear, blue sky. The sight board shimmered in the haze and the whole ground was postcard-still, except for the occasional scampered running of the batsmen and the converging fieldsmen. Bat hit ball with the steady, slow tick-tock of a metronome, for the time signature that hung over the afternoon, Spin reflected, was decidedly *adagio*. He let his body go loose, felt his weight sink into the canvas, and idly ran his fingers along the trimmed grass as if floating in a sea-green pool. Somewhere out there, beyond the town, beyond the sheared wheat and barley fields of the surrounding countryside, beyond the deep lanes that led from village to village, the world was spinning into noisy change with breathtaking abandon. But not here. The ground, the clubhouse, the trees, the very sky itself were all exactly as he remembered. Nothing had changed. He had always come here to see his friends play in his student years, and he now felt for all the world as if he were still watching the same games he watched then. The same muted cries out on the field, the same soft clatter of polite applause, even the same players.

Somewhere on the green fields of another time, the youthful Spin was idly tossing a cricket ball in the air, its seam revolving in flight like Newton's apple. The same sun that had warmed him then, warmed him now, but for the first time that day clouds were forming over the town. He ought to go, for the day would turn chilly if he left it too late. But suddenly he barely had the strength to raise his head, let alone lift the weight of his useless frame. And walking—walking was out of the question. The exhaustion of the last few days was finally hitting him with the force of the nasty, sharp, rising ball that had just struck one of the batsmen out on the field, for there was a young quick out there, and he was, as they say, getting amongst them.

His eyes stayed on the field, his mind drifted off, brass heart, brass torso, arms and legs pinning him to the chair. He stared into the distance. So close. They were so close to each other. Then her arms were around him again, encircling him ever so briefly, and they touched. And in that moment he was joined once again to the only human being who had ever had the power to wipe the indifference of the world away and make him feel, beyond all doubt, that there really was someone out there after all, that he was, and he paused internally before pronouncing the word: connected.

Once again, this impossible happiness rose up in him, happiness he'd long assumed he'd lost any right to feel. But there it was. And it wouldn't go away. Had he really come all this way for a brief, solitary embrace and the satisfaction of receiving a short glance from the daughter he had never known, before watching her go out into the world, complete and ready for life? Quite possibly. Those two specks of happiness that he had never expected, and which had blown his way, somehow, ridiculously, seemed enough. Enough for a fragment to feel part of a whole again. There was joy in those specks. The deep green of the playing field, the trees surrounding it, the white-clad players, the spectators, the clubhouse, all shimmered under the summer sun as if he were twenty-two once more, and the day held the promise of going out into life for the first time all over again—and getting it right this time. He contemplated the possibility of the heart simply bursting, and expiring with what? Joy? And it seemed to him that it might be the sweetest of deaths.

The players strolled from the field for tea and the change of innings. He closed his eyes tightly, and kept them closed while his lips moved, silently lingering on each treasured syllable, Mo-mo-ko, as if he had once again assembled the parts of a picture puzzle he had carelessly scattered when he had been too young to know what he had been looking at.

It was then that Spin was suddenly roused from his reverie by the sound of someone calling his name.

'Professor Bowler?'

Spin looked up, not sure if he weren't finally insane. But there, standing on the very boundary line upon which his student friends had once christened him, was a young Japanese woman, dressed in a turtle-neck sweater. She was staring at him, quizzically, the question still in her eyes. Then, she repeated herself.

'Professor Bowler? It is you? Isn't it?'

'Yes, yes.' Spin stammered into speech. She offered her name, and he rose from his seat, lightly, almost floating, the heaviness in his legs, his whole frame, no longer an impediment. She was calling to him, as if through a fog, and he responded happily to her voice.

'We met, you remember? In Melbourne. I came to see you.'

'Yes,' Spin replied, drifting towards her, her features becoming more familiar the nearer he approached until he stood before her, close, nodding, 'of course.'

'You were helpful.'

'Was I?' he answered, pleased by the words. 'Why have you come? It is *you*, isn't it?'

The question amused her. 'I live here. Sorry, *we* live here. That was my boyfriend out there getting amongst them. He was one of your students.' She smiled. 'He warned me you were hard to pin down.'

'You were visiting, then?'

'Yes.' And then she looked around at the gathering clouds. 'Well, time I got going.'

'Yes…' he nodded '…time, indeed.'

And so she smiled again, and walked away along the white line of the boundary. Then she turned, a movement almost choreographed in its perfection, pulled back the sleeve of her sweater and waved. Faded, upon the sounding of the horn; her eyes, at once innocent and knowing, ignorant yet completely aware of the effect that she had. With her back to him she followed the wide curve of the boundary, becoming smaller and smaller until she disappeared from view. For the third time in as many weeks she'd given Spin her name, and for the third time in as many weeks he'd immediately forgotten it, as he always did with students.

At his feet was an old match ball. With the ease and alacrity of a young man he bent down and plucked it from the ground, swift and clean. Instinctively, he began tossing it in the air and catching it, one-handed, as it fell. Up and down, up and down. 'Hey. That's what we'll call you. Spin. Spin Bowler.' There was general laughter along the boundary line. His friends were calling. And Spin lingered, ready to follow their young voices, with steps as light as air, into that future where Momoko's room surely waited.

He returned to his chair, the old match ball in his hand, and sat down again, gazing out over the ground. He tossed the ball into the air, up and down, up and down, an entrancing, sweet ache in his brass chest, while the afternoon light faded and the sky thickened. Day gave way to dusk, stumps were drawn and the players filed quietly from the ground. The ball suddenly plopped to the ground and nestled in the grass. His body slumped and the chair took the full force of his weight. Those three syllables, Mo-mo-ko, hovered round and about him, then pealed off into the twilight, and the steady, metronomic click-clack that had hung over the day came to a sudden stop.

It was only when the last of the players locked up the clubhouse and prepared to leave that somebody noticed that the odd gentleman in the straw sun hat hadn't moved for some time. Surely, someone suggested, they should wake him. And so two men broke briefly from the small group and edged towards the slumbering figure.

At first they quietly informed him that play was over, but he remained impassive. Then one of them prodded him gently and his arm fell, slack and heavily, to the side. They called the others over and all stood around the slumped figure in the deck chair, pondering the awkward question of who on earth to contact.

Read all about it...

MORE ABOUT THIS BOOK

MORE ABOUT THE AUTHOR

WE RECOMMEND

2

Read all about it...

QUESTIONS FOR YOUR READING GROUP

1. Does the Japanese student who prompts Spin's odyssey really exist?

2. What role does the disapproval of others at the fact that they are "fraternising" play in the development of Spin and Momoko's relationship?

3. In Puccini's *Madam Butterfly*, Lieutenant Pinkerton abandons Butterfly, leaving her to her fate. Can we see Spin as a Pinkerton who *does* return?

4. If so, is Momoko a Madam Butterfly who chooses *not* to die following her lover's betrayal, therefore breaking the colonial mould?

5. Was Momoko right to conceal her visits to Yoshi from Spin?

6. Do you believe that Spin was "one who had loved, not wisely, but too well" (page 268)? Does his treatment of Momoko mean that he did not actually love at all?

7. Naomi is puzzled that her mother wishes Spin was there (page 242), and Momoko herself ascribes it to disliking "unfinished business." Are you convinced that this is the only reason?

8. Do you find Naomi's reaction to Spin when she finally meets him surprising, given her knowledge of the past and what he did to her mother?

Read all about it...

9. Are Spin's actions throughout the book those of a weak man?

10. Do you believe that Spin and Momoko have found peace by the end of *The Lovers' Room*?

HOW LITERARY THEORY INSPIRED
The Lovers' Room

This may be of limited value, but the inspiration did, in fact, come from reading a book on critical theory – Terry Eagleton's *Literary Theory: An Introduction*. It's his bestseller "bluffers guide". In it he gives – and I think he's that rare beast, a very readable theorist – a brilliant snap-shot description of FR Leavis, the whole Leavis philosophy and its impact.

One paragraph in particular – and I can't quote it because I haven't got my copy with me – says something to the effect that if, as Leavis stresses, literature/high culture is meant to make the reader a "better person", then, when the commandants walked out of the death camps after having committed the crime of the century, reciting Goethe and whistling Mozart, it appeared a few questions had to be answered. The assumption was always tenuous, and could not be taken for granted. It struck a chord with me.

My Eng Lit degree was done along strict Leavis lines (the canon, no studying of translations etc.), many of my teachers were former students of Leavis. I didn't read Eagleton till I went back to uni to do my MA (which I never finished). By then the new theory – which challenged all my assumptions – had arrived. It was quite exciting. And through fiction I saw a way of re-examining everything I'd been taught – which opened up the whole question of literature and the individual, literature and society, and the "function" (if any) of it in rela-tion to society. From there I thought, well, why not take a young Leavisite (the literary equivalent of a missionary), put him in a

Read all about it...

crucible-like situation that tests his beliefs and see what happens. So, I could look at large questions, but, at the same time, have a specific focus. That may sound cold, but I identified with Spin, and having set the whole story in motion, also set a lot of other things in motion as well.

I realise this may be of very limited value (people either get up and leave the room immediately or promptly fall asleep whenever anybody says the word "theory") but that was the way it happened.

Read all about it . . .

AUTHOR BIOGRAPHY

Born in Melbourne in 1949 and live in Melbourne with my partner and our son. Attended high school and La Trobe University, where I eventually completed a degree in Literature and History. I taught in high schools and played in a rock band in the 1970s, usually about three to four nights a week in pubs (often "beer barns" that housed up to a thousand people), doing Eagles and Doobie brothers covers. You can only take so much of that, so I left the band and formed my own, doing original songs.

By then I decided I wanted to write – so I sold my Rickenbacher for an electric typewriter, packed my bag, and went and lived in a small French village just outside of Perpignan and wrote a play about TS Eliot, his first marriage and the writing of *The Waste Land*, thinking that nobody would be interested in so specialist a topic. A year later – back in Melbourne – someone told me about a play called *Tom and Viv*, which had just opened in the West End. The theatre company that had planned to do it dropped the play from the season – but ABC radio drama did produce it.

I eventually stopped writing plays, became a theatre critic but kept writing novels. I also taught fiction at RMIT in Melbourne and at Melbourne University. These days I write books, write book reviews for the *Melbourne Age*, jog, go to cricket training as much as possible and share in looking after my little boy. Writing – through residencies – has allowed me and us to live in different parts of the world – mostly Paris, Pont-Aven (Brittany) and Venice.

Read all about it...

STEVEN CARROLL ON WRITING

What do you love most about being a writer?

I don't have to go to work. Of course, writing is work. Often very hard, exacting work. But it's also a lot of fun. And I mean fun in a broad sense. Even with sad – or saddish – books such as *The Lovers' Room*, there is fun involved. I'm sure Proust – for all the seriousness of his project – was also having fun.

Where do you go for inspiration?

Books can come from reading other books or from life. But, really, there are no rules here – as there no rules for most of writing. Apparently Somerset Maugham once said that there are three golden rules to be observed when writing fiction – fortunately nobody remembers what they are. It should also be added that the whole notion of inspiration is over-rated. Most writers who go to a mountain top and sit around waiting for the thunderbolt of inspiration are still sitting there.

Where do your characters come from, and do they ever surprise you as they write?

There are no rules here either. They come from life, from books or a mixture of both. And I suppose they should surprise you. But I suspect because it takes so long to write a novel (two or three or four years) the characters evolve slowly over a long period of time. Almost incidentally. Or nonchalantly. At the end of the book you may very well look at them and wonder where on earth they came from. When, in fact, the prosaic truth probably is that they were slowly evolving the whole time. You were just too busy writing the book to notice.

Read all about it...

When did you start writing?

I was a Johnny-come-lately to writing, after having very wisely mis-spent my youth in rock bands in the 70s. It was hard to sell my Rickenbacher (pretty much the same one John Lennon used) but it had to be done. I actually came to writing through painting, then music. First plays, then novels.

What one piece of advice would you give a writer wanting to start a career?

Write regularly – three or four sessions per week (each session about three or four hours) and aim to produce a thousand words a session. Do not waste too much time re-reading what you wrote the previous day – writing is about production. Word production. The very best you can come up with. That requires discipline and a clear head.

Read all about it...

MY TOP TEN BOOKS

This is not in any order:

Marcel Proust, *Swann's Way*

Vladimir Nabokov, *Lolita*

Somerset Maugham, *The Razor's Edge*

George Eliot, *Middlemarch*

Alain Fournier, *Le Grand Meaulnes*

Graham Greene, *The Third Man* (novella and film script)

Tom Stoppard, *Plays*

George Johnston, *My Brother Jack*

TS Eliot, *Poems*

F Scott Fitzgerald, *The Great Gatsby*

Read all about it...

A DAY IN THE LIFE

Very simple. I live in inner-city Melbourne. I have a small study in the back yard and after breakfast and after taking my son to school I go to my study and write for three/four hours. I usually aim for a thousand words a session. I have a regular non-fiction book column with the *Age* – a Melbourne broadsheet newspaper – and in the afternoons I try to get a review done. Afterwards, I'll go for a run, or off to cricket training and in the evenings, after a hard day's write, it's not uncommon to sit down at dinner with my partner, Fiona (also a writer) and share a bottle of bold Australian red.

STEVEN CARROLL'S FUTURE PROJECTS

Read all about it...

The Love Song of Lucy McBride

When thirteen-year-old Lucy McBride hears the haunting music floating in through her window, she falls instantly in love. And when she sees a post-war picture of the cellist, Fortuny, she is sure her heart is lost forever.

As she gradually learns to play the cello, Lucy grows from an awkward teen into an accomplished musician and a seductive girl. When the opportunity to study in Venice arrives, Lucy travels to meet Maestro Fortuny, and begs him to become her teacher. But the idol she has kept on a pedestal for so many years is now an old man and the roles of who idolises whom will be dangerously reversed...

A haunting and powerful novel of seduction, music and passion, *The Love Song of Lucy McBride* will be available from MIRA® Books in 2008.

If you enjoyed *The Lovers' Room*, we know you'll love...

Kommandant's Girl by Pam Jenoff

Overnight, Jewish eighteen-year-old Emma Bau's world is turned upside down when Germany invades Poland. And after only six weeks of marriage, her husband Jacob, a member of the Resistance, is forced to flee. Assuming a new, Christian identity, Emma finds work at Nazi headquarters and as secretary to the charismatic Kommandant Richwalder, she vows to use her unique position to gather intelligence for the Resistance – by any means necessary.

Everything Must Go by Elizabeth Flock

To those on the outside, the Powells are a happy family, but then a devastating accident destroys their fragile façade. When seven-year-old Henry is blamed for the tragedy, he tries desperately to make his parents happy again, but as he grows up, he questions if the guilt his parents have burdened him with has left him unable to escape his anguished family or their painful past...

Angel's Rest by Charles Davis

It is 1967, and eleven-year-old Charlie York lives in Angel's Rest. His town is a poor boy's paradise – until a shotgun blast kills Charlie's father and puts his mother on trial for murder. When reclusive veteran Hollis Thrasher is also linked to the death, Charlie must embark on a dangerous midnight journey so that the truth about what he witnessed that fateful day can finally be revealed.